Unchain
My Heart

Sharika Esther Sharma comes from a diverse background: she is half Indian and half Dutch, was born in Washington DC and has lived the majority of her life in India.

After graduating from Woodstock International School in Mussoorie, Sharika went on to acquire her Bachelor's degree in Mass Communication and English Literature from the University of San Diego, California. Returning to India, she wrote articles on latest archaeological discoveries for *Asian Age* and *Education Times*. She has written for television and was part of a production for Star Plus channel. Sharika travels between her homes in Delhi and Mumbai for work.

Her first book, *Monkeys in My Garden: Reflections from A Life in Isolation*, was published by Om Books International in January 2022.

Unchain My Heart

SHARIKA ESTHER SHARMA

RUPA

Published by
Rupa Publications India Pvt. Ltd 2023
7/16, Ansari Road, Daryaganj
New Delhi 110002

Sales centres:
Prayagraj Bengaluru Chennai
Hyderabad Jaipur Kathmandu
Kolkata Mumbai

Copyright © Sharika Esther Sharma 2023

This is a work of fiction. Names, characters, places and incidents are either the product of the author's imagination or are used fictitiously and any resemblance to any actual person, living or dead, events or locales is entirely coincidental.

All rights reserved.
No part of this publication may be reproduced, transmitted, or stored in a retrieval system, in any form or by any means, electronic, mechanical, photocopying, recording or otherwise, without the prior permission of the publisher.

P-ISBN: 978-93-5702-051-0
E-ISBN: 978-93-5702-067-1

First impression 2023

10 9 8 7 6 5 4 3 2 1

The moral right of the author has been asserted.

Printed in India

This book is sold subject to the condition that it shall not, by way of trade or otherwise, be lent, resold, hired out, or otherwise circulated, without the publisher's prior consent, in any form of binding or cover other than that in which it is published.

*I dedicate this book to every woman
on the path of self-discovery*

Contents

1. Victory — 1
2. A Bridge Once Crossed — 6
3. Reflection — 15
4. A Tea Party — 21
5. The Old Man and the Tree — 29
6. Pride and Pain — 37
7. Organza — 39
8. A Brother — 47
9. Ali Mansion — 53
10. A Regular Day — 68
11. A Wedding — 84
12. Breakfast in Bed — 106
13. Star Power — 109
14. Thailand — 114
15. (No) Piece of Cake — 123
16. Sea Rock — 131
17. Clarity — 138
18. Paradoxes — 143

19. The Tuxedo	150
20. Dystopia	158
21. A Resolution	163
22. A Discovery	168
23. Black Gold	176
24. A Bittersweet Farewell	206
25. Power Outage	213
26. In a Quagmire	219
27. Natural Light	224
28. In a Limbo	230
29. Devastation	232
30. Reformation	235
31. A Blossom	240
32. Swan Song	242

Acknowledgments   245

1
Victory

Tremulous, diamanté collar askew, coiffure windswept, she waited in the storm.

Cameramen on cranes ditched their high perches; the flashes of light in the sky rendered the shutterbugs twinkling on the ground obsolete. Holding her umbrella firmly, Alya's attendant guided her through the cluster of artists and security personnel jostling for space. The actress had no animosity towards the rain, but while endlessly imagining this night, she had never envisaged the possibility of anything untoward—natural or human—overshadowing her victory. A chill ran down her spine despite the warmth and pride in her heart as she whispered, 'What a bummer.' The coveted Filmfare statuette was hers, but she was fretting about the lightning, rain and crowd jostling her into dropping it and losing it forever.

She tried to wiggle out of the tangle of famous bodies as politely as she could, eyeing the procession of cars picking up the stars. The crowds behind the barricade suddenly went hysterical. Photographers who had managed to shoot but a few hazy pictures of a sea of umbrellas encircled some entity moving towards the edge of the red carpet. Alya strained to see through the gaps. Who could it be? Then she felt foolish for not having guessed already. It was not some entity but the entirety. It was Pops, the godfather of Bollywood, an actor so legendary that his divinity was the subject of televised debates. Temples were dedicated to him, wherein life-sized replicas sitting in glib repose were bathed daily in cow's milk. Pictures of Pops were priceless and pictures with him, more so. In a tick, Alya shifted from first to fifth gear, air-kissing a darling here, elbowing a staffer there, cutting towards the storm of flashing lights on the red carpet with a one-point agenda—reaching Pops before his silver Bentley reached him.

Alya was confident about her navigational skills in the sticky waters of filmdom. A decade in the business had made her a mistress of the art of multitasking. Wading towards Pops, she unzipped her clutch and produced a compact powder and a lipstick. She wiped the kohl that she was sure was running down her cheeks with the rainwater, possibly taking a false eyelash with it. To be photographed with smudges on her face was something an A-list actress could in no way allow. Alya dabbed off the smudged kohl on her face with the powder puff in her compact and applied a coat of raspberry red on her lips. And, voilà, she was camera ready!

It was a secret, though not a well-kept one, that Pops who appeared to be ever-so-youthful and agile was actually the opposite. He was, in fact, a breath away from being whisked to the infirmary at all times. Alya's impulsiveness almost became her undoing when she finally reached him; she bumped into the septuagenarian actor, nearly knocking him over. Both ended up clinging on to each other for support—albeit for different reasons.

When Pops saw his car arrive, he dashed to it with deftness that he generally reserved for such occasions. But Alya was yet to exploit her opportunity. Aware that every camera in Mumbai was focussed on them, she waved goodbye to the living legend in a grand, remarkably imperial, flourish despite being no more than two paces away from him. Only an expert could have identified it as the trademark wave of the charismatic, world-famous Princess Diana. Alya was good at picking up attractive traits from people she considered more impressive than her and making them her own. Searching the web till her knuckles stiffened, she had found the most fetching wave—a clear-cut winner—and made it her own. She always did her homework. She believed in preparation.

By the time the storm passed, the cameras had captured multiple photographs of the two stars waving goodbye to each other. Making a mental note of another mission accomplished, Alya headed to her car, which was next in line.

∞

In the privacy of her Range Rover Sport, the actress heaved a sigh of triumph and relief. Abandoning social decorum, she leaned her head against the half-open window and spread her legs; the drizzle pattered against her face; the cool breeze relaxed her senses. Alya was enjoying the moment.

As her car drove along, ribbons of smoke wafted out of Alya's lips as she finally smoked the cigarette she had been craving since receiving her award. She peered out of the window at the high-end boutiques lit in the waxing night. Mannequins in embroidered skirts and floor-length gowns seemed to stare at her from the storefronts, smiling broadly. Alya smiled back. Across the street from the designer stores, she saw a tea stall with a billboard featuring an attractive young woman sipping soda. 'That's me!' Alya said to herself, giggling with delight. Seeing herself on billboards and big screens, in magazines and on TV, was her greatest thrill. It was what she had wanted since her childhood. And now, it was happening. It was real. A bus whizzed past and there she was again, smiling with her immaculate teeth for a popular toothpaste brand. Alya laughed—the irony of every one of her teeth being capped was not lost on her. She was in a good place and she was feeling it.

The car stopped at a traffic light. Alya's attention turned to an abnormally large sewer rat running from a hole in the divider to a more secure shelter. It scampered over a pair of bare feet as it went, feet that moved towards her car, feet that belonged to a nine-year-old street urchin cradling a baby in her arms.

'*Dedo paisa* [Give me money],' the girl said, thrusting the infant's grimy hand past the heroine's open window. 'You are so pretty, may you get a good husband,' she went on, shaking the baby's hand. This was a common sight in Mumbai, but the gaping wound on the baby's half-shaved head was not so common. Alya tried to ignore the sight and the thought that the drizzle, which felt like snowflakes on her face, must feel like salt on the infant's wound. Its rag doll head flopped back and forth dangerously as the girl jiggled it to get a response from the rich lady before her. Alya guessed that the infant must have been heavily doped with opium. She tried not to let it unnerve her, but the sight was cruel and hard to ignore.

Anger overcame her joy. *Why does this have to happen to me right now? Why can't I just enjoy my victory?* she thought. She knew that if she gave money to the girl, it would end up in the pockets of those who put her on the streets in the first place. She had been taught in school that Mahatma Gandhi discouraged the patronage of beggars for this reason. She reached for the half-eaten bag of rice crackers and bottle of orange juice beside her on the seat. These she could give to the girl. Realizing that the infant didn't stand a chance, her anger morphed into helplessness. The light changed. The car rolled forward. She tossed the bottle and the bag at the girl. The suffering was behind her and there was no looking back.

'No looking back' was the foremost belief in Alya's rulebook. She had this motto etched onto her brain and could act on it on command. So much so that not looking back had become a reflex, one that never failed to do the job of instantly desensitizing her, of not letting anything grim make a lasting impression. It stopped the black ink of helplessness from dripping into her mind. 'Look at the larger picture' was another one of Alya's favourite nuggets of wisdom. Looking at the larger picture at all times enabled her to do things she may not have normally done.

Alya rolled up her window, as the humidity had sapped her. She chided her driver, 'Bikam, switch on the AC, *aur jaldi chalo* [Hurry up]! How long does it take to get to Sea View?'

2

A Bridge Once Crossed

Alya's feet were aching from standing in heels and her Spanx was making it difficult for her to breathe. As she entered her apartment, she was puzzled by how dark it was inside. *Why are the curtains drawn? Is Karan in the house?* An unfamiliar sound coming from the living room alerted her to the possibility of an intruder. *Has a stalker broken in?* Alya's feet froze and knees locked. Before she could muster the courage to decide what to do—fight or flight—the lights came on with a resounding cheer, 'SURPRISE!'

Karan was the first to emerge, saying, 'Congratulations, babe!' Then, Jayant and Barbara appeared in her field of vision. Bobby and Monica were standing beside them. Karan kissed her and gave her a glass of champagne. He proposed a toast, 'Here's to the winner of the night, woman of the moment, my girl, Alya!' Everyone raised their glasses and partook in the sweet taste of success.

'Bartender, shots!' yelled Karan's best friend, Bobby, over the sound of the music, adding, 'Ten minutes in the darkness can bring out the devil in a man.' Then, he turned to Alya and said, 'Let us see the trophy!' She'd tucked her award under her arm, fearing that an intruder had broken into the house.

She hesitated, not yet ready to share her glory, but now that everyone was inquisitively demanding to see it, she held it up for them to see.

'That's one hot mama!' Bobby remarked on seeing the svelte statuette.

'Watch out, Bob,' the lissom model, Monica, who was Bobby's girlfriend, warned him. 'You're making me jealous,' she kidded. Then, leaning over a coffee table covered with shot glasses, she hollered, 'Bring out the tequila!'

Alya wasn't expecting this excitement at the end of the evening. She had hoped to be in bed by now. Jayant's wife, Barbara, knew that she wasn't big on surprises. Barbara watched mostly foreign language films—she was French Canadian—but knew the ins and outs of the Indian film industry through her husband. He had worked with Alya for years. Barbara congratulated the actress.

'Thanks, Barbs. How are the kids?' Alya responded.

'They're good, honey.' Alya liked it when Barbara called her 'honey'. It had a pleasant ring to it. As a child, she used to enjoy practising foreign accents like Barbara's.

'What are you ladies chatting about?' Jayant joined them.

'We were chatting about your children. How they've grown, how time flies, and how it is truly miraculous, Tondu, that you managed to produce such cute kids!' Alya teased Jayant.

Miracles were indeed happening for Jayant. Aside from having fathered adorable children, he was reaping the rewards of his hard work. Not even his stained teeth—from the cups of chai and Classic cigarettes that saw him through his early days in Bollywood—could embarrass him into not grinning. 'You've done well, Al; very well,' he said.

Shaking the statuette, Alya replied, 'I'm going to put this in the safe.'

'Where are you going, doll?' Karan caught up with his girlfriend as she started cutting through the crowd.

'I'm going to my room.'

'Don't be long,' he told her, with a pat on her buttock.

∞

Alya stood quietly for a moment in the stillness of her room as the accomplishment of the night dawned on her. After stashing her prize in the safe behind her dresser, instead of feeling a sense of satisfaction, of completion, of things coming full circle, she sensed a void opening up inside her. The pregnant pause was disturbingly unlike any in her years of acting. She couldn't understand the reason behind it. She had won, so why this void? An unnerving question was then birthed by the void, a question mired in apprehension: *Is this the beginning or the end?*

The party outside was getting raucous. *What are they celebrating—my victory or their own lives?* Alya went to the balcony of her twenty-fifth-floor apartment. Leaning against the parapet, she drank from the glass of champagne that she had been holding in her hand since it had been given to her. It had lost most of its fizz.

Above the placid waters between one island and the other, suspended by hollow concrete pyramids strung together with shiny beams of steel, hovered the Bandra–Worli Sea Link. Alya gazed at the bridge. It had brought her to the emerald archipelago; if you were on this side of the bridge, you had made it. The value of her apartment had skyrocketed since the completion of the Sea Link, adding to her wealth and gratification. But that day, the bridge didn't evoke the sentiments it normally did when she looked at it. The clouds had lifted and she could see the islands of Mumbai on either end of the bridge. She was familiar with both ends.

On the opposite end were the streets that had enabled her journey across. The map of a particular neighbourhood, at a considerable distance, unfolded before her eyes. It was one of the many colonies in Mumbai located on the edge of a gutter. Alya tried to shrug off the memory, but it stuck to her like a life-sized leech, a creature that lurked in the turbid waters of the colony's dreaded gutter.

⸻

Alya balya bo balya, banana fana fo falya, mean mine mo malya, Alya. As she recollected the rhyme, Alya was drawn down memory lane into a hovel.

The young woman singing the rhyme removed a pot of yellow dal from a single-burner stove, placed it beside a bowl of rice on a plywood counter, which was chipping at the corners, and said, 'Food is ready.'

In her mind's eye, Alya saw herself sitting on a sofa, leafing through a thin spiral-bound script. Her friend's slender fingers, dry around her filed nails, stirred the soupy dal one final time. 'You've been sitting there and reading for more than an hour,' she said, stepping towards Alya. 'It's not a film script.'

'Eisha, stop looming over me. You're a giant in this hobbit house.'

'And what are you? The hobbit?'

'You take up so much space, chica. It makes me nervous when people stand so close, breathing down my neck.'

'True, true. I'm a tall gal. What can I do?' Eisha responded, turning to the kitchenette and spooning equal portions of the dal and rice into two bowls. 'Let's eat.'

The girls dug into their food, sitting on the dilapidated but cosy couch. 'What's taking you so long to read the script? Only your legs have to show in the ad,' Eisha told Alya.

'I'm reading to get familiar with the scenario. Is my character reclining? Is she sitting? Is she standing? Is she walking?'

Eisha then kidded, 'What if she's doing splits?'

'If you weren't so damn gorgeous, Eisha, you'd make a good clown.'

'I'd love to be a clown,' Eisha said, crossing her eyes and sticking her tongue out, making Alya laugh and laughing with her. Their peals of laughter mingled with the sounds of their colony: the hiccups of a passer-by outside their window—a cut-out in the mud-and-brick wall covered with a faded floral curtain—the sawing of a plank by the carpenter next door making cabinets and picture frames for residents of the high rises across the train tracks; and the incessant barking of the stray dogs who had found a plaything in the heroin addict who'd strayed into their slum.

'Work doesn't fall into your lap, chica,' Alya told Eisha, as she watched the latter roll a joint. 'You have to go out and grab what you want by the horns, by the ears, by the balls, any way you can.'

'I'd rather sit here, smoke a joint and wait for Lady Luck to come knocking than run around the city sucking up to other wannabes. Besides, I'm not sure how long I'll hack it out here.'

Eisha lit the joint and passed it to Alya and said, 'It'll help you relax.'

Alya closed her eyes and took a drag. 'I may be four years

older than you but you'll always be the undisputed queen of living-it-up street.'

'Four years is not much.'

'Four years is a lot,' Alya retorted, then, returning the joint to Eisha, added, 'I have to go and shave my legs for the shoot tomorrow.'

'Don't slip into the gutter while you're at it.'

'I'll try not to,' Alya replied wryly and stepped out into the alley.

The girls shared an Indian-style toilet with their landlady and her son. The landlady had been the wife of a master fisherman who owned a fleet of traditional fishing boats. He was a good man who lost his life trying to rescue a man from the sea. He left his fleet and three shacks to his foul-mouthed wife and no-good alcoholic son. The landlady was a shrewd businesswoman; she knew that her tenants were young strugglers who could barely afford basic necessities, including clean drinking water. So, she'd ration pitchers of filtered water to them in return for petty favours.

As she stepped out, Alya dodged a motorcycle. The bike-riding heroes of the slum charged at the women in the alleys to get cheap thrills from watching them jump out of the way. Alya was used to their behaviour, but the cloud of dust that their bikes left in their wake was harder to get used to or get rid of. The omniscient *azaan* that rattled the slum at regular intervals throughout the day served a peculiar yet practical purpose for the girls—it was the only clock reminding them five times a day to rid their room of dust. A fight had broken out at a nearby shack; punches were thrown and bottles broken. Alya lowered her head, hunched her shoulders and walked on. Someone fell against a heap of pots and pans with a resounding clatter. A mother screamed. A child cried. She kept going.

When she reached the toilet at the edge of the gutter adjacent to the colony, she found it occupied. She knocked on its rickety door. 'Bugger off, I'm taking a shit,' she heard a slurred voice coming from the inside.

'How long will you be, Ajay?' Alya asked.

'All night.'

A scrawny, shrivelled arm reached across from behind her and banged on the toilet door, accompanied by a gravelly voice that shouted, 'Out, you useless bum or I'll have you dragged out as you are!' It was the landlady. Handing Alya a package with an address scribbled on it, she said, 'Drop this off tomorrow.'

'I have an important assignment tomorrow, and—'

'It's urgent.'

Alya decided neither to argue with her landlady nor to ask what was inside the package. All she wanted was to shave her legs for the shoot. The fisherwoman filled her lungs with the putrid fumes from the gutter before spewing a barrage of Marathi profanity at the toilet door as it flung open and out came her son. Sniggering and stumbling, he tried to grab Alya. Anticipating his move, she sprang out of the way, leaving him teetering at the brink of the gutter. 'Go on, fall in there! What fun the rats will have eating you up,' she taunted him.

The landlady pulled her son away from the edge of the gutter. 'Don't come home tonight,' she screamed at him as she kicked him on his behind and sent him scampering into the innards of the slum.

Handling the landlady's parcel, a razor, a bar of soap and a towel in the dimly lit and unevenly floored bathroom was a juggling act fit for a circus. Alya splashed water onto her legs from a bucket in the corner and started shaving. When she was done with one leg and was halfway through the other, she lost her footing and fell. The razor slashed her shin. It was a circus act after all: one with blood.

'What happened?' Eisha asked Alya when she limped back into the room, 'Let me see.' She had been unfolding the sofa-cum-bed, preparing to sleep. Alya was leaving soapy and bloody footprints as she stepped towards the bed. 'My God, that's a deep cut,' Eisha exclaimed seeing the blood. She pried the towel out of Alya's hand, wet it under the tap in the kitchenette and wiped the wound. 'Crap! We don't have antiseptic,' she shouted, rummaging through odds and ends on the shelf above the bed. 'What do we do?' she wondered aloud, and then said, 'I'll rub Vaseline on the cut and then tie a cloth around it. That should stop the bleeding.'

Even as Eisha pressed a scarf on the wound and wrapped it around Alya's leg, she didn't whimper. Eisha shook her by the shoulders and called her name. 'Alya! Say something, you're scaring me.'

But for the tears rolling down her cheeks, Alya's face was a blank screen.

'Please don't cry. I know it must be hurting like hell,' Eisha pleaded, trying to be responsible for the first time in her life. 'Can I get you something?' she asked Alya, although they had no money.

There was nothing anyone could do or get to ease Alya's pain because it had nothing to do with her leg. The pain was coming from the profound sense of loss of a golden opportunity. Her tears had nothing to do with her leg, blood or life in a slum. Alya's wound was on the inside. The tears she was shedding were for the loss of a chance at doing something that could have been the beginning of everything.

∞

Returning to the moment, Alya removed her stilettos and stroked her foot against the shin of her wounded leg. The scar was still there. She decided to go back inside the house, to distance herself from the memories of her days on the other side of the bridge, a bridge now crossed, when a set of warm arms took her into their embrace. The soothing smell of Paco Rabanne; the caress of fine cashmere; the touch of tender skin; of hands unaccustomed to labour, which had never rinsed a plate or washed a shirt; were the most comforting things she could ask for. Enveloped in Karan's embrace, she said, 'I don't want to think about it.'

'Think about what, babe?' Karan asked.

'Anything,' she responded, grabbing his collar and pulling him towards her. She nibbled at his chest and cupped his groin with her hand. She pulled his hair and sunk her teeth into his shoulder. Karan was immediately aroused, disarmed by female aggression and the intoxicants he had consumed. He lowered his lips to the nape of her neck and huskily whispered, 'Alya, people are waiting for you at your party.'

Pushing him into the room, she said, 'I want to party in here.' He looked at the door. It was too late. He was on the bed already.

The music from the party and the music of the lovers' moans merged deliriously, ascending past Alya's balcony towards the sky above the Sea Link, to merge with the terrific sounds and secrets lingering there.

∞

3

Reflection

Movie Mania, *Nightlife* and the popular *Jackie Funwala Show* were buzzing with news of the Filmfare Awards. In their cheery little home in Chembur, Reena and her mother were sitting in front of the TV set, watching Jackie Funwala, a popular TV anchor who had two shows on air, hosting the biggest red carpet event of the year in India. Flipping her locks around, in a dance of wig, sparkle and spritz, Jackie looked especially lovely that night, or so Reena thought.

Reena's mother, fondly called Dolly aunty by her daughter's friends, was a diehard Bollywood junkie. Reena had to watch what Dolly wanted to watch because Dolly would rather die than surrender control of the TV set. That the set was in the sitting room, where the family spent most of its time, further diminished the chance of Reena getting a hold of the remote. Thus, she was a captive audience of TV's titillation at 10.00 p.m.

The Jackie Funwala Show was the one entertainment news show Reena tolerated because Jackie, according to her, had more spunk than most of the divas of Tinseltown. She was irreverent and fearless; her ruthless tongue cut through the hard-boiled egos of macho men like a knife cutting through butter: many heroes had been slain by her.

'Sugar plums, don't you think she looks fab? Alya's got such spirit, such...*pizzazz*,' Jackie said, swiping at the screen with her pointy nails.

Dolly was so absorbed in the show that she pricked her finger while sewing a floral garland for the Devi Ma idol, which had been in the family for generations. Ignoring her injured finger, she said, '*Dekh, Reena, Alya bahut achi lag rahi hai, na* [Look Reena, doesn't Alya look beautiful]? She looks pretty. *Aur ye Jackie bhi mast hai* [And this Jackie is really good too]. He is such a good entertainer.'

'She's not as pretty as a lot of other actresses, but, granted, she looks nice here. And mom, Jackie prefers to be referred to as she.'

'Arre, he, she—what difference does it make?'

'To her it does.'

Despite being witty, talented, fashionable and fun, Jackie was only on the brink of being accepted. It was a state Reena related to. Although she was an educated, able-bodied girl from a regular, middle-class family, she felt different.

Watching the parade of beauties sashaying down the red carpet, she thought, *They flaunt, they flirt and they get what they want. What justice is there in this world?* Questions like these led to repeated battles between Reena and her higher self.

'Oh look, Laila and Abbas Ali have arrived,' Jackie said, breathlessly patting her chest. 'Bollywood's power couple!'

As much as Reena admired Jackie's courage, effervescence and otherness, she was beginning to get on Reena's nerves. 'Mom, haven't you had enough? Can't we watch something else?'

'It's Filmfare, *beta*. It doesn't get better than this.'

'Yeah, mom, for you it doesn't get better than this. I'm going to my room. Call me when dinner's served.'

'Okay, beta.'

Reena stopped in front of the mirror in her room to look at her reflection. Reena and the looking glass shared a complex relationship. Although she hated what she saw in it, she couldn't stop looking anyway. She noticed her acne scars and hoped that they'd be less prominent the next time she checked, which, inevitably, would be the next time she walked past a mirror.

Reena drew the curtains and put on a pair of pyjamas. She planned to spend the rest of the evening snuggled in bed with a book, her preferred pastime on the weekends. She'd gone through phases of fancying authors and experimenting with genres until she had developed a fondness for serious literature. Her current book of choice was a particularly challenging read by a Nobel laureate. Reading was not only a hobby for Reena but also an excellent escape from her father's whining about her being single in her thirties. She didn't blame him for it; the predicament was hard to accept for an orthodox South Indian patriarch. Books came to the rescue; they immersed her in the lives of others and, in so doing, circumvented the monotony of her life.

After reading for an hour, Reena noticed that the words on the page were getting jumbled and forming new words with unrecognizable sounds and no meaning. It was her suspected dyslexia—a condition exacerbated by tiredness. To stop the letters from betraying their intended meanings, she started reading slower.

In this regard Reena was unlike her sister, Keya, who had been a model student from the start. She had never brought home a letter of complaint from teachers who were unable to deal with children with varied ways of thinking. She was drawing flawless lines of kohl on her eyelids and weaving French braids when Reena, four years elder to her, was struggling to even tie her shoelaces. Reena still struggled with footwear, tending to wrap her sandal straps the wrong way round. At work too, she struggled, confusing the letters 'b' with 'd' and 'u' with 'v', whereas Keya was on scholarship at a prestigious university in America.

When the author launched into a five-page description of his protagonist, Reena got bored by his infatuation with his own creation and gave up on the book. She opened the second drawer by her bedside table and pulled out a bar of chocolate. Biting into it, she hummed sensuously and then looked around to make sure no one had heard her [knowing well that no one had]. She ate with breathless intent, letting the molten chocolate coat the insides of her mouth. When the bar was gone, she licked the last traces of it off her lips. Reena was in a private world of sensory pleasure when the mobile rang, rudely interrupting her.

'Hello,' she said, answering the call.

'Hi, Rin-rin,' a voice on the other end of the line said.

'Oh, hello Sunanda,' Reena responded.

'What are you up to?' Sunanda asked.

'Umm...nothing. How was your trip to Bali?'

'Oh, was that a *trip*!'

'I'm sure it was. Sunanda, could you please return my bag? The one you borrowed last month for the concert?'

'Chill, Rin, I'm not running off with it.'

'I need it for an event I'm attending—'

'Yeah, yeah, of course, I'll get it back to you. Call me if you want to catch up for drinks, okay?' Sunanda cut Reena short.

'Will do,' Reena said, and then after cutting the line, loudly said, 'Will not!'

Reena had dropped her old group of friends, who used to waltz into her wardrobe unannounced to 'borrow' her things, only for her to never see those things again. The 'friends', however, she used to see too often. They used to make plans to dine at a restaurant, go watch a movie or drink at a bar and, somehow, uncannily the bill would always end up in Reena's lap.

Dropping the old crop had stripped her calendar of many social engagements. However, this decision had not affected her disastrously, not even the loneliness it entailed. Reena had her perfectly legal feel-good fix to all her problems: it's not for nothing that chocolate is called a woman's best friend. She reached for the book again but then decided to get the *Cosmopolitan* hidden behind the mess of clothes in her cupboard—a possible result of cocoa on her oestrogen levels.

'Now *this* goes better with chocolate,' she said, jumping back into bed and turning the pages to a naughty article in the middle of the magazine. It was about the G-spot. Holding the magazine inches away from her nose, lest her reflection in the seemingly omniscient mirror reveal her sexually charged expression, she read voraciously.

The article spoke of ways to stimulate the G-spot—the lubricants, postures and devices that helped with it. 'But hey, I did that backwards position,' Reena said to herself, scrutinizing one of the diagrams alongside the article, 'it didn't work.' She remembered her encounter with the naval captain in London. She had been visiting her uncles, aunts, grand-uncles, grand-aunts, their grandchildren and grandchildren's children with her parents there.

It kept slipping out, she remembered. The thought of the romp got her excited. She started thinking about that guy—not the captain, but the one who she had shown a renovated three-bedroom flat that her father's company had put up for sale. He and his wife were starting a family. When Reena had taken the soon-to-be-father to see the prospective burrow, he had become more interested in getting in her pants than in making the purchase of a lifetime.

'You're not married,' he had said. 'There's nothing stopping you from having some fun. Just lie there and let me pleasure you. I'll do whatever you want.'

It hadn't been a bad idea, in retrospect. Reena reached for her phone and was about to dial his number when she was suddenly and irrevocably confronted with a dilemma, the dilemma, of choice. *Should I? Shouldn't I?* Her eyes roved the room and, despite her best intentions, settled on the miniature painting of Kali hanging on her wall. Her friend Malini had made it for her on her birthday.

When Reena had confided in Malini about the married man, she had said, 'He's bored with his wife and wants action on the side. But girl, be careful. You've got to make up your mind about what you want. You can't be looking for a good man to marry while you have a bad man to screw.'

Startled by the knocking on the door, Reena dropped the magazine on the floor. Regaining composure, she returned it to her cupboard and went back to the family room, heaving a sigh of relief as she went, thankful for the call to dinner that saved her from the burden of choice.

4

A Tea Party

'No, I will not have it. And your mother has also had it with you,' Eisha's father said.

He put on the derisive look he had practised beforehand and continued, 'You get yourself thrown out of school, and then instead of making up for it by taking your correspondence education seriously, you run around like a stray child.' He was out of breath and bothered. Despite his best efforts, behind their round spectacles, the kindness in his eyes was betraying him. It was only when his focus shifted from his daughter to the bony finger he was shaking at her that his derision grew earnest, as if he was reprimanding himself rather than her for being so unmanageable. 'People must think you are an orphan. I'm sure they say, "Where are this girl's parents?"'

Eisha's mother, standing behind her husband, petting her miniature dog, nodded in agreement.

'Nobody knows when you leave or where you go,' the father's upbraiding got louder. 'For God's sake, you're only seventeen! No, I will not permit it,' he declared.

The mother nodded again. If the pooch had been a person, he would also have reacted like a younger brother—laughing at not only the frequency of the rant but also the one-sidedness of the whole argument because, no matter how much energy her father exerted in battle, the seesaw of power always favoured Eisha. The altercation would end only when she decided it was over. Then, she would skip down the stairs with her father's car keys in hand. It was no different today.

Stepping out of the house, Eisha drove her father's car to her favourite haunt—her friend Jayant's house. Jayant lived with his sister, Mukta, on the top floor of a three-storey building in a charming neighbourhood of New Delhi. He was twice Eisha's age, although similar to her in many respects. Jayant had a talent for finding opportunities in the most inopportune situations and a knack for getting his fingers into many pies. Although, at this point in his life, these pies had more crust than filling, it mattered little to him. Jayant was innately confident and calm. He knew that life was about to change. New opportunities would arise.

When Eisha approached the siblings on their rooftop garden, Jayant was talking to his sister, his hand under his shirt, rubbing his flat stomach, 'Delhi is beautiful in December. One can stay outside all day.'

'Yeah, Jayant, I'm sure you'll do just that,' Eisha joined the conversation, '...and I'll join you in doing it. But first, I have to go inside and make a phone call.'

'Alya's already on her way,' Jayant said, pre-empting Eisha's call.

'Not Alya. Malini.'

'Sure, but who's Malini?'

Eisha made her call and returned to the siblings sitting on one side of the rooftop amid a plethora of indigenous plants. Bulbs, bells and ribbons were artfully attached to the bamboo fencing behind them. Creepers twisted their way up a weathered umbrella, reaching for the straw bird dangling from a spoke. Everything about Jayant's home hinted at his creativity. He loved life and was fascinated by the things it had to offer. When he made money from one avenue, he stopped to enjoy the sights and smells before moving on to the next stint. He played golf, cooked and practised yoga. It was this laidback liberality that attracted young people to him—Indians and foreigners alike. He had a way of making people feel at ease.

'What's up, girl?' he asked.

'The usual,' Eisha responded, dropping into one of the cane armchairs Jayant had bought at a garden fair at Pragati Maidan. She nodded at Mukta but got no response. Mukta's eyes were fixed on some invisible spot on the coffee table. Eisha wasn't offended by her unresponsiveness. She was immune to Mukta's vacant stare, so much so that its familiarity was comforting.

'What's up, chica? What's up chico?' Alya asked, entering the balcony just as Jayant was passing a joint to Eisha, 'Sparked up already?' The armchair creaked as Alya dropped into it.

'*Chee, chee*, Alya, I know you have a bad stomach, but in public?' Eisha joked.

'Very funny,' Alya responded sarcastically.

'From where did you pick up these words "chica" and "chico"?' Eisha asked Alya, curious about the lingo.

'From a Spanish model in a movie I watched. It's what she called her friends. It means baby girl and baby boy. Cute, huh?'

'Yeah, alright.'

'So, tell me,' Jayant asked Eisha, 'who is this girl—Malini?'

'Who? What?' Alya said, trying to catch up with the conversation.

'She's just a girl, I guess, a rich one. Her father's a big...

something. Bouncers literally bounced out of the way when we went out the other day. She has her own jeep.'

'How old is this chick?' Alya said.

'Twenty-one, I think,' Eisha replied.

'Same as me.'

'I've called her here to hang out with us.'

'Right now?' Alya asked sceptically.

'Why not' Jayant asked, 'It looks like you have a girl crush, Eisha.'

'You should know better, Jayant. I'm strictly into guys. Not you though—other guys,' Eisha clarified snidely.

'Don't break my heart,' Jayant pretended to be hurt.

Sensing a shift in Mukta's gaze, Eisha quickly passed her the joint.

'So, Al, how does it feel to graduate?' Jayant asked.

'I thought you knew…I dropped out,' Alya informed Jayant.

'I didn't! What are you planning to do now?' Jayant asked.

'Act, maybe,' Alya replied.

Just then, the doorbell rang and Eisha sprang up from her chair. 'That must be Malini!'

'Yippy!' Alya exclaimed, sarcastically.

Eisha brought the new girl and introduced her to the group: 'This is Malini.'

'I'm Jayant, welcome!'

'Hello,' Malini said.

'I'm Alya.'

Malini greeted Mukta; though Mukta didn't answer, everyone noticed the change in her posture. Mukta's head was turned towards the new girl and she was watching Malini intently. A mild smile, imperceptible to the newcomer but highly evident to the rest of the group owing to its general absence, was playing at the corners of her chapped lips. It was the first time Alya had seen Mukta smile. She *had* to get a better look at this girl who had even caught Mukta's attention. Malini was tall and sinewy, but not in a towering or masculine way. Her movements were slight, with a feline grace. She was polished and sophisticated beyond her years. Her taste for the Bohemian—she was wearing a Batik blouse and a Bob Marley medallion—offset these bearings. They were looking at her and the more they looked at her the more her green eyes drew them in, framed as they were by her symmetrical face and raven black hair.

'Malini, please sit,' Eisha said, pulling up a chair, just as Jayant's skinny, middle-aged cook, wearing an old pair of Jayant's shorts two sizes too big for him, entered the balcony.

'Would you like to have tea?' Jayant asked his guests.

They nodded in the affirmative.

'*Paanch cup chai aur samosae* [Five cups of tea and samosas],' Jayant told his cook, who ran back to the kitchen barefoot and silent.

Lighting the joint that had gone out, Alya looked at Eisha and asked, 'So, how did you two meet?'

'We met at a friend's house,' Eisha said. Mukta reverted to staring into blank space. Alya passed the joint to Jayant. 'Malini has a farmhouse with a garden and a pond, where wild ducks from the Yamuna take refuge at night,' Eisha added.

'Come home for lunch before I return to college after the winter holidays,' Malini said to the group.

'We really should. It'll be fun,' Eisha said.

'Yes, it will! We can have a picnic under the mango tree by the pond,' Malini agreed, motioning with her hands for emphasis. Alya noticed the expensive watch on her wrist. The new girl suddenly became irksome.

The cook returned from the kitchen carrying a tray with teacups, a kettle and a plate of samosas. Steam rose from the masala tea as Jayant poured it into the cups and urged his guests to help themselves to the samosas. Mukta's gaze turned to the crispy snacks on the plate. She picked one up and, biting into it, sat up straight. This made Eisha sit up too. Alya folded her arms and placed a leg on the table, preparing for a typical Mukta meltdown. The sheer unpredictability and volatility of the atmosphere created by his sister turned Jayant into a statue that could aptly be called, 'Man with Cup and Kettle'. It was a matter of seconds between Mukta taking a bite of the samosa and then spitting it out. 'What kind of shit samosa is this?' Mukta yelled angrily. Jayant overcame his momentary paralysis and continued pouring tea into the cups.

'This weasel you've adopted here can't make a decent roti and you've got him making samosas?'

'No, Mukta,' Jayant replied, passing a cup to Malini with practiced calm. 'The samosas are from Haldiram.'

'They're yummy, aren't they?' Eisha asked, trying to lower the rising temperature on the rooftop garden, 'Haldiram has good stuff.'

'Who the fuck is Haldiram?' Mukta demanded rudely.

'Haldiram's not a person. It's a shop. Everyone in Delhi knows it,' Eisha said.

'She knows it too. Mukta, go inside for a while. You'll feel better,' Jayant told his sister.

'Why should I go inside? You go inside. This is my house as much as it's yours. I'll do what I want, when I want to. I'll stand or sit where I want to and when I want to,' Mukta said, her voice rising in anger.

'Did you say "shit where I want to"?' Alya said, finding humor in the unfolding scene.

'Alya, please, don't make it worse,' Eisha cautioned.

Malini sipped on her tea.

'This is *our* house,' Jayant said, reaching for Mukta's hand, 'Relax now. Take it easy.'

'Take it easy? You take it easy!' Mukta answered back, snatching the plate of samosas from Jayant and throwing them one by one at him.

'They're samosas, Mukta, not water balloons. It's not Holi,' Alya said, laughing.

Jayant got up, walked to the door leading to the stairs to the ground floor and said, 'Come on girls, let's go.'

Eisha, Alya and Malini followed, as did Mukta. When everyone but Mukta had made it through the door, Jayant pushed the door shut on his sister and locked it. Guilty as it made him feel, he knew it was his only available restraint.

'It's okay,' Eisha said, putting her arm around Jayant, who was a head shorter than her. Stroking his hairline—which was significantly receded for a man not quite middle-aged yet—Eisha told him to let it go.

'Malini, I'm sorry you had to witness this scene on your first visit to my house,' Jayant said.

'Hey, no worries. Every family has its anomalies,' Malini said.

None of them knew what that meant, and it didn't matter. Jayant was relieved she had been unperturbed by the incident.

'What a mad hatter!' Alya quipped.

Pointing to the park across the street from the line of houses, Malini said, 'What a pretty garden.'

'How about a stroll?' Eisha asked Jayant.

'That's a good idea,' he said, the prospect reviving him.

As they walked around the park, their chatter excited the rhesus monkeys living in the Mughal-era ruins skirting the block. As the balmy December afternoon transformed into a cool evening, lights came on in the surrounding homes. Parrots and crows started flying back to their nests. All was wintery wonderful. But not so much for a set of parents elsewhere in the city, wound up in anxious knots, awaiting the return of their runaway daughter.

5

The Old Man and the Tree

Reena suffered few dilemmas of choice when she was seventeen; she did whatever she wanted and was impressed by whoever she encountered. Reena and her friends were getting more exposure than ever before, thanks to liberalization. But, what they weren't getting more of was pocket money. With funds too limited to pursue other, more wholesome, recreations, pitching in to buy a packet of hashish was the only worthwhile leisure activity they could think of.

Everyone that was cool smoked hash. They gathered on rooftops or in parks, the mangroves or even at the Gateway of India. If you happened to have a buck and wanted a bang, Goa was all the rage. Running off to Goa, with its white sand beaches and laid-back vibe, was the coolest thing to do; and that's exactly what Reena did.

She casually strolled up to the local ATM one day and withdrew a fat sum from her father's account (how she knew his password remains a mystery). Then, she hopped onto a bus with Sunanda, Bobby, Priya and Avi—and off they went to Goa. The further the bus got from Mumbai, the more distant her problems—over-protective parents, perfect prissy sister, the day she attempted to guzzle a litre of drain cleaner after failing her board exams, the city full of mirrors—seemed. Nothing and no one could bother her where she was going. Reena was embarking on an adventure.

Goa was green, but Reena was seeing more of it than there was thanks to the pizza the group had eaten with magic mushrooms as a topping after getting off the bus. The mushrooms heightened her perception of colour. Legally, she'd done no wrong. The hallucinogenic fungus was not a banned substance. Bobby and Sunanda had scored the mushrooms from a hippie who had sourced them from a picturesque plantation in Ooty, where they grew imperceptibly in the moist mud under the shade of the mist-fed tea leaves.

After the hearty, drug-infused meal, the group decided to trek on a broad path, traversed by the local crowd—fishermen with nets, women carrying baskets of fresh catch, skimpily clad foreign tourists and Romeos in dark glasses ogling at the skimpily clad tourists. After a couple of hours, when the mushrooms had really kicked in, the teenagers became lone travellers on a narrowing path. Giant plants clawed and caressed them as they made their way to an unknown place. A golden light, obstructed by criss-crossing branches, dappled the forest floor and played hide-and-seek with the ghostly shadows in the undergrowth. Reena stopped to marvel at the sheer beauty of a leaf. She touched the leaf and it spoke to her, its silver veins beseeching her to sit and admire it for all eternity. Walking through this marvellous nowhere, forgetting who or what she was, Reena became one with nature. Twilight fell. The last of the butterflies seemed to disappear into clouds of sparkling pixie dust. A deafening cacophony of crickets claimed the forest. In the black of night, the group arrived at their destination—The Tree. Bobby, the eldest of the group, was their undeclared leader. When he suggested that they camp under The Tree, the others agreed.

So the purpose of the nearly seven-hour trek had been to reach a circular opening in the forest, the size of a football field, and shelter beneath The Tree. Reena had never seen such a mothership of a tree, even in a science fiction movie. They pitched their tents among the tendrils tumbling from The Tree and anchored them into the earth.

There they were, with the hippies they wanted to live among. It was true, paradise was not lost. Just as they finished pitching their tents, a man with piercing blue eyes and a white beard till his navel emerged from the maze of tendrils with his silvery hair swishing behind him. He gazed at Reena and smiled. Then, he parted the roots and returned from whence he had come. The group followed him.

The sanctum of The Tree was immune to the elements—nothing could get through, not rain, light, hail or mist. The old man sat down on a velvet cushion in a circle of rugs on the ground around a fire. The travellers sat on either side of him. He leaned over a brocade bolster and opened a toolbox of knick-knacks and pulled out a totemic stone object. The object, a *chillum*, had birds, insects, flora and fauna engraved on it. At the centre of the organic profusion was the symbol of the cosmic sound, 'Aum'.

The old man filled the chillum with a mixture of hash and tobacco. He chanted, '*Bom Shiv Shankar,*' and took deep drags of smoke from the chillum. He held the smoke inside his lungs for a few beats and then blew it out in the shape of a dragon that passed over Reena's shoulder and disappeared into the expanse beyond. The whites of his eyes changed shades and finally settled on a glazed red hue. The travellers availed of the pipe until they were all cocooned in a delirious fog.

None of them could recall how long they sat there, staring at the tongues of fire lapping at the locks of The Tree, gaping into its infinite canopy, ogling at the roots beneath their feet. Reena couldn't remember when she fell asleep or whether she ate.

She awoke the next morning to the sounds and smells of breakfast cooking on a crackling fire. Avi, the quietest of the lot, was making pancakes. The teens had come prepared. They had carried basic provisions and three sets of clothing in their backpacks. In the early afternoon, revived and refreshed, they took a walk around The Tree. The forest folk were washing clothes and hanging them up on lines to dry, they were decorating their tents, braiding hair and making necklaces with beads and semi-precious stones. Children were swinging on a plank tied to a branch with ropes of hemp while their parents relaxed in hammocks.

Who are these people? Where have they come from? Reena mused, knowing only that they were the friendliest folk she'd ever met. They offered no introductions and asked for none either but when they spoke, it was with a friendliness befitting people sharing a common planet. Reena pictured herself living here, among these people, under this tree. The simple life appealed to her. After exchanging some niceties, the people told the teenagers about a pristine beach just a kilometre away. They left to find it.

∽∞∽

The line between the forest and the beach was so distinct that it blinded the group as they stepped out onto the beach. When Reena had adjusted to the change from cool and dappled forest to hot and glaring beach, she saw the vast expanse of sea, sand

and sky, with fluffy clouds unfurling like a silk-screen print before her. She watched her friends rush past her and dive into the water. The ocean was beckoning her; she could hear it. She wanted to go in. If only she could swim.

Kicking up clods of wet sand, chasing crabs and poking at the starfish scattered on the shore, Reena relinquished her self-consciousness—that feeling of being watched and judged as if she were onstage. Out of sight, down a bend along the beach, she flung off her clothes and charged into the water stark naked. With every step she took, the sand rushed away from under her feet with the alive and moving water, while the current pulled her forward. Reena had never felt so wanted. Like a fish that was stranded on the shore, dry and breathless, she strained towards the horizon, her body tingling and shivering against the lapping waves. When her toes could barely touch the seabed, she surrendered to the ocean and let her body float. Reena was deaf to the chatter in her mind when she saw them—a family of dolphins springing out of the water as if propelled by an invisible force. To see dolphins, not fifty feet away from her, in their natural habitat was awe-inspiring. She was convinced that God was watching her. She felt special. 'I *am* somebody,' she proclaimed to the world and to herself.

༺☙༻

The group went to the shore every afternoon from then on, and at night they ate with the tree-dwelling folk. This remained their routine for the rest of the week until, after consuming the last of their mushrooms on the beach while watching the sunset, they returned to a party under The Tree.

The community considered the full moon to be sacred, and they commemorated it each month with a celebration.

Reaching the periphery of the settlement, Reena's group came upon effigies of gods and goddesses as big as the floats from the Republic Day Parade. Lanterns were hanging from the high branches of The Tree, revealing the tangled pattern of its organic roof. The triplets that scoured the woods for beetles to gift to their parents wore straw hats covered with multicoloured sponges while their mother, dancing beside them, wore a purple dress with a necklace made of fluorescent grasshoppers. She was the fairy queen and they, her elfin offspring. Everyone was in costume. Lords and jesters roamed around The Tree, while the Wolf and Little Red Riding Hood sat on a bench, watching the marvellous world.

Reena danced barefoot on the cane mats spread on the uneven ground until the soles of her feet were numb. The gods smiled. The gods frowned. *Did they frown*? She would never know. Her mind was playing games. The lanterns were leaving trails. The Wolf was chasing Little Red Riding Hood around the trunk of The Tree. A clown made a lewd gesture. *Why did he do that?* When she looked again, he was dancing gaily. Reena reminded herself that she was in a magic mushroom world, where clouds could become dinosaurs and clowns perverts.

So wildly was her head grooving to the music that she could have easily missed the old man, but so grounded was his form in the midst of the movement that he was hard to miss. Reena wasn't sure if it was his appearance that had stopped her or his stillness. Dressed in the likeness of Lord Brahma he was standing before her, watching her with serenity and stillness while she watched him with the chaos of her mind. His gaze shifted to the opening in the wilderness from whence they had come and, as he did so, the iridescence around his sapphire eyes disappeared. The unsavoury men that loitered at the cafés rimming the forest had found the place and were spreading like a sickness: forcing themselves on the women, rummaging through belongings wrapped in neat bundles, disseminating unrest as they rampaged through the commune. Reena's head spun.

What happened next may never be known, while what happened after that cannot be forgotten. A blinding light awoke her; not the light of the heavenly beach. A loud noise stunned her; not the cacophony of the birds and crickets of the forest. Water was splashed on her face; not a friendly splash from a fellow tree-dweller waking her up for a cup of coffee. It was muddy water splashed by a passing rickshaw at a crowded intersection in broad daylight that brought Reena back to her senses.

Rushing past a red light, an even larger and more unwieldy vehicle charged at her. She was unable to spring out of harm's way in time. Inches from severing her leg at the ankle, the truck veered away. Reena lifted herself up onto her blistered feet, faintly recollecting dancing on rough mats spread over uneven ground the night before. *Or had it been the night before that?* She couldn't recall. She turned a corner in search of a familiar landmark and came upon a menacing street dog defending his turf. Pinned against the wall with the dog barking at her, she asked herself, *Where am I? How did I get here?* Questions floated like chunks of debris in the waters of her mind. *I'm starving! Where are my belongings? My head is about to explode. My money...where is it?* She reached into the pockets of her denim shorts and found ten rupees. All the panic buttons in her mind were pushed to a nuclear capacity at that moment. She tried to make sense of the fragmented images in her head—not an easy task for a brain fried on hallucinogens.

With ten rupees to her name, no idea where she was and, more importantly, how she got there, Reena decided to do the only rational thing she could think of—call Dad.

6

Pride and Pain

She watched her father from across the desk in their office, wishing she could share the surge of love she was feeling for him in her heart. He had been so patient with her, so forgiving. Looking up from his work, he noticed the expression of serenity on her face and took the opportunity to tell her what he had been waiting to say for a long time. 'Beta, you have to stop getting angry at the clients. They'll run away and we'll end up losing business that we can't afford to lose—and that's no fun.'

Reena felt the tenderness in her heart reducing as she said, 'Dad, they're a bunch of unprincipled cheats.'

'At this level they're all the same, understand that. We're small fry. We have to make the most out of the people we get. That's the challenge.'

'I can't promise anything, but I'll try.'

The phone rang and Reena picked it up, 'Yes, Mr Chandrashekhara,' she said, glancing at the calendar on the desk. 'Yes Sir, we have three flats that meet your needs. Does Thursday work for you? Okay. Done. I am forwarding you the address of the one in Khar. That's right… We can take it from there. Thank you and goodbye, Mr Chandrashekhara.'

The father looked at his daughter with pride. Despite her shortcomings and past follies, she was doing well; she was helping him run the family business. Even so, his burgeoning pride was pricked by pain. She was in her mid-thirties and not yet married. The situation was not only embarrassing but also of grave concern. What if he failed to find her a husband?

Lord, if only my dear girl were married. Nothing would make me happier. If she were married, I'd be free of my biggest responsibility. If she were married, I'd be free to live and die.

7

Organza

California, no time to party [...] In the city of LA [...]
Keep it rockin...

The club was thumping with the catchy tune. It was holiday season, a Friday night, and the first anniversary of Organza—the swankiest club in town. Malini and Eisha had many reasons to celebrate. They had become close friends. So close that Eisha stayed at her house whenever Malini came home for semester break from college. They walked around the pond, swam in the pool and played with the dogs in the lawn. They shopped for tribal wear at Janpath and went for high tea at the Imperial Hotel. Malini was back for summer vacation. Now that Eisha was nineteen, the daytime vanishing acts that she used to pull on her parents had become blasé. She was now a pro at making nocturnal disappearances that took her to places that they couldn't dream of, such as the charged, taboo environs of a nightclub.

Seeing them approach, the bartender let out a low whistle. Delhi was famous for its gorgeous women, but the ones coming his way were in a whole other league.

'What can I get for you ladies?' the bartender asked.

'What will you have, Eisha?' Malini asked Eisha.

'I'll have what you're having,' Eisha responded.

'Let me see. How about a Cosmopolitan? They can get sweet though,' Malini said, thinking aloud. 'Scotch and water on ice... Yup, that'll be it.'

'Coming up,' the bartender said, starting to mix their drinks.

They turned to the dance floor packed with people moving to hip-hop, a musical genre most of them had developed a taste for only recently. A disco ball was spinning overhead, casting shards of light that bounced off metallic pillars and replicas of Ming vases standing against walls dressed in blue silk. Malini was familiar with the liberated vibe and unapologetic opulence of clubs abroad. Watching her friend so enthralled was giving the night's outing new worth and meaning. Organza was a first in the country. The club was swanky, played good dance music, had an exhilarating atmosphere and somehow, inexplicably, was the only club in the city that managed to stay open beyond the legal closing time of 1.00 a.m.

'Your drinks, ladies,' the bartender said, pushing their glasses towards them across the bar.

> I'm too sexy for your body [...]too sexy for your body
> [...]the way I'm disco dancing. I'm a model, you know
> what I mean, and I do my little turn on the catwalk [...]
> on the catwalk, yeah, I shake my little tush on the catwalk.

As the music continued playing, the friends hopped onto the dance floor. Everyone was drawn in by the popular track—everyone but the 'range rovers'. These were the people who—no matter where they went, what they did or who they did it with—were always on the prowl. Eisha was scanning the room with military precision. The only song that appealed to her when she was this tuned in was 'I Need a Man'. And she was not seeking just any man, it was a particular type of man: well-connected and wealthy, attributes most attractive to Eisha. The hot number dancing beside her, trying to get her attention, hadn't gone unnoticed. But he could never make the cut—not with his ripped jeans and bedhead; unless he was an international rock star.

Eisha had trained hard to hone her skills. It took her minutes to identify a potential candidate. He was tall, well-dressed and, as a bonus, part White. She knew she had to be careful though; experience had taught her that appearances could be deceiving. There were many good-looking and well-dressed boys out there without a penny in their pockets—male versions of her. She had to make sure he was not one of them. She watched him get a drink at the bar and noticed a platinum American Express card slide out of his snakeskin wallet. Malini was too engrossed in the music to notice Eisha put on her most provocative expression. It was when their eyes locked that she noticed that the candidate was not as good looking as she had previously thought. His nose was off-centre, leaning enough to the right to make it distracting. It was also difficult to tell if she had, indeed, caught his eye; the poor sod—well, not exactly poor—was dreadfully cross-eyed. But Eisha was not going to let negligible obstacles dash her hopes. She turned up the intensity of her gaze. Now, she was sure she had caught his eye. He was standing motionless on the dance floor, his nose pointed in her direction. What Eisha failed to notice, absorbed in her manoeuvres, was that she had managed to get someone else's attention too—a woman who was livid on seeing another female trying to steal her meal ticket.

'Eisha, want another drink? Eisha?' Malini asked her.

'Umm, err, yes,' Eisha replied distractedly.

Malini put a cigarette between her lips as they waited for their drinks at the bar. Before she could light it, a velvety voice said, 'May I?'

Malini lifted her head, and replied, 'You may.'

The man lit the cigarette with his Zippo and then, lighting his own, introduced himself, 'I'm Gaurav.'

'I'm Malini, and this is my friend, Eisha,' Malini responded.

'Pleasure,' Gaurav said.

Eisha noticed the fine fabric of his tailored suit. He wasn't wearing a tie and the top button of his white shirt was open, giving him a crisp yet informal look and a sneak peek at his chiselled chest.

'Are you two sisters?' he asked.

'You could say that,' Malini replied, blowing smoke away from him.

The women looked nothing like each other, but they exuded an uncanny resemblance that often confused people. The way they dressed and did their hair and make-up was similar. It had come to this: if Malini lined her eyes with blue, Eisha did too; if Malini wore high-heeled shoes, Eisha did the same. Even their steps appeared to be synchronized when they walked together. Eisha's tendency to emulate Malini was not a mystery to Malini. She didn't mind it. She saw Eisha as the sister she never had.

'Are you from Delhi?' Gaurav asked.

'Yes, we're from here. And you?' Malini responded.

'I went to boarding school in England and just graduated from MIT.'

'Are you here on holiday to see your parents?'

'Not exactly,' Gaurav said. 'I've returned to join the family business.'

'Ah, I see. Thank you for the light, Gaurav,' Malini said, putting out her cigarette. 'It was good talking to you,' she added, settling the bill before she left.

The women in the Ladies Room were powdering their noses in more ways than one. Some were gossiping on the daybed while others were waiting in queue for the cubicles. 'Didn't you find that guy…interesting?' Eisha asked Malini as they waited in line.

'He has potential,' Malini responded.

'He liked you,' Eisha said.

'I don't want to get into a long-distance relationship. I've been there, and it was messy. You know how the saying goes, "once bitten twice shy",' Malini explained.

'What're you talking about, Malini? He's loaded!'

'I still have two years left at college,' Malini told her. 'I'll be open to new beginnings when I get my degree and am back for good.'

'Okay, up to you,' Eisha shrugged it off.

'Imagine the fun we'll have!'

'Yes, I'm looking forward to it.'

'But hold on, aren't you moving to Bombay? You mentioned something like that,' Malini asked.

'I'm thinking of trying my luck at modelling. Alya's already there. We'll be sharing the shithole she's rented in some shitty colony,' Eisha explained.

'She's really going for it. Kudos to her.'

'Her mother isn't happy about her Bollywood dreams. She's not supportive of the decision.'

'Alya's a tough girl. I'm sure she'll succeed.'

'Yeah, maybe.'
'When are you leaving?'
'In about six or seven weeks.'
'Are you excited?'
'Bombay is happening, they say, so I guess I'm excited.'
'How do your parents feel about it?'
'For once, they're not stopping me.'
'I'm sure they think it'll make you more responsible,' Malini said affectionately, but it came across as condescending to Eisha. 'I mean…it'll help you become independent.' Guilty about unintentionally offending her, Malini added, 'I'm sure it'll be an enriching experience.'

'Gosh, that took long!' Eisha exclaimed when their turn to use the lavatories finally came.

Music blaring, heads spinning, arms thrashing—Organza was reaching its climax. Bodies rubbed against each other and the smell of sweat mingled with that of alcohol as the temperature rose. Catching sight of her man amid the pandemonium, Eisha employed every move in her repertoire to get his attention—writhing to the rhythm of the music with a seductiveness that could put the finest belly dancers to shame. Raising her arms above her head and drawing circles with her hips, she performed for him and, in so doing so, provoked her competitor—who had been staring at her with hatred so intense that it could have drilled holes in her if she'd been any closer. Malini headed to the door leading out to the patio. Eisha followed her, glancing over her shoulder and giving the man a 'come-hither' look as she went.

Outside, the Ashoka trees were swaying in a mild breeze and bowls brimming with scented water offered them a welcome respite from the crowded club. They got themselves bottles of water and, leaning against a lamp post, engaged in light banter. Eisha saw her man come out onto the patio. It was the opportunity she had been waiting for and she was not going to let it pass. Taking sweeping strides, she went up to him. But, just as she was about to make his acquaintance, a flash of crimson flew at her from the darkness.

Eisha flung her arms up with all the force her inebriated frame could muster. The creature fell off, but was back in a snap. With concerted effort, she detached herself from her attacker again. The platinum blonde in a red bomber jacket and leather pants was a tough contender. She attacked Eisha with renewed fervour, intent on causing maximum damage.

Malini was convinced that she was on some kind of hardcore drug, like methamphetamines. 'Please, if we've wronged you in any way, I beg for your forgiveness,' Malini pleaded with the attacker. The woman was beyond pacification. Shoving Malini aside with inhuman energy, she dug her claws into Eisha's scalp and grabbed a fistful of her hair. Although the woman was smaller than Eisha, she seemed to have acquired the strength of a rogue elephant.

People gathered around, watching Eisha being dragged by her hair over the gravel walkway. She was trying to get up, but her tight skirt was making it difficult. Malini attempted to untangle the woman's fingers out of her friend's hair. The fingers loosened only to get a better grip.

'Oxana, baby, stop it,' her boyfriend finally found his voice. Someone in the crowd screamed. A drop of blood was trickling down Eisha's hairline to the middle of her forehead and along the bridge of her nose. A few drops more and three streaks of blood partitioned her face and turned her blouse into a macabre piece of abstract art. The man pulled his girlfriend off and away from Eisha, even as the crowd stared at her crying on her knees in the gravel.

'Don't give them the pleasure of seeing you cry,' Malini said, helping her up. 'Come on, let's get the hell out of here.'

Holding her friend in her arms, Malini cut through the crowd. She was unable to understand, for the life of her, how a night that started so agreeably could have gone so horribly wrong.

8

A Brother

The plump leather couch Alya had installed in her office for taking power naps was providing little relief to her sore bottom. Reclined, Cleopatra-esque, she commanded, 'Pull down the blinds!'

'You're wearing dark sunglasses,' Jayant responded.

'I know,' Alya said, adjusting her Prada shades, 'it's still too bright.'

Jayant squeezed half a lemon into the concoction he was making to help his boss recover from her hangover. 'It's my specialty—an orange and aloe energizer with a stick of celery. It'll take the edge off the soreness of all kinds.'

Alya licked her dry lips and took a sip of the juice.

'I don't remember you having much alcohol yesterday,' Jayant commented.

'I was drinking with lover boy in my room, chico,' Alya responded.

'I don't want to ask you what you were drinking,' Jayant joked.

'Don't be crass.'

'Cocktails, I mean.'

'Jayant, seriously, I don't have energy to kid around.'

'Al, there's work to be done. It has just been parties and fun since the Filmfare Awards. You have a big day ahead of you. Your schedule, in fact, is crammed for weeks.'

'Shoot.'

'You have three directors to meet this week, five narrations, an interview, a dinner engagement and a photo shoot for a fashion magazine.'

'What about the gig in Lucknow?'

'I got a call this morning from R.R. Gupta. Your performance at his daughter's wedding has been cancelled.'

'Cancelled? Why?'

'All the star appearances have been cancelled.'

'What about the ₹30 lakh they paid me in advance?' The prospect of returning the money troubled Alya more than her hangover and sore bottom combined.

'You get to keep the money. The *gutka* king's offices were raided this weekend by the income tax department. He's feeling the heat. He wants to avoid more attention, so he's cancelled the star appearances at the wedding. Everybody gets to keep the advance.'

'Have you sent pictures of my holiday in South Africa to the publicist?'

'It's done.'

'Karan's not in any of them, is he?'

'Of course not, I sent the ones of you feeding the mother and baby giraffes and some of you scuba diving with the *firang* instructor. Very nice.'

'"Very nice" is not important, Jayant. People need to see that Alya is compassionate, adventurous and experimental.'

'I know. Image is everything. They will.'

'Moving on, what's on the agenda for today?'

'You have a dental appointment at 3.00 in the evening, a meeting with Minty Bose at 6.00 and dinner at Laila and Abbas Ali's house.'

'That means I'm free for the next two hours.'

Jayant double-checked the calendar on his smart phone. 'There's a famous saying: Be careful what you wish for because you just might get it,' he said.

'Yes, yes. I know. I'm a star. I have no time—least of all for myself.'

'You said it.'

'I'm perfectly fine with that. Now, chico, I have to go,' Alya said, rising with some effort, 'I'm meeting Vishal at his hotel.' She paused before the mirror and applied blush on her cheeks and gloss on her lips, then, straightening her back and flipping her hair to one side, waltzed out of the office with the vitality of a woman half her age. Jayant smiled. That was Alya. She was good at what she did—make believe.

༄༅

'Papa said you wouldn't come,' the toddler said, running into her aunt's arms, 'I'm so happy you did.'

'You told her I wasn't coming?' Alya asked her brother.

Vishal shrugged his shoulders.

'Papa said you were busy.'

Alya opened her handbag and pulled out the freckle-faced doll with strawberry-blonde curls she had bought at the Charles de Gaulle Airport and said, 'Look who's come all the way from Paris for you!'

'Thank you, *bua*,' the little girl said.

Alya kissed Vishal, her sunglasses brushing against his cheek, and commented 'Soni's grown.'

'She's so much like you. Her poor mother has to hear it from everyone,' Vishal replied. The siblings laughed mischievously. 'Mom was looking at your childhood pictures the other day and she said it too,' he added.

'How is mom?' Alya asked, removing her sunglasses and setting them on the table. 'How are things back in Australia?'

'You helped us with the business. Thanks to you, it's all good.'

'Glad to hear it.'

'Alya, I know how independent you are,' Vishal told his sister as they sat down to talk, 'but I see it as my duty, and my privilege, to be honest and direct with you. May I?'

'Men nag too. I read it in a magazine, Bhai. Really, it's a fact and you're the proof.'

'You've achieved everything you set out to—'

'And now it's time to start thinking about starting a family—isn't that what you're going to say?' Alya interrupted Vishal.

'Something like that, yes.'

'It'll happen when it has to happen.'

'Sometimes we have to make things happen. Difficult choices are a part of life. You know that better than anyone.'

'Relax, Bhai. Don't worry. You'll get indigestion. As they say, "*Hajmola khao, khush ho jao* [Eat a Hajmola and be happy]".'

'It's smart to prioritize your career, of course, but what if you keep going and then look back one day and regret not shifting gears? That's my concern. Just for a bit, think of giving some importance to other matters—of the personal kind. I don't want you to have regrets.'

'Papa, I want milk,' Soni interrupted.

'Alright, sweetheart.'

'I want chocolate milk.'

'We'll have to see if they have chocolate milk,' Vishal

responded, getting up to look at the minibar.

Alya watched little Soni tie a napkin around the doll's strawberry curls with her uncoordinated fingers. She had a round face with a pug nose and sparkling, lively eyes. Alya loved that the girl resembled her; something about it made her heart swell with a hitherto unknown emotion. Suspecting that it could be a game changer—a potential speed breaker in her road ahead—she picked up the day's edition of the *Bombay Times* from the table in front of her. It was a clever diversion, but one that turned out to be nearly as unsettling as the untoward emotion. At the bottom of the front page, she read the headline, 'Danny's Drive to Save the Mangroves.' Beside the article was a photograph of a ruggedly handsome man, standing in thigh-high gumboots in Mumbai's endangered mangroves.

'There's no chocolate milk,' Vishal told his daughter, giving her a glass of regular milk instead, 'Sugar's not good for you anyway...'

'Bhai, did you place this here?' Alya demanded, waving the newspaper at him.

Vishal feigned ignorance.

'You wanted me to see it,' Alya continued.

Vishal didn't reply.

'Why are you doing these immature things?'

'What happened with Danny? I thought you loved him,' Vishal said.

'It didn't work out, okay? I'm with Karan now.'

'Then why not move it to the next level?'

Just then, they heard loud voices coming from outside the boutique hotel. Parting the curtains, Alya saw a crowd of at least eighty people gathered at the gates; fans who had discovered that she was inside. The bell rang. It was her bodyguard. 'I should get going, Bhai,' she said.

Soni was playing with her aunt's sunglasses, putting them on and taking them off the doll's face. Alya gently pried them out of the child's hands and kissed her goodbye. Putting the glasses back on, bodyguard in tow, she strode out of the room. Vishal entered the elevator with her.

The crowd at the gates went berserk on seeing the actress come onto the porch. Her car was waiting for her, but she didn't get in. She stood beside it, waving at her fan club of whistling youths; housewives and maids taking a break from their soap operas and chores; and office bearers out on a late lunch break. Receptionists, doormen, hotel guests—everyone was overcome by inertia at the sight of the superstar. Alya blew kisses at the crowd. Emboldened, people pushed past the guards and into the compound. The lucky ones who made it through were gifted a scribble by the actress. Vishal saw his sister blushing due to the attention. Her bodyguard urged her to leave, but she didn't move; intoxicated by the adrenaline rush. 'Ma'am, we really should go,' the bodyguard warned again. People were getting rowdy.

Vishal was heckled and shoved by fans trying to get to his sister. 'Goodbye sis,' he called out to her and turned to go back inside the hotel, 'Take care.' His voice was drowned in the madding crowd.

9

Ali Mansion

The ocean around Bandstand was hungry. It smashed the fading rays of the sun against jagged rocks and devoured the quivering shards of light that were falling back onto its waves. Like yin and yang, the coupling of the restful sky and raging waters created a unique harmony, similar to the various neighbours that constituted the neighbourhood on Bandstand's shore.

A purple S-Class Mercedes whizzed along the coastal road, contributing to the drama of the terrain, making weekend revellers lose interest in nature and marvel at the genius of mechanics. A Hummer zoomed by, followed by a Rolls Royce Phantom. The swanky cars were headed to Laila and Abbas Ali's mansion. Less a mansion and more a monument, the Bandstand address was the embodiment of India's ever-growing might in film-making; a testament to how the earning power of home-grown stars was fast catching up to their Hollywood contemporaries. Indian stars towered over the public sphere—above politicians, cricketers and corporate tsars. They made more than magic; they had the power to change perceptions.

Despite the young cocks relentlessly pecking at his heels, Abbas Ali—no spring chicken—was still the undisputed, incomparable, ruler of the roost. He was the reigning champion of Bollywood. The actor was not only dazzling on-screen but also a marketing wizard who had single-handedly turned himself into a bona fide brand. But, as is well known, there's no pressure like the pressure of being on top. How long Abbas stayed supreme was to be seen. He wasn't breaking a sweat though. Not yet. He was at the peak of his game as was his house at a height on Bollywood Boulevard.

The iron gates of Ali Mansion opened at the flip of a switch and the cars lined up outside were allowed in. To the throngs perpetually gathered at its gates, it was a mystery: Was the house like the Neverland Ranch, a garish place of worship or the Mumbai Bar Dancer's Association? Did the Alis' have a leopard as a pet, a terracotta warrior or ivory elephants? The mysteries of Ali Mansion were known solely to the privileged few allowed entry and speculated about by those who were disallowed.

Alya stepped out of Karan's Lamborghini, resplendent, an image of chiselled perfection. Dr Chopra's lipo wand had created a flawless masterpiece out of Alya. It was not without reason that Dr Chopra was called Mumbai's Michelangelo. Placing his hand on the curve of Alya's back, Karan led the impeccable woman past the teak doors and into the house. He was familiar with the place. There was no place Karan, debonair man from one of the founding families of the city, was not familiar with or welcome to.

Ali Mansion had many exceptional features and objets d'art, but the most outstanding of these, known to be a reflection of Abbas's extraordinary personality—his alter ego—was Flapjack. He was no ordinary robot of wire and steel, wheeling around the house serving olive hors d'oeuvres and titbits on toothpicks.

Flapjack was a self-aware, state-of-the-art robot made of cosmetic cartilage and silicon flesh. He was programmed with the latest artificial intelligence. He had expressions and a sense of humour. Alya watched him amusing guests with wisecracks, even as they clamoured to shake his hand. Flapjack was wearing blue suspenders strapped over a black satin shirt, patent leather brogues and a bowler hat from Bond Street. He reminded Alya of Johnny Depp in *Edward Scissorhands*. The robot was an expensive piece of technology, costing an arm, a leg, two kidneys and a heart, sure to make the Hollywood actor he resembled blink in amazement. That he came at such a hefty price was only logical; he was designed to satisfy *all* of Abbas's needs, wherever and whenever they arose. Superstar Ali had always dreamed of two things: one was a robot he could call his own and the other was a trip to the moon. He chose Flapjack.

'Dah-ling Alya!' Laila Ali greeted the actress. 'You've lost weight.'

'Thanks Laila, you shouldn't be talking. No one would guess you have three children! You look like a supermodel.'

'Aw, that's sweet.'

Laila held Flapjack by the arm and commanded him to tell her husband that she'd be with him shortly.

'Yes Ma'am,' the bot answered and left to do her bidding.

'Feel at home,' Laila told the couple.

Karan and Alya went to the lawn and sat beside a stream gurgling over moss-covered rocks and into a pond with lilies. Karan lit a cigarette. As much as Alya wanted one, she would never be seen smoking in a place like this; in the presence of acclaimed directors, producers, agents, actors, corporate honchos and their glittering wives and some would argue, people with a more dubious character, like escorts and dons.

'Why do you care about what people think?' Karan asked, offering her a cigarette.

'You can afford not to care, Karan, but I can't,' Alya responded.

'You're a star. You don't need to care either.'

'I do.'

'Suit yourself.'

'I'll sneak out and have one later,' Alya said, slipping a cigarette in her purse.

'Life's about having a good time.'

'I *am* having a good time.'

Laughter rang through the air. Alya recognized its high-pitched nasal tone from the TV. Jackie Funwala was in the house.

Jackie's favourite segment on her show was the 'Latest Initiates to the Surgical Wand'. The show, which was supposed to be about the craft of film-making and the calibre of actors' performances had no place for the ruthless and random segment, but Jackie couldn't help herself. She couldn't resist making the divas and macho men of Tinseltown tremble at seeing their pictures dissected and critiqued by a coterie of cosmetic surgeons. She claimed that the segment, and even the programme at large, was 'purely scientific; based on expert analysis'. However, this was contested [anonymously] by the gifted glitterati. *Read My Lips*, Jackie's other extravaganza, featured equally shudder-worthy segments. It explored—in embarrassing detail, replete with candid camera footage—the liaisons of famous stars, inviting a battery of astrologers and psychics to foretell the future of the couples. It was gospel, beyond the gilded gates of their golden enclosures there was nothing the stars feared more than the feisty frolicsome Funwala. The Alis greeted her together as she entered their house with unapologetic pomp, extending her hand for Abbas to kiss.

Waiters in spotless white gloves, with trays laden with champagne, weaved around producers talking shop; directors discussing plots; and starlets striking poses, their gowns coming alive as they danced about. There was a seating arrangement in the shape of an eight in the living room with the glass doors leading out to the lawn; its twin ovals were adorned with floral bouquets and sea corals. The decorations were serving as partitions between the stretches and curves of the couch. Bored with flattery from designers wanting to make clothes for her and society doyennes hankering after her for their next party, Alya settled down. She was feeling the weight of slow-burning exhaustion caused by her rigorous work schedule and constant dieting. Her friend Suzy came and sat beside her, but instead of allowing her the rest she sought, Suzy embarked on a commentary about her latest collection, the gown she designed for Laila Ali to wear to the IIFA Awards, performance fabrics and wardrobe malfunctions.

'...The model's boob popped out of her dress while she was walking the ramp,' Suzy informed her.

'What did she do then?' Alya asked.

'She plucked a flower from her hair and pressed it against her nipple and kept going as if the incident was an intentional part of the show.'

'Clever girl.'

'The gown was ill-fitting. Clients don't have that problem with my clothes because I pay close attention to fit. A similar incident happened involving a costume at a photo shoot on a beach in the Maldives...' Suzy went on but Alya switched off. She visualized herself floating, like a disembodied entity, over the glittering, posturing, yammering people in the room. Spying on people was her hobby—how they touched their bodies while they spoke; how they stood, motionless, with their shoulders hunched and fingers clenched; how they shook their heads; and how they gestured furiously with their hands.

But, again, her attempt at snatching a personal moment was disrupted; this time by a burst of conversation coming from the other side of the partition in the couch. 'The manor in Edinburgh is old. We've had that for years, for generations. The villa in Gstaad is our most recent acquisition. I can't stay more than three weeks in this hot and humid city!'

Alya guessed the voice belonged to a woman in her mid-fifties. She was likely to be wearing an obese ruby set in a gold ring around her finger. Alya was certain that fidgeting with jewels was an unconscious habit for the lady with the robust chords and insatiable appetite for leisure. She was the type that actresses most feared—the type that gossipped incessantly.

A shrill laugh rose from a different part of the couch, similar to the one Alya had heard earlier in the evening. 'No, sugar lips,' it *was* the one from earlier in the evening, 'those aren't saddlebags attached to her rump under that dress, they're her hips. Someone, please tell that mare, "Cookies-n-Cream, lose the baby fat or you'll be permanently locked in the shed, missing every chance to race to the red carpet".'

That Jackie can be so mean, Alya thought.

Jackie was on the other side of the couch with Ponti—her dummy in more ways than one. She talked so much that Ponti wasn't listening to her half of the time.

'My, my, what have we here?' Alya almost twisted her neck into the shape of a pretzel to see what Jackie was talking about and witnessed the unfolding of a romance, the likes of which Jackie was personally familiar with.

Could the rumours be true? Did Abbas swing both ways? Alya speculated silently. Abbas and another famous, and much younger, actor, Tony were sitting so close together that they could have been conjoined twins. They were sharing a cigarette, Tony's hand rested on Abbas's knee as he whispered into his ear what Jackie knew and Alya guessed could only be sweet nothings. If Alya had been on the other side of the couch, she would have seen Jackie blush—a rare sight. It wasn't the pink ostrich-feather stole—which she had inherited from her maternal uncle—framing her face along with her instinct to be a real woman that were bringing out the pink in her cheeks. Alya was bewildered by the nature of the friendship she was witnessing. Jackie was not: when Tony's hand moved, she knew that he was caressing and that the pair was canoodling. 'Tony, you lucky bitch,' she muttered, 'Abbas, my George Clooney, turn that mojo my way!'

She turned to Ponti and asked him if he thought the rumour was true. 'Do you really think there is an elite club with an exclusive membership to a secret den in this mansion?' Succumbing to the throes of her imagination, her grey matter getting greyer, her fantasies running amok, her mind revisited the uses and abuses of every sex toy she had come across in Amsterdam, bought or invented, the visuals all fusing together to form a titillating slideshow in her head.

When Tony got up to leave, two pairs of eyes were on him. And when Abbas pinched his bottom as Tony stepped forward, the prying eyes nearly fell out of their sockets.

Alya was delighting in the charade, straining to hear Jackie's remarks on the novel romance: all the gossip in the world paled in comparison to this sparkler. But there was nothing to be heard. Jackie was mum. Alya then realized what prompted the uncharacteristic silence. Jackie had witnessed a huge Bollywood exposé, one she could not speak of on TV. Talking about such a big revelation without a glimmer of proof was a risk she was not willing to take. But it still wasn't the real reason for her silence—a gossip show needed no proof to back its allegations. The reason for it was that the news would be hard on the sensibilities of the masses. It had only been a month since gay sex had been decriminalized. No leading homosexual actor or actress had come out since. That made the affair not only scandalous but also potentially destructive. It could destroy Abbas Ali's career and demolish Tony's prospects. For now, Jackie was thankful the public appreciated her as they did. That was big enough of them. She would stay mum. She would maintain the status quo. She would continue touting Laila and Abbas Ali as the ideal Bollywood couple. And maybe, one day, when she was done with the razzmatazz, retired and writing a book to keep the boilers running, she would let Bollywood's juiciest secrets rip.

'Jackie-la.'

'Yes, Ponti.'

'How come Pops and Dude didn't come tonight?'

'*In sab ke apne camp hain* [All of these people have their own camps].'

'Oh,' Ponti said, clearly not understanding the dynamics.

'Do you remember when you were in school?' Jackie started elaborating, 'everyone belonged to a group—'

'I didn't. No one wanted me in their group,' Ponti interrupted Jackie.

'I know, Ponti. That was in the past. Now, you belong to

the coolest and most feared group, so you need not worry. It's the same as school in the film industry. The big stars have their own camps. Most talent gets caught in their crossfire. Those who don't pick a camp, or can't, risk being left out. *Yeh sab ek doosre ke patte kattein rehtae hain, Ponti. Samjhe, beta* [All these people keep trying to pull each other down, Ponti. Understood]?' Jackie explained this complicated nuance of the film industry to Ponti with a tenderness few knew she was capable of. Alya had to pinch herself.

'What would happen if you swallowed uranium? You would get atomic ache,' Alya heard Flapjack joke over the hubbub of the crowd.

'Jackie Funwala, I'm a big fan! I love your shows,' another voice entered the conversation.

'Hi Dorothy, are you looking for Oz?' Jackie said, her voice slurring. The vodka cranberries she'd been drinking through the evening had started getting the better of her.

'I'm Kimi,' the young woman replied.

'Oh, I'm sorry. I thought you were Dorothy, you know, from *The Wizard of Oz*? Honey, it's those pumps. You've got to lose those cheap red shoes if you want to make it in this town,' Jackie chastised.

She was contradiction personified. Within the span of five minutes, she could be as sensitive as a nun and as cruel as a pimp.

'Um, okay,' Kimi responded.

'Changing your name to Kimi was a good idea though. That'll help. "Kimi"—I like it, original and catchy.'

For Alya, the sing-song voice rang a bell too close to home. It belonged to a small-town girl with big dreams. She turned to Suzy, who had continued with her monologue regardless of whether anyone was listening to her.

'...You have to stand out in a crowd. You have to see to it that you are seen. *That's* fashion,' she said. Alya debated if Suzy or Jackie was more astute.

'What do you get if you cross a centipede and a parrot?' Flapjack interjected. 'A walkie-talkie.'

'Sugar plum, if you weren't made of plastic I'd jump you,' Jackie said, presumably to Flapjack though the robot was far from being the only one in the room with synthetic parts.

'What do you get if you cross a cat and a lemon?' Flapjack continued, unaffected.

'What, sweet pea?' Jackie responded.

'A sourpuss.'

'Are you making insinuations, tin man?' Jackie asked, unamused. Alya, however, was endlessly amused witnessing someone rub Jackie the wrong way.

'Absolutely, I agree with you,' Alya heard the woman with the robust chords and ruby ring say, 'She's much better off with him. That other guy she was with, the environmental activist... What's his name?'

'Dharmesh Pawar,' came another female voice.

They're talking about me! Alya realized. Her already overworked ears now strained to elfin proportions to hear the women's scuttlebutt.

'Yes, yes, Danny! What a loser. Not a penny in his pocket and forever making noise about construction in marshes and what have you. My husband hates the fellow. He's a pain in the neck. Slugs and slush are his claim to fame,' strummed the robust chords.

'Actually,' the other woman replied, 'Alya was his claim to fame.'

'Luckily for her, good sense prevailed. Karan comes from a solid background. She can walk around with pride. Let's be honest, actresses have a shelf life. They reach their expiry date before they know it.' Together they cackled.

Alya wanted to disappear, more out of shame and confusion than embarrassment. The last time she had been at Laila and Abbas Ali's house for their annual Christmas luncheon, a few years back, had been with Danny. Gift-wrapped boxes had been stacked on the carpet under a tree embellished with shiny trinkets and tinsel and children had pranced around the boxes like happy ponies as their mothers talked about nannies, first-class schools, vacations and latest acquisitions. Alya had earned enough to afford all the things they had been speaking of, on her own. And yet, she recalled looking at Danny and wondering if he really was *the one* for her. At that point, the seed of discontent had taken root in the soil of their relationship. She still had no idea why. Had it been because she had doubted if she could spend forever with a man of modest means? If she had married this man, would she have been able to maintain her status in society after her career was over? And, most pertinently, could she respect a man whose bank balance was less than her own? As she remembered those doubts, Alya pondered over one final question—why did the woman calling Danny a loser bother her so?

Alya's thoughts were interrupted by Flapjack asking, 'Why did the ghost go to the astrologer? Because he wanted to see his horoscope.'

The ruby fetishist bumped into Flapjack as she got up and said, 'Excuse me.'

'Your sister's a nice girl,' he responded automatically.

'Why, thank you. How adorable!'

'Everybody likes her—twenty thousand flies can't be wrong.'
'Be gone, rude chunk of machinery.'

Jackie laughed so hard, she nearly gagged. She was enjoying being entertained rather than having to entertain. Alya, on the other side of the sofa, wasn't paying attention to anything anymore. She was still reeling from the flagrant dissection of her private life by the two rich ladies.

'...And that's the season's fashion forecast,' Suzy concluded.

'Your commentary on the ins and outs of the garment industry has left me thirsty,' Alya told her.

'Thirsty?'

'For a model's favourite sin.'

'Yeah baby, that's what we're talking about!'

'Let's go get some bubbly.'

The pair snuck out to a private part of the garden with their glasses of champagne, where Alya could have her drink with the cigarette that she had resisted since arriving at the mansion. After hearing the voyeuristic deliberations over her relationships, there couldn't be a better time for it. She savoured the cigarette like it was life support.

Then, Suzy and Alya got more champagne and walked about to take in the sights. The alcohol was doing its job. People had loosened up. Hands were straying on bare shoulders and backs. Hopping onto the dance floor inspired by the movie *Saturday Night Fever*, Alya said, 'I want to dance like John Travolta.' Striking the classic Travolta pose, she shouted to Suzy over the music, 'Come join me!' Suzy jumped on next to her, hopping on the squares and lighting them up. They held hands and spun around, forming a blinking Hula-Hoop of rainbow colours beneath their feet. Finally breathless, Alya stopped and looked for her boyfriend. 'Where's Karan?'

'We've just started. Where are you going?' Suzy said, peeved.

'I'm going to get Karan,' Alya said, stepping off the dance floor. 'But first, I need to use the washroom.'

'I'll come with you.'

'No, it's okay. I know where it is.'

Alya blew kisses at familiar faces as she walked along in her flowing gown—a witty pretension at concealing her dwindling control. Not many people knew of the washroom under the staircase in the hall. She was relieved not to have to wait in queue. She had reached the corridor to the washroom when the door flung open and out stumbled a couple, laughing so hard that they had to cling to each other for support.

The woman was clearly of European descent. Alya could tell by her chestnut hair—it wasn't the bleached variety sported by many of her friends and colleagues, including Suzy. She was tall and buxom, a genuine stunner. She rubbed her nose with her forefinger and let out a sniffle. It was a dead giveaway. The couple had been doing lines of cocaine in the toilet. That came as no surprise to Alya; on occasion she'd done so herself. Feeling like an eavesdropper on a private moment between lovers, she half-turned to head to the other washroom, when she caught a glimpse of the man's face. It was Karan.

The chant began even before her heart rate increased. *Fight or flight? Fight or flight?* Getting a hold of herself, becoming conscious of her breathing, she arrived at her choice. *Flight.* Causing a scene at a party like this one would irrevocably harm her image. She hadn't come this far to flush her career down the toilet. By the time the lovers became aware of the world around them, Alya was gone.

Leaving the party at the stroke of midnight to avoid the awaiting horrors, Alya lifted her beaded gown and ran down the corridor, calling her friend to ask for a ride. Flapjack was posted at the teak doors. When she passed him, he asked her, 'What animal can you never trust?'

'I don't want to know,' Alya responded.

'A cheetah,' Flapjack delivered his punchline.

Alya saw Suzy's car come through the automatic gates. Miraculously, she had made it out without running into anyone. Almost. Just as she was stepping out, a tap on the shoulder caught her unawares.

'Yes?' she asked, turning around.

'Alya, wow! What an honour it is to meet you. I've seen all your movies,' a girl said to her in an excited voice.

'Would you like an autograph?' Alya asked in a mechanical response.

'I just wanted to meet you.'

The girl was pretty, though a little rough around the edges. She was wearing a cheap dress and a pair of red shoes. Alya remembered Jackie's taunts about the shoes. So, this was that girl.

'You are an inspiration to me,' the aspiring actress told Alya as she was getting into Suzy's car. 'I want to be like you. I want to live a life like yours.' Gripping the tinted window to stop her idol from fleeing, she said, 'Tell me what it takes!'

Alya was about to answer. She was good at coming up with answers. She must have given a thousand interviews in the course of her career. But when she locked eyes with the girl, she lost the ability to speak. Those eyes were not only full of fire and drive but also the frustration of not having guidance. They craved knowledge but because they had none, they were bewildered. They were desperate eyes and, yet, in them shone an indescribable innocence. Alya recognized those eyes. She had once been that girl. The recollection made an avalanche of emotions break away from the mountain of ice she had built in her heart. They came hurtling at her, threatening to shatter her armour and bury her under their weight. The starlet stepped away from the window. Alya raised the tinted glass and, cutting herself off from the disconcerting reflection of her distant past, fled the scene.

∞

10

A Regular Day

Reena worshipped her sixteen miniature lingams on a Monday morning, not because that's what Hindu women did to get a good husband but because she had been attracted to the lord of the mountains since childhood. The ritual that started as a way of expressing her love for the divine had become a means of bringing discipline to her life, above and beyond work. Her self-control was getting stronger and her partying had reduced to a more reasonable frequency, leading to a sharper sense of responsibility. Whether these changes were a result of the lord's blessings or of having to wake up that much earlier on a Monday morning, Reena didn't know and nor did her parents. However, everyone noticed the difference that practising a ritual had made to her personal development.

Each of the sixteen lingams had been gifted to her; one by a dying aunt from her ancestral village on the Karnataka–Kerala border. This aunt saw Reena as a younger version of herself, who could act as a conduit to further the family legacy of lingam worship. Another lingam had been gifted to her by a hermetic priest living on Elephanta Island off the coast of Mumbai. Yet another, her mother had given her on the day she had graduated from high school. She had found one lingam in the Tungabhadra River while holidaying in Hampi, half-submerged in silt. Each one was special. Each had a story. Reena valued them more because of it. The last of the sixteen had been a birthday present from Malini. Made of quartz, it was from the holy city of Rishikesh.

'Wait Reena, don't run like that,' her father called out, seeing her pick up the rava idlis off her plate and drop them into a Ziploc bag. Reena dashed for the door with a thermos of filter coffee in one hand, the bag of idlis in the other and a beige purse hanging from her shoulder.

'Eating breakfast on the go is bad for digestion.'

'Half the world has breakfast on the go, Dad.'

'That doesn't mean you have to.'

'It's okay, Dad.'

Giving her an envelope, he said, 'Here, take this.'

'What is this?'

'It's a picture and profile of a boy I've found for you.'

'Now *that* is something that *will* give me indigestion.'

'You may like the boy.'

'Dad, shouldn't you stop referring to men between thirty-seven and forty years of age as boys, even if they have a lot of growing up to do? Enough. Let it be,' she said, wanting to go on ranting at her father and ask him to butt out of her life, but she stopped short because she knew that his words were well intentioned.

'What harm is there in it, beta?' Reena's mother joined the conversation while clearing the breakfast dishes 'No one's forcing you. Meet the boy. If you don't like him, don't meet him again.'

'Take it, na. I found him myself after searching the net for hours,' her father pleaded.

'That's reassuring.'

'He'll be waiting for you at The Bistro at 6.00 in the evening,' she heard her father say as she slipped the envelope into her purse and bolted out of the house.

Reena's driver hadn't shown up to work. She was apprehensive about driving herself. Discerning signals, indicating when she was going to turn, looking in the rear-view mirror and watching out for disorderly pedestrians, all at once, was a lot for her to handle. She had three sites to survey that day and they were all far apart.

Mr Chandrashekhara had made a down payment on the apartment in Khar. But for a few minor repairs, it was ready to be handed over to him. Reena arrived at the site in good time to check on progress, only to discover that the workers hadn't shown up.

What the hell! She thought angrily as she phoned the foreman and demanded, 'Where are the workers?... What?... What are you talking about? What kind of festival is that? I've never heard of it. Okay. So when will they show up?... Tomorrow? Excellent. A whole day wasted.' Reena hung up the phone, exasperated.

A dislodged lamp was hanging from a wire sticking out of a hole in the ceiling. It dangled above a broken tile that had made a depression in the floor. A puddle had formed in the depression where a cockroach was taking a dip, nibbling on ants and mites that happened to float past, making the most of his circumstances with an enviable air of contentment. Inspired by the critter's resilience, Reena left for her next destination.

On arriving at Mr Chogule's office, she was directed by his secretary to a stuffy waiting room at the end of a corridor. Sweating, Reena patted her face with a tissue paper and sat there for an hour before she was summoned into the boss's cabin. This treatment of her had been deliberate. He owed her money.

'Yes, Ms Reena Subramaniam,' an irate Chogule said when she walked in.

'Sir, I've come to ask you for the pending remuneration for my company's services. I've called your office every day for the past week but—' Reena started.

'You've been paid the full amount,' Chogule interrupted her.

'Mr Chogule, I have the paperwork,' Reena retorted, though she knew it was useless. Nobody did business in white alone; black money played a major role in most real estate transactions because paperwork only told part of the story—business had to be based on trust. Resultantly, a lot of dog-eat-dog deals were happening.

'Mr Chogule, I look forward to working with you in the future. We must, however, first complete the financial—'

'Ms Subramaniam, I owe you nothing. I have important meetings to attend. Please leave.'

'Mr Chogule, let's be decent human beings and conclude our association on a positive note. Pay me the remainder of the agreed-upon remuneration and—'

'LEAVE,' Chogule thundered.

Reena had suspected it would come to this. She would have to resort to the 'Backstreet Boys'—that's what she called them. She'd been part of the family business for nine years with her father, who had been nearly broken by it. But when it was her turn to go through the gamut of begging for what she was rightfully owed, she was determined to find a solution. After witnessing a scene similar to the one that just transpired in Chogule's office, her driver had come forward to help. He had urged her to avail of the services of a group of boys in his slum, who were members of a chain-snatching gang—a common phenomenon in Mumbai. The juveniles rode around the city on motorbikes, snatching handbags and gold chains from unassuming pedestrians. If paid, they were willing to commit other petty crimes too. Reena found an effective solution to her problem in them, and they a legitimate part-time employer in her. The job was easy. The boys had to show up at a given address, at a specific time and misbehave. If that failed, as it sometimes did with stubborn businessmen like Mr Chogule, the Backstreet Boys called upon *their* backup—the eunuchs of the slum. Dressed in their finest saris, they showed up at the culprit's office and created a hideous raucous: clapping, singing, dancing vulgarly and, if necessary, lifting their saris to expose themselves. The arrangement worked beautifully. Nine out of ten times Reena got her dues.

'Mr Chogule, You *will* give me my money,' Reena said emphatically.

'If you say so,' Chogule responded dismissively.

'Oh yes, I do.'

Having lost her appetite in Chogule's office, Reena drove to her next destination with her packed lunch sitting on the passenger seat untouched. While waiting at a traffic signal, she remembered the envelope her father had given her in the morning. *What the heck,* she thought hating to admit that she was curious. She was about to open her purse when the signal changed and she had to turn.

Reena had scarcely crossed the intersection when a heavily dented car overtook hers and blocked her way. The driver got out of his vehicle and came towards her. She pressed the auto-lock button and thought, *Where's a traffic cop when you need one?*

The driver pounded on her window with his fists and yelled, 'Bitch, you cut me off. You scratched my car.'

'There must be something wrong with the signal. I'm sorry if you think I cut you off,' Reena said.

'You owe me damages. Give me five thousand rupees!' he demanded.

'My insurance will cover the damages.'

'Bitch, give me five thousand,' he insisted, kicking her car and punching its windows. Reena slammed her foot on the accelerator and drove past his car, nicking its rear fender. The man grabbed the handle and ran beside the car even as it gained speed. Reena drove faster and faster, until he was forced to let go.

Reena's final destination was the construction site of a building in upscale Worli. Assuming the gentleman waving at her from a mound of dry cement powder was the architect—an acquaintance of her father's—she had come to meet, Reena made her way to him through an obstacle course of forklifts, concrete trucks and giant excavators in her three-inch heels. The elderly man in a yellow helmet watched the woman in a pantsuit and pumps coming towards him through all that dangerous machinery. For any woman the site was hostile territory, especially so for one as petite as Reena.

'Good afternoon,' Reena greeted the man upon reaching him, seemingly unaffected by the chaos around her. 'I'm Reena Subramaniam. I'm here to see an apartment.'

'Follow me,' the man said.

They stepped into an elevator and within moments were on the twenty-seventh floor of the building. 'Interesting, the lift opens directly into the apartment,' Reena said.

'It's Sky Tower's USP. Each floor has just one apartment,

either a three-bedroom or a four-bedroom flat. They all have 800 square foot balconies.'

'When will the building be ready?'

'It's almost done. The penthouse is on the seventy-fifth floor. Do you want to see it?'

'I'd like to discuss rates first.'

'That'll take time.'

'Approximately how much is this apartment?'

'The price of an apartment depends on the number of bedrooms it has and the floor it's on—the higher you go the more expensive it gets.'

'Can we meet again to discuss rates?'

'My time is precious. Besides, almost all the flats are sold. It won't be easy to buy one at this stage.'

Something about the way the architect was looking at her from under the rim of that ugly helmet was making Reena uncomfortable. When she first saw the elderly gentleman, she had considered calling him 'uncle'.

But this uncle, to her growing unease, was remarkably fit compared to any uncle she had known. A draught blew through Sky Tower, catching Reena unawares, throwing her off balance. The architect leapt forward and grabbed her.

'Let go of me,' Reena said, pulling away from him.

'I'm only trying to help you,' he scoffed at her.

Stepping back, Reena noticed that the window frames on either side of the flat had not been fitted with glass yet.

'As I was saying, my time is precious,' the architect told her, his helmet tilting to one side, 'I could convince the builder to sell you an apartment, and at a good rate, if you make it worth my while.'

The nagging suspicion that the person in front of her was

not the one she had spoken to on the phone grew stronger. Maybe this man was the builder's secretary: an old-school employee in the habit of taking cuts from potential buyers. 'I'll give you a seven per cent commission,' Reena said, guessing he was in some way associated with Sky Tower but certain he was not the architect she had come to meet.

'It can get lonely up here,' the imposter said, coming closer.

Reena's options were running out fast, teetering on the edge of the glassless frames beyond which there were no gunny bags waiting to break a fall; only steel beams and mean machines. 'I'll do something for you if you do something for me,' he continued in his predatory tone. Reena bolted to the lift but was slammed midway by another gust of wind blowing through the building. This one knocked her down. If she had wondered why the man was behaving like a crazed animal, she wondered no more—he was standing over her with a protrusion in his pants.

Reena tried to think quickly while he struggled with his belt. She drew her leg up to her chest and jabbed her heel into his knee. He buckled over, his yellow helmet dropping to the ground. Reena sprang up with the agility of a gazelle being hunted by a leopard. He grabbed her leg and pulled her towards him, too aroused to let go of his opportunity. Clawing at the uneven ground, she tried crawling away from him. With one push of his hand, he pinned her down and flipped her onto her back, yanking open the buttons on her blouse. 'You're a free woman, aren't you?' he said, seeing the butterfly tattoo showing from under her white bra. Reena was in no position to see the ridiculousness of the statement—she was too busy wriggling to free herself of him. 'Why resist? It's not like you haven't done it before,' he said. There it was, the misogynistic line so commonly used by molesters to justify their acts. Reena kept kicking until her heel struck something hard. 'My ankle!' he screamed, reaching for his foot. She got up and dashed to the elevator and kept punching the call button until it arrived.

Within minutes, Reena was back in her car with the doors and windows securely locked. Clinging to her steering wheel, pervaded by a sense of being trapped in not only her car but also her life—adrenaline, thirst, emotions and exhaustion overwhelming her—she lost consciousness.

When she awoke, she couldn't recall at which point her car had become more of a refuge than a mode of transport, and when exactly had her life turned into a scramble to make ends meet. Work and parents, parents and work, over and over, round and round.

Is there no escape? Reena thought helplessly, and then remembered the envelope. *No, I don't want to think about a man right now, not any man.* Then, her father came to mind. If she went home without meeting the prospective bachelor from the envelope, he would be upset—very upset. She wouldn't hear the end of it.

The thought of upsetting her father more than he already was about her marriage prospects, or lack thereof, incited Reena's muscles to act. She reached for her purse and pulled out the envelope. Praying that the bachelor belonged to the harmless-looking category of the male species, she drew the paper out from its cover and examined his picture. 'He seems pleasant enough,' she said, with measured relief. *Could this be the prince that whisks me away to the world of marital bliss?* Raising a cloud of dust, Reena's tyres spun on the gravelly road of the construction site and turned onto the smooth tarmac of the highway.

The Bistro was a lively café near Prithvi Theatre, the epicentre of Mumbai's theatre scene. Owing to the eclectic personalities dropping in from the neighbourhood around it, the café had a creative and unpretentious vibe; making it an ideal setting for the kind of meeting Reena was about to have.

To enter a place in search of someone in a crowd is always strange; more so if that someone is not a friend but a perfect stranger; and strangest of all is to discuss something as intimate as marriage with a total stranger. This was unpleasant for Reena, though she had done it more than she wished to remember or liked to admit.

On such occasions, she used to tell her sister that she was going on a blind date. But she knew that this was a white lie. A blind date was a rendezvous set up by mutual friends. What she was doing was meeting a random person who had made himself available online, a shopper's paradise where everything was up for sale. The bold new world was about selling, and Reena was looking for a human to take home. But she wasn't dreaming up a wedding dress yet. She knew that, like many things advertised on the internet, what met the eye was often far from the truth.

Reena pretended to be reading the menu as she used her peripheral vision to search for the mystery man from the envelope.

He found her first and asked, 'Are you Reena?'

'Yes, I am,' Reena replied.

'I'm Dewan,' he introduced himself.

Reena discreetly looked him up and down. He was wearing black trousers with a brown belt and a pastel blue shirt. He was clean-shaven and his hair was combed.

Not too shabby, she thought, relieved he wasn't potbellied, short or wearing a toupee—or worse, all three.

'You look different in the photograph that your father posted.'

Where had she heard that before?

'Quite different,' he emphasized.

'It's an old picture,' she replied.

It wasn't an old picture—it had been photoshopped.

'Are you coming from work?' he asked, settling down.

'Yes,' she responded as they ordered coffee.

'What do you like to do in your free time, Reena?'

'Well, I like to read. I like spinning—'

'Spinning?' Dewan interrupted her.

'It's a group exercise similar to aerobics. It's a choreographed cardio workout using stationary bicycles.'

'So, you go to the gym,' he said, checking her out.

'Three times a week. Do *you* like to exercise?'

'I walk at Joggers' Park. I find the smell of Indian gyms nauseating. Even the so-called fresh air by the ocean here is sickening. It stinks like rotten fish.'

'That's because they dry the fish outside, near the beach.'

'You're wearing your blouse inside out,' he said.

'Excuse me?' Reena asked, a little embarrassed.

'Your blouse, it's...'

'Um, yes... I was in a hurry.'

'You live with your parents, I was told. Do you have siblings?'

'I have a sister. She's studying abroad...'

'Then, you're alone at home with your parents?'

'Pretty much.'

'Do you own the house you live in or is it a rental?'
'It's our house.'
'That's good,' Dewan said, stretching his legs.
'You lived in America for twelve years, it was mentioned in your profile,' Reena started probing.
'Yes, I did.'
'How does it feel, being back in India?'
'One can never get used to the garbage on the streets. The city is so damn dirty, with stray dogs and beggars everywhere, but it's still so expensive. I'm actually thinking of moving to Coimbatore. That's where my parents live, in our ancestral home. I'll save a whole lot of money.' Listening to him, Reena visualized a dilapidated wooden roof caving into a crumbling brick house in the middle of a coconut grove stretching as far as the eye could see.

'How many bedrooms do you have in your house?' he asked her.

'Excuse me?'

'How many bedrooms do you have in your house in Mumbai?'

'Three.'

'When we marry, I mean, if we marry, we can put the house up for rent and move your parents into a one-bedroom flat. It'll be easier for them to manage. They won't be needing so much space once you're gone.'

Reena took her shot of espresso.

'You'll move to Coimbatore with me,' he informed her.

'I like Mumbai,' she calmly responded.

'Don't worry, you'll have no problem adjusting. My parents are good people.'

'I'm sure your parents are wonderful.'

'It doesn't matter if you don't cook. My mom is a great cook.'

Reena was already planning her escape.

'Coimbatore is cleaner than Mumbai. What's not to like about it?'

'I'm sure there's everything to like about it.'

'Once we've moved, you can continue working. I don't expect you to sit at home.'

Of course not, you intend to work me to the bone, is what Reena really wanted to say. Instead, she said, 'That's nice.'

'There's no problem, then. The deal is done.'

'No problem at all. Excuse me, Dewan. I have to run. We have relatives coming over for dinner tonight. My parents want me to be home in time to receive them or else it won't look good.'

'No, it won't look good at all.'

'Let's meet again this week,' she said, taking her purse off the back of the chair, 'I'll call you tomorrow.'

'I'll walk you out.'

'No, thank you Dewan, I'll see myself out. Please, enjoy your coffee,' she said, hurrying out.

Reena made the final journey of the day back home, a place getting less attractive with each passing day, but one she had no choice but to return to. Parking her car, she reached into the glove compartment and took out a drawstring pouch she kept there for emergencies.

What makes him think marriage is something you broker? she thought angrily, opening the pouch and pulling out a lighter and the only vice she still allowed herself to indulge in. *Marriage can't be a deal struck between two people and, that too, a deal heavily in favour of the man. What about my views, Mr Dewan, whoever you are? Do they matter?* Huffing, she declared, 'I hate men!' It was a sentiment she felt strongly, particularly after the day that she had had—although her body needed more convincing.

'Okay. That's it. I've had enough,' she said to herself, rolling her window down to let out a cloud of marijuana smoke, 'I'm getting myself a dildo.'

Just then, Mrs Venkataraman walked past her car. 'Oh, hello, Mrs Venkataraman,' Reena greeted her neighbour. 'There are so many pests out here, don't you think? I've fumigated my car with this new repellent, Dido. You should try it. It's more effective than Hit in getting rid of pests,' Reena tried to cover up.

'*Theek hai, beta* [Alright, child]. I'll try it,' Mrs Venkataraman said, waddling on.

Reena felt her car closing in on her. She wanted to scream. She wanted to cry. She wanted to go to the salon and chop off her hair. Then, her mobile rang.

'Reena, are you on your way home?' It was her father. 'Don't hurry if you're still at the café,' he added hurriedly.

'No, Dad, I'm home,' she responded.

Reena didn't notice how high she was until she stepped out of the car. She had lived in the same building for as long as she could remember and it still took her five minutes to figure out how to open the iron gate of the lift; and she was grateful for it—grateful to be sufficiently numb in all the right places. It made her as ready as she could be to face her father.

'How did it go?' Reena's father asked the moment she stepped into the house.

'Hello, dad,' Reena responded, trying to stay calm.

'Hello, beta,' Reena's mother, Dolly, called from the kitchen.

'Has he also rejected you?' Reena's father asked.

'Thank you for asking me how my day went.'

'What's the response?' her father prodded.

'Where do you find these guys, Dad? In the waste bin of the world?'

'Ah, so it didn't go well. Put the blame on me.'

'The guy was sacked from his job in America, probably laid off during the recession. He hates the city. He has no proper income or idea of what he wants to do or where he wants to live. Yet, his wish list is endless. Wow, I didn't know homeless guys had wish lists too.'

'Yes, they do, and you can't make it even on *their* lists.'

'I don't want to make it on their lists.'

'At this rate, you'll never marry.'

'So what if I don't get married! What is a wife in this culture but a glorified servant! "Bahu" is a curse word in my mind. It means cooking, cleaning, caring for in-laws and children and still having to look presentable for that mostly unsatisfying, one-sided fuck.'

'Reena, how can you speak to your father in that way?' Dolly chided.

'The culture you're talking about doesn't apply to you, Reena.' her father said, 'we're a middle-class family.'

'Oh, so that happens only in low-income families, is it? Do you know that India has the highest rate of suicide among women in the world, ranking only after a couple of poverty-stricken African nations?'

'This is exactly the kind of talk that has landed her where she is,' Mr Subramaniam told his wife.

'And where is that, Dad?'

'Stop it now, both of you,' Dolly scolded them.

'Say whatever you want, Reena, it won't change the fact that you're thirty-five and unmarried,' Mr Subramaniam said conclusively as the pressure cooker in the kitchen whistled, reminding Reena of her munchies. Luckily—the only lucky thing in her day—her mom happened to be cooking a sumptuous feast.

'Ma you went to an Art of Living class today, didn't you?'

'How did you know?'

'Call it a hunch.'

There was only one photograph in Reena's parent's bedroom; it was of Sri Sri Ravi Shankar, founder of the Art of Living Foundation. Something about the spiritual guru made him irresistible to his devotees. Watching her mother flit about in the kitchen, cooking desserts and singing melodies from the movies, Reena knew it was no drug that had got her high. Reena considered becoming a Sri Sri groupie, so that she, too, could levitate through life with a perpetual smile on her face. But that would not do it for her. What Reena wanted was a real man and she was willing to go through dirt and jerks to get him. No matter the challenges life threw at her—testing circumstances, her father's high expectations, treacherous experiences with lecherous men—she would not be deterred from her quest. Reena wanted happiness; not the floating-on-a-cloud kind of sublime joy one gets from faith. She wanted the real and tangible joy of being with a man, living her life with him and making a home and a family with him. Was that too much to ask for?

11

A Wedding

'Twenty-one and married, that's what you're going to be by the end of the night, chica.' Alya said.

Eisha was sitting with a group of women under a cluster of trees at Fairy-tale Gardens, every bit the fairy-tale bride. Her hair was tied in a long braid adorned with fragrant flowers. She looked as lovely as the day she had caught the attention of her husband-to-be, an NRI, who had alighted upon the Indian shores in search of the loveliest lady in the land.

Pointing at her friend, Eisha said, 'What's that?'

'What's what?' Alya asked.

'What's that in your teeth?'

Alya ran her tongue over the front of her teeth. 'Is there something stuck in them?'

She was a recognized face, on her way to becoming a celebrity; rubbing her tongue over the front of her teeth was making her look ridiculous, surely. She didn't want the sight to make a lasting impression on the other women. Then again, food stuck in teeth looks stupid too. Either way, she was looking stupid or ridiculous and that bothered her.

'You've been chewing on those leaves you brought from the hills to lose weight, haven't you?' The guffaw accompanying the question was specially funny, as it was coming from a woman dressed in the finest bridal wear that money could buy just minutes from taking her marital vows.

'You're a clown,' Alya said, realizing that Eisha was joking, 'and you'll always be one, with or without the costume.' Hugging Eisha, she whispered, 'Congratulations.'

'To you too.'

'For what?'

'For becoming the new Cola girl. The ad is everywhere. You're famous.'

'I'll need a film to get famous. I'm working on it, I'll get there.'

Eisha's Delhi friends were eager to get to know Alya. Ranjita Mamgai was the first to introduce herself. Her sister, Romila, was next.

'Nice to meet you,' Alya said.

'I'm Sunayana and this is my friend, Reena. We're from Bombay.'

'Hello.'

Waiters offered them succulent chicken and paneer tikkas. 'I'm hungry,' Eisha said, popping a tikka into her mouth.

'Unbelievable!' Alya told her, 'In another five minutes, life as you know it is going to change forever and all you can think about is food.'

Reena helped herself to a paneer tikka. She was famished. She had skipped the in-flight meal. Sunayana used to be a resident of Delhi until she was fifteen. Just before her sixteenth birthday, her father, an army officer, had been transferred to Mumbai. She and Eisha were old school buddies. As for Reena, this was her first visit to the capital and her first Punjabi wedding. She was entering the second year of work in what her father reminded her daily was the 'real world', just in case she forgot that 'life was about taking responsibility for yourself' and slipped back into 'living in a fantasy'. When Sunayana invited her to attend a wedding in Delhi, she agreed without a fuss, deciding that a little fantasy in the right measure didn't harm anybody. The weather in the capital at this time of the year was ideal and, judging by the hors d'oeuvres, the food delectable. Biting into another succulent tikka, Reena resolved to make the most of her holiday.

'Sorry, I'm late,' a young woman in an ivory sari joined the group, mildly breathless, stray hairs from her bun falling to her face.

'Want a tikka?' Eisha asked the woman, offering her one.

'Hello, Malini,' Alya said.

'Hi, Alya,' Malini responded.

Looking more anxious than usual, Eisha's mother came to inform them that the groom had arrived. 'Girls, you have to start moving to the *mandap*,' she said, her pocket pooch—bathed, blow-dried and wearing a scarf around his neck—firmly pressed against her chest.

Eisha needed help getting up; her bridal ensemble weighed fifteen kilograms. Malini stepped forward to assist her but a small army was already attending to her.

People gathered on both sides as the bride and her entourage began their slow march to the mandap. First among them was Eisha's father; a double scotch on the rocks in his hand and tears filling his eyes behind his round spectacles. *What bittersweet irony*, he thought with a tormented smile on his lips as he watched his daughter pass by. Eisha's father was facing a predicament faced by every bride's father. His daughter was leaving home and he had no control over her future. When Eisha used to run around like a stray puppy, he used to keep wishing she'd settle down; but now that she was settling down, he wished it wasn't happening so soon. He had paid a fat packet, which he could scarcely afford, for the Fairy-tale Gardens. He wanted his daughter to be happy. He was sure she would be. Robin Chauhan was a handsome, polite and affluent man. Eisha had known him for a month—theirs had been a quick courtship. Now she was going away with him to live in a country on the other side of the planet.

Robin was seated in front of the sacred fire in the mandap when his bride was ushered in and settled down beside him. The couple's immediate family members took their respective seats on either side of them. Extended family members and friends were designated to the outer circle.

People entering the sacred space of the mandap were required to remove their footwear. In the course of the ceremony, it was customary for a sister, cousin or friend of the bride to steal the groom's shoes. To get the thief to return his shoes, the groom would have to fulfil a challenge or present a monetary reward to the culprit. When everyone's attention was focussed on the ceremony, the shoe thief got to work.

It had been difficult for Eisha's parents to find a good priest at such short notice. They were usually booked months in advance. When priests inadequately trained in Sanskrit were hired to conduct ceremonies, their chanting tended to sound more like babbling, as was the case with the priest conducting this ceremony. Faced with the prospect of sitting as mute spectators for two hours, watching the pair cast oblations into the sacrificial fire while listening to the drone of a deficient priest, everyone but immediate family members discreetly decamped to the bar at the far end of the lawn.

Robin had many cousins, most of whom were eligible males. Ranjita and Romila strategically positioned themselves at the bar. Others from Eisha's group joined them shortly. The only friend of the bride missing in action was Alya. She was in a bristly bush, hiding the groom's shoes.

'Eisha looks like an angel tonight,' Ranjita said.

'Her blue contact lenses are gorgeous,' said her sister.

'She is breathtaking, indeed, but I'm not wild about the lenses,' Malini remarked. 'I would have preferred seeing her eyes as they naturally are on her wedding day.'

The sisters drew in their breaths to respond to her but stopped on seeing Sunayana lighting a cigarette. Wrapped in nine yards of fabric with a *bindi* the size of a pigeon's egg on her forehead and a cigarette between her lips, she made a picture too disturbingly bold to ignore. Oblivious of—or perhaps inwardly delighting in—the negative attention she was getting from them, Sunayana blew a mouthful of smoke towards the sisters and asked them, 'When is the after-party?'

'Shouldn't you know that by now? It's on the night after the reception,' Romila replied, 'at the penthouse suite of the Hyatt.'

Ranjita and Romila belonged to a prominent family of investment bankers and, though everyone knew it, they still acted hoity-toity. Perhaps they wouldn't have behaved in such an uppity way if they knew that class was an inherent and not inherited attribute. Attitude was a shield they used to stop anything but what they wanted to hear from reaching them.

'They don't have champagne,' Ranjita said.

'The groom's family is hosting the reception and the after-party,' Ranjita replied. 'They'll have champagne at both the events.'

'Anyone want scotch?' Malini asked the group.

'I'll have one in the next round,' Reena said.

'Alright,' Malini said, getting herself a drink, and then she asked Reena, 'Is this your first visit to Delhi?'

'Yes.'

'I hope you're having fun.'

'I am. Are you an old friend of Eisha's?' Reena asked.

'Pardon me?' Malini said distractedly. She had just noticed Jayant crossing the lawn with his arm around a white woman. Mukta was not with them, likely a conscious decision on his part. If she threw a tantrum here it would be difficult to subdue or ignore. Catching up with the couple, Alya jumped onto Jayant's back, covering his eyes with her hands. He was least expecting an ambush but was quick to guess who it was.

'Are you an old friend of Eisha's?' Reena repeated, bringing Malini back to their conversation.

'Old enough,' Malini responded.

'Hi there,' Jayant greeted Malini as he reached the group with Alya in tow.

'Hello Jayant,' Malini replied.

'Where have you been? I haven't seen you for what, two years?' he asked.

'I was interning over my summer breaks at college.'

'That's a long time away. Well, I'm sure your parents came to visit you.'

'No, they were busy.'

'Okay, um...'

'I'm happy to be back. How are you?'

'On top of the world. Meet my wife, Barbara,' Jayant said, pointing to Barbara, who was standing next to him.

'You're married! Congratulations!' Malini exclaimed before

turning to Barbara and saying, 'Nice to meet you, Barbara.'

'Likewise,' Barbara responded.

Malini introduced Reena to the couple. Sunayana had disappeared at some point during the conversation.

'I can't believe Eisha's getting married. She's just a baby,' Jayant said.

Alya wasn't interested in their talk and declared, 'I deserve a drink.'

'Why is that?' Jayant asked her.

'Because...' Alya started, with a conspiratorial expression.

'Because you've been up to mischief. I can see it,' Jayant guessed.

Alya smirked.

'Come on, spill the beans,' Jayant prodded.

'I've hidden the groom's shoes,' Alya whispered in his ear.

'You fiend!'

'They'll never find them.'

Jayant stepped away from the conversation to get a scotch for himself and white wine for Barbara and Alya. He returned to the group with the glasses and said, 'This occasion calls for a celebration. Here's to Eisha.' Jayant raised his glass as he said this and everyone followed suit.

The groom's cousins were growing louder and more boisterous in the background. They weren't the only ones getting intoxicated. On her third drink, Reena was enjoying the entertainment—watching the Mamgai sisters flirting with the bachelors.

Someone called out, 'Who's got the groom's shoes?' Ranjita nudged the young man beside her and said, 'It wasn't us.' The ceremony had ended and guests were pouring onto the lawn. Sunayana emerged from the shrubbery followed by one of the groom's cousins. People stared at her as if she was the shoe thief. Reena knew she wasn't—she was going into the shrubbery with the young man for an entirely different reason.

Eisha's mother was observing her daughter's friends to guess who had taken the shoes. She saw that people were spreading out. Some went to the bar, others were dancing and still others started having dinner. Then, noticing Alya, she approached her, saying, 'Beta, the groom needs his shoes. Come to the mandap and ask for your *shagun*.'

Alya responded to this by ducking behind Jayant.

The pooch, whose furry head was peeking out from Eisha's mother's handbag, craned his neck to see where Alya had vanished. Eisha's mother repeated, 'Beta, come on.'

'Aunty, how can you be so sure that I've taken the shoes?' Alya demanded.

'Let's just say,' Eisha's mother replied, putting her hand on Alya's arm, 'I've earned my grey hair.'

As the two women stepped towards the mandap, Romila yelled, 'Look! Aunty and Alya are going to the mandap. Alya stole the shoes! Let's go and see what happens.'

∽∞∼

'We've got 97,000 rupees,' Robin said, offering Alya the grimy fifties, hundreds and crisp thousand rupee notes that his father, cousins and uncles had pitched in to raise.

'Is that the best you can do?' Alya said, driving a hard bargain.

'I forgot about the shoe-stealing tradition or we would have carried more cash.'

'You should have done your homework.'

'It's all in good spirit. Here, take it,' Robin said.

'Alya, please, return the shoes,' Eisha pleaded.

Guests were forming a circle around them. 'Why isn't she returning the shoes?' Reena asked.

'She's demanding three lakh for them, that's why,' Romila replied, looking like she was about to explode with joy.

'Three lakh?' Reena asked, incredulously.

'The whole family has pitched in but they still can't make the cut. Everything's already paid for, you see, so no one's carrying much cash tonight,' Ranjita said.

'Does Alya need money?' Reena asked, unable to understand Alya's motive, 'The bride's her best friend, isn't she?'

All eyes were on Alya. The charade would go on until she decided it was over. Seeing Eisha's anguish almost made her give in, but then Minty Bose entered the scene and bolstered Alya's fervour.

Minty was a whale of a man in more ways than the obvious. He was a notoriously shrewd film financier. Robin's parents received him at the entrance of the venue and escorted him in.

'That's Minty Bose,' Jayant said, scampering up to Alya.

'Are you talking about *the* Minty Bose?'

'Yes, I am.'

'Could it really be him?'

'Do you have any doubts?' Jayant asked, gawking at Minty.

Oblivious of the effect the newest guest at her wedding was having on her friend, Eisha whined, 'It's supposed to be in good fun.'

Eisha's whiny requests brought Alya back to the subject of the shoes. 'Oh, um, what do I do about the shoes?' Alya whispered to Jayant. 'I guess I should return them.'

'No,' Jayant whispered, 'all eyes are on you. And the ones that have just arrived are the most important ones. They have

to stay on you. Seize the moment. It's yours for the taking.'
Jayant was aware that associating with the aspiring actress could be beneficial to him in the future. If he guided her towards success—which meant big money in Bollywood—he could do well for himself. Also, Alya was a friend. He always did what he could to help his friends.

'You clever fox, you. I'm going to hire you some day,' Alya said.

'Eisha, chica, your groom has to abide by tradition.' Alya continued with the game, 'Tradition demands that he cough up cash.' Saying this, she shot a look at Minty and knew she had his attention.

The groom's cousins milled around her—begging, flirting, flattering—doing whatever they could to make her give in. Alya prevailed, refusing to accept the disparate notes they were offering her like gifts to the divine.

Ranjita and Romila were enthralled. For once, the occasion of a friend's wedding made them joyful rather than jealous. As for Malini, she had no part to play in the events and was finding them too disagreeable to want to be a part of either. With discretion, she left the venue. For the Mumbaikars, the eye candy, liquor and music were good enough to make them stay. Feeling a bit tipsy and thereby unusually confident, Reena went up to the star of the wedding and asked her the question causing an itch at the back of her throat.

'Alya,' Reena said.

'Yes? Sorry, I forgot your—' Alya began.

'Reena, that's my name.'

'Yes, of course, Reena.'

'I wanted to ask you something.'

'Shoot.'

'Why are you doing this?'

'Shh! Keep your voice down.'

'I want to know why you are continuing this, whatever it is, on your friend's big day.'

'Dear girl, it is also *my* big day. Every day can be your big day, if you are ready.'

'I don't understand.'

'Being in the right place at the right time is half the battle won. The other half is having all eyes on you. If you're not the centre of attention, you don't exist. And if you don't exist, you don't have a chance to begin with. The question of a chance being lost or found becomes redundant. It never was yours.'

'Ah, attention. I get it. No, I mean, I don't get it. I wish I got it.'

'How does one draw attention to oneself? Watch, you may learn something. But first, get a drink of water, girl,' Alya instructed Reena, returning to addressing her retinue. 'Gentlemen, have you come up with a solution?'

'We've collected 150,000 rupees,' the groom said.

'You only have another 150,000 rupees to go then. Come on, Mr Chauhan, you don't look so hard up,' Alya said. Her suggestive language and pugnacity were sending shock waves through Minty as she had planned. The more he watched this feisty female play her game, the more riled up he was getting.

'You're the bride's friend, beta,' Eisha's mother said, forcing the wad of notes into Alya's hand. 'Let it go,' she pleaded.

'May I have my shoes now?' the groom said.

'You're cold,' Alya replied.

'What?'

'Since you couldn't give me what I asked for, you'll have to find the shoes. I'll give you hints,' Alya explained.

One of Robin's cousin's had an idea that would not only save the groom's face but also infuse light-hearted fun into an evening on the cusp of going sour. He huddled the men together.

Sensing sabotage, Alya demanded, 'What's going on?' Hoisting Robin onto their shoulders, the men took a few steps towards a relatively deserted part of the lawn. 'Alright, you're getting warm,' Alya said. The women followed the cheering group, as did Jayant, Barbara, the bride, her mother with the pooch in her bag and, of course, Minty, shifting his mass from one leg to the other as he trailed behind them. When the search party guessed its way to Alya's grove, they dropped to the ground in search of the shoes that had, over the course of the night, become a treasure.

Minty watched these good-looking wealthy people digging and grovelling in the mud like scavengers. That Alya had got them doing so was arousing to him. They still hadn't met, but Minty recognized a kindred soul. They were two competitive, hungry survivors, even conquerors, in a concrete world.

'Alya, tell us where the shoes are,' Eisha's mother asked her.

'Alright, *Jeeja ji*, I'll give you your shoes,' Alya said to Robin with her gaze fixed on Minty. Parting the thorny bushes where she'd hidden the shoes, she declared, 'Here they are, Jeeja ji.'

'All's well that ends well, right?' Eisha said, relieved it had just been a game Alya had been playing to amuse her guests.

Once the show was over, Jayant introduced Alya to Minty. 'Minty ji, Alya is an actress. She's the new Cola girl.'

'It's an honour to meet you,' Alya said.

'Hello ji,' Minty said.

'She wants to act in films,' Jayant continued, 'your guidance at this point in her career would be greatly appreciated.'

'Yes, yes. I will guide her. Alya ji, I have very much enjoyed being in your presence tonight,' Minty said. 'Are you going to attend the party at the Hyatt?'

'Eisha is an old friend, so I wouldn't miss it for anything,' Alya replied.

'*Theek hai*, then I look forward to seeing you there,' Minty said before turning and leaving.

The hunt for the bridegroom's shoes had galvanized the youngsters. They noisily explored the site where the shoes had been as if more treasures were to be found there. Reena was the only one who could clearly see who the real winner of the night was—the winner who had found the treasure she sought: Alya. Her prize had not just been the shagun for the shoes.

∞

'Up there,' Sunayana said, pointing at the penthouse suite. Reena looked out of the car window and saw tiny figures moving in an electric glow on top of the building. 'It's the last party. Eisha and Robin are leaving for their honeymoon tomorrow.'

'There aren't many people at this one,' Reena said.

'The hotties will be there, that's all that matters.'

So what? None of them are interested in me. Reena was about to say but she restrained herself, not wanting to sound despondent. Appreciating the technicolour lights raging against the night, she said, instead, 'Nothing's going to stop me from having fun!'

∞

The groom's handsome cousin with the Californian lilt to his voice raised his glass and said, 'To the newlyweds.' Sunayana couldn't get enough of him or his accent, nor could Ranjita and Romila and a bevy of female friends of the bride. He was exotic for these parts. But this whole affair was beginning to bore Reena and make her uneasy. The night was about celebrating a union, the merging of souls in wedlock. There was an abundance of all things lustrous and impressive but something was still missing, something important. She couldn't tell what.

'Hi Reena,' Malini said, approaching her.

'Hello Malini, nice to see you,' Reena responded.

'What a pretty dress you're wearing!' Malini said, stepping back to get a better look.

'My sister got it from Milan.'

Reena asked a passing waiter for a Long Island iced tea. 'What about you, Malini? What will you have?'

'I'll have a gin and tonic,' Malini told the waiter. 'It's not my usual drink but it'll do for tonight.'

'Long Island is not my usual drink either,' Reena said, 'but isn't that the trend around here?'

'What is?'

'Nothing is what it's supposed to be,' Reena observed.

With the drama of his wedding behind him, Robin was in the mood to celebrate. He was dancing with his bride, satisfied that the girl was his. The deal was sealed.

Meanwhile, the Indian clan from abroad was raving about the couple's reception: 'I loved Daler Mehndi's cloak and beaded turban'; 'I don't think I've ever seen my parents move like they did that night.'

'I can't get over shaking Bill Clinton's hand,' Romila said. 'Shaking his hand was the highlight of my night.'

'I bet it was the highlight of your life,' Alya jibed. 'Have you washed your hand since?'

Hearing Alya's jibes, Malini laughed. Reena nibbled on a chipped nail. Nobody could make out Sunayana's reaction, if she had one. Hanging from the arm of her favourite among the groom's cousins, she had a grin on her face that she couldn't rub off, least of all for the Mamgais.

Guests were spreading to the corners of the venue. Some wandered onto the terrace and others congregated in corridors, rooms and closets, involved in conversation, dance and mischief. Seeing Eisha by herself, Malini seized the opportunity to share a moment alone with her old friend, not sure when or if another would arise.

'I want you to know that I'm going to miss you,' Malini said.

'I'll miss you too,' Eisha responded.

'I hope you'll return here often.'

The impregnable cloud of unresolved matter—words that should and should not have been said, falsities and truths misunderstood—hung heavily between the former best friends. There had been a time when they had been inseparable. It had just taken one phone call to change that.

⁂

Three weeks before Malini had relocated to Delhi from the US, she had gotten a call from Eisha. 'Guess what?' Eisha had asked, 'I'm getting married.' When they had spoken barely a month before that call, Eisha had not mentioned so much as a boyfriend or a date. The friends had only chatted about Eisha's dalliance with a foreign traveller while on holiday in the hills.

'Aren't you happy for me?' Eisha had said, not hearing sounds of excitement coming from the other end.

'I'm too surprised to be happy,' Malini had replied.

When Malini finally returned, Eisha's wedding preparations had been in full swing. The latter had only met her once, and thereafter, Malini had been excluded from all wedding-related errands and activities. When Malini had received the invite to Eisha's wedding only a day before the marriage, she had been convinced that Eisha had misinterpreted her initial reservations as envy. In truth, Malini wanted nothing more than to embark on a satisfying career, rediscover her country and bond with family and friends. Marriage was nowhere on her agenda.

⟞⟝

As the two friends stood together in awkward silence, Eisha's husband and a few of his buddies joined them. Convivial conversation led to talk of the Kalra family. 'You mean the ones in petrochemicals and…something?' Eisha asked.

'Yes, petrochemicals and steel,' Robin's friend replied. 'I know Gaurav Kalra. I met him at a nightclub. He wanted my number. He was back home to join the family business after a long time abroad,' Eisha said.

Her husband's buddies started looking at Eisha in a different light. She'd been around. She'd seen life. Somehow this side of Eisha had not come across before. The Kalras were a far more powerful family than the Chauhans. If Gaurav had taken an interest in Eisha, it confirmed that she was a good catch. Her husband was proud.

Malini listened to and watched this interaction in disbelief. She remembered that night at Organza when Gaurav had introduced himself to her, not Eisha. But Eisha narrated the incident with such conviction that it made Malini doubt her memory. Eisha didn't meet her eye, and a tingle in her gut told Malini that even if Eisha had, she wouldn't have seen her so much as blink or twitch. Eisha had told the lie so many times that she had come to believe it.

On the other side of the room, short, dark and intoxicated Reena was mouthing the lyrics: 'I'm so horny, horny, horny, horny, I'm so horny, for love'. Dancing to the catchy number without shame or guilt, she became a subject of scorn. Her behaviour provoked Ranjita and Romila. How could someone like Reena dare to be rapturous when they denied themselves not only rapture but its expression as well. It was unpalatable, intolerable and foolhardy to them. When Reena tripped over her nine-inch heels and fell on the carpet, they got more than what they had wished for. She had been foolish—getting drunk while wearing heels so high.

'What a runt,' Romila proclaimed. Above her, Reena was seeing a spinning vortex of quintuplet and septuplet Mamgais—a dizzying, devilishly befuddled nightmare. People gathered around her. Someone tried to peek under her dress. She got up and tottered to the terrace.

In another part of the venue, Jayant and Alya were in conversation.

'Jayant, where have you been?' Alya demanded. 'You've come late to every event.'

'We had a family emergency,' Barbara said, looking tired. 'I've got to eat.'

'Go ahead, dear, I'll join you in a few minutes,' Jayant told his wife.

'So, chico,' Alya said, when the coast was clear, 'is Bose coming tonight?'

'He should be here any minute.'

Outside, on the balcony, where food was being served,

Barbara took a plate and got in line behind Malini, Reena and Sunayana.

'Hey, Reena,' the Mamgai sisters hollered, coming out onto the terrace. 'I'm surprised you're not having a bazooka kulfi,' Romila said, getting in line behind them.

'What kulfi?' Reena asked.

'Bazooka kulfi,' Ranjita repeated, tittering. 'Those ice creams over there in the shape of—'

'You know better than us,' Romila finished her sentence.

Reena glanced at the dessert counter and saw phallic ice creams standing in circular holders on a tray. She needed to go to the washroom but had thought of putting it off till after dinner. The Mamgai sisters' taunts made her reconsider.

The toilets in the bedrooms of the suite were occupied, so Reena went to the one in the hall by the entrance of the penthouse. It took a while to do the needful, always a challenge for an inebriated woman. Men didn't have to tackle a dress, stockings, high heels and a bag, all at once, while doing their business. Considering her poor coordination, Reena performed superbly.

Confident to appear before the world again, she opened the door to return to the buffet, when she saw Alya in the corridor outside straightening her dress, smelling her breath in the cup of her hand and fluffing her hair. This was the most confident woman Reena had ever encountered; what could be making her so nervous? Something was afoot. She waited and watched from a crack in the door. Just as it seemed that nothing was going to happen, Jayant appeared. He whispered in Alya's ear. She nodded. Then, he put something in her hand and went back inside the suite. Ambling up the hotel corridor, Reena saw the big man from the wedding. 'What a stylish leather jacket you have on,' Alya told him. Looking at the man's girth, Reena guessed the jacket must have taken two cows to make—a vile thought for a vegetarian. Alya led him down the corridor. When they disappeared out of sight, Reena stepped out of the washroom and turned towards the terrace, but her unruly feet refused to obey and took her down the corridor behind them.

Reena saw Alya stop outside a room at the far end of the floor. She unlocked the door and went inside. *So, it was a key that Jayant had put in her hand*, Reena thought as she saw the fat man go in behind her. Looking around to make sure that no one was there, Reena pressed her ear to the door.

Inside the room, Alya dimmed the lights but Minty was far too solid a structure to avoid. When his daunting mass approached her on the bed, she held her breath, and when he rested upon her, the air was involuntarily pushed out of her. She saw stars; not of the type she had envisioned herself becoming one day. He pulled off her underwear and hiked her dress up to her neck. It was a most repulsive feeling—to have this absolute stranger enter her inner being.

Bose kept thrusting while Alya strained beneath him for snatches of air, her eyes fixed on the ceiling, her mind trying to pin her goal. *Look at the larger picture. Look at the larger picture. Look at...* Minty's material reality crippled the chance of any other picture coming to the fore. Trapped under his whopping weight, consumed by it, seconds stretched to minutes and minutes to hours. The pounding of her body had reached the point of becoming unbearable when Minty hit the spot and, finding his momentum, doggedly drove towards his objective. As the pace of his movements increased, her head was awkwardly cupped in his armpit. Gagging on wet armpit hair, a shaft of meat sandpapering her dry insides, she felt disgusted, humiliated and sickened by what was happening to her, but she refused to give up. *Stick to the script. Stick to the script, Alya,* she thought to herself. This was not going to deter her from her mission—not even this. *I've come this far. I'm not going to let it be for nothing.* Her lungs were in lockdown mode, craving oxygen. She refused to give them the breath of life they needed, sacrificing herself in a bid for her higher goal. Minty achieved his singular objective. Grunting like a wild boar, he rolled off her. Finally, she breathed.

Outside the room, Reena heard the grunt loud and clear. She had heard too much; more than she should have, more than she had imagined she would or wished to have heard. *Beautiful people are a persecuted lot,* Reena thought. For the first time in her life, she asked herself if it was really that bad to be ordinary. *Whatever I am, however I am, I'm okay with being me.* People were collecting at a nearby lift. Reena unstuck her ear from the door and returned to the party.

'Have you seen Alya? We're about to cut the cake,' Eisha asked Reena, who chose to remain mum. The cake was a five-tiered confection with a bride and groom in a sugary embrace, peering down from their marshmallow-covered pinnacle at a pair of doves perched at the bottom tier. She wished Alya could have made it for the momentous finale. The cutting of the cake not only marked the end of her wedding celebrations but also signified a new beginning—the beginning of a life of luxury, glamour and freedom.

'Reena, where have you been?' Ranjita asked her when she saw her back at the suite.

'Hope you're not too late,' her sister added.

'Late for what? I'm here for the cutting of the cake, aren't I?'

'The bazooka kulfis,' Ranjita said, 'Grab one, quick. They're melting fast.'

'I have something to say,' Reena replied.

'She has something to say!' Romila exclaimed.

'What might that be?' asked Ranjita.

'You both need those bazookas more than I do,' Reena said.

The sisters had bullied Reena to no end over the past few days and she had patiently tolerated their jibes. This unexpected rebuttal was surprising not only to them but also to Malini.

'Did I miss something?' Malini asked, surprised at Reena's newfound confidence.

The newlyweds cut the cake and fed pieces of it to each other. Eisha had been drinking from a bottle of Dom Pérignon champagne. Tipsy, she started behaving like her silly old self again—making dirty jokes and singing Bollywood songs in a squeaky high-pitched voice. Her accent got heavier. She burped, crossed her eyes and said, 'I'm sorry.' She laughed and her friends laughed with her. The groom's cousins mimicked the bride's antics and accent, mocking the local addition to their family. Embarrassed by his bride, Robin announced, 'Next time you meet Eisha, she'll be a changed woman.'

Malini was offended on Eisha's behalf. She turned to Reena and said, 'What does he mean by that?' Then, turning back around, she said aloud, 'I hope not.'

Reena's professional interactions over the past year and, on a micro level, what she had witnessed in this one wedding weekend had her questioning the very notion of authenticity. She respected Malini for having the courage to rebut Robin's declaration about his wife and for being unafraid to speak her mind regardless of the consequences. *There's nothing more inspiring than a single person standing up; one person standing up can inspire a hundred, a thousand, or a hundred thousand,* Reena thought, her faith in humanity restored. She felt strong again.

The day had been momentous not only for Eisha but also for Reena. It was the day she decided that she, for one, would be authentic, no matter how hard it was in the contemporary age. She was not going to use or be used by anyone to get what she wanted. Karma, dharma, whatever it's called—she chose it. She decided to live her life by it. This was her vow to herself that night. To remain silent or to speak up, to be weak or to be strong, to be true or untrue—these were the choices life demanded and only she would make those for herself.

12

Breakfast in Bed

Those days were grand. Everything had potential. Her new break, her talent and her love all had potential. Alya's career was at that moment of suspension that came before a thrilling ride—when the heart flies up to the head and fills it with anticipation. Beside her on her way to the top was her partner, confidante and best friend, Danny. He was an upcoming activist in an emergent, environmentally conscious Maharashtra. He was a passionate man who had his own aspirations but wasn't loud about them, pursuing his interests with quiet determination. Romantic road trips, evenings watching movies in bed and leisure time with friends had become distant memories for the go-getting couple now that the dreams they had shared many moons ago were seeing the light of day.

Danny was feeling nostalgic, sitting at a table at a fancy restaurant overlooking the Gateway of India. 'It seems like ages ago,' he said, looking out the window.

'What does?' Alya asked.

'When we used to walk along the promenade, look at the lights on the boats floating on the water and eat food sold by the street vendors. Remember?'

'Oh yes, back when we couldn't afford restaurants like this one, back when I endlessly talked about famous freaks in showbiz, and how I wanted to be one, and you, well, you spoke about becoming a crusader for the crows.'

'The migratory flamingos, darling.'

A waiter discreetly interrupted the couple to take their order.

'I miss walking along the promenade with you,' Danny told her. If they did it today, they'd be mobbed.

'With the good comes the bad,' Alya reasoned stoically.

Danny would have liked to spend more time with his girlfriend but when he was free, she usually wasn't. He accompanied her, at times, on one of her networking sojourns. He had gone with her to Laila and Abbas Ali's annual Christmas luncheon. It brought him cheer to see children running around with their toys, bringing a semblance of normalcy to an otherwise ostentatious affair. Kids, Danny could do with.

'Happy birthday,' he wished her, kissing her hand.

'Shhh,' she hushed him.

'What is it?'

'I hope you aren't going to mention my age.'

He laughed.

'I'm sure everyone's eavesdropping on us.'

'No one can hear us, honey,' he said, 'What a funny bone you have.'

But she was dead serious. They went back to his apartment later that night. Danny had every intention of making sweet love to his woman on her big day but it wasn't easy. The number of phone calls interrupting the session would have thrown off any man. Luckily for Alya, Danny was as passionate in bed as he was about his work.

The next morning, Danny woke up as early as the birds

he enjoyed watching. He went into the kitchen and prepared a bowl of porridge with chopped apples and sliced almonds. He boiled an egg and poured freshly squeezed orange juice into a tall glass. Danny enjoyed going to Crawford Market to buy his own produce, and he didn't mind people gawking at him—this handsome, broad-shouldered man—tenderly holding a plum between his thumb and forefinger, testing its ripeness, wholeness, readiness, willingness and every other trait before committing to it. When Alya woke up, he was fully dressed and serving her breakfast in bed.

'Good morning,' she said, stretching her arms above her head.

'Good morning, Señorita,' he said, 'how are you today?'

'As well as I can be.'

'I'm heading out. Don't forget the awareness drive at Charkop on Thursday. It's World Wetlands Day. We're expecting a significant turnout.'

'Danny, I've just woken up.'

'My team has informed the media that you're coming. Your attendance will give the campaign the exposure it needs.'

'I'll be there. I promised already, didn't I?'

'See you later,' he said, kissing her on the forehead. 'Stay as long as you wish.'

13

Star Power

On the face of it, Charkop was a lush forest resounding with birdsong. Some say that the lone hill that was surrounded by water had been there for millennia. Above the hill was a sight rare to come by in Mumbai—an expanse of open sky. Charkop was the kind of place that could bring peace to the most troubled souls. If only it survived to serve that purpose.

'I know it's not easy to take time out to come here and show that your environment matters to you,' Danny said, standing in his trademark gumboots on a plywood podium erected on a barren patch of the forest that had once been covered with mangrove shrubs. He was addressing a gathering of about two hundred people, a third of them media persons who were there for only one thing and it wasn't the forest.

'Mangroves act as a buffer for our coastal cities against flooding caused by storms at the sea or the ravages of tsunamis,' he said into the microphone, addressing the gaggle of casually dressed teenagers carrying backpacks and garbage bags. These were smart kids, intensely aware of the most urgent need of their times. Danny was their Clean Guru, the Messiah of Mangroves, an environmental Indiana Jones who they envisioned cracking a whip across the backs of the political sand mafia, land sharks and other nefarious violators of forest-related and coastal regulations. To them, it was cool to challenge the establishment. It was cool to demand accountability from politicians. They were tech-savvy, well-connected and a click away from an invisible universe of information they could access at will. And will was something they were full of.

'Mangroves are being destroyed at an alarming rate by debris dumping, poaching, illegal encroachment and construction. The government is incapable of stopping the menace. Heck, they're in cahoots with the perpetrators! I'm speaking to you, the youth of Mumbai, because it is you who will have to face the ecological consequences of this devastation. You *have* to get involved. You *have* to get your hands dirty. Unite and clean up. That's how you can pressurize the government into taking responsibility. Embarrass them into action!' Danny said emphatically.

Cheers rose from the ranks of the young crusaders even as a troop of policemen joined the gathering from behind. Undeterred by their arrival, Danny continued, 'Charkop is home to 131 species of birds, 14 species of reptiles and mammals such as...can anyone take a guess?'

A girl raised her hand.

'Yes?' Danny said, looking at the girl.

'Jackals?' she answered.

'You're absolutely correct, young lady.'

'Have any of you seen a jackal?'

The policemen grinned.

'Just the other day,' Danny said, staring at the apathetic officials, 'three flamingos were shot dead in broad daylight in this creek, right where we stand. Did anyone do anything about it?' Danny demanded.

The youngsters booed and jeered, making the uniformed men visibly uncomfortable. One placed his hands defiantly on his hips; another scratched his crotch; and yet another, with stained teeth, spat half a cup of tobacco juice that had sloshed around in his mouth for a quarter of an hour on a teenager's white Converse.

'When is Alya arriving?' a TV correspondent asked the volunteer handing out lemonade in paper cups. In response to his question, starting with a muttering at the back of the crowd, pandemonium began to spread. Cameramen ran helter-skelter. She had arrived.

Dressed in a peach shirt and blue jeans, the actress moved through the desolate mangroves like a seed of hope. The paparazzi clambered over each other to take pictures of her. When they got too close, her bodyguards pushed them aside. A photographer slipped and fell into the creek. It didn't matter. One picture of a superstar was worth a thousand of an activist's words.

Alya stepped onto the platform, took the microphone from Danny, and said, 'Hello everybody, how are you today?' Shutterbugs flashed. Birds scattered. 'Girls and boys, listen to what this guy has to say. He knows what he's talking about.' That was it. Her speech was done. She stepped off the platform.

'Alya, Alya! Give us a shot with the teens,' a photographer shouted from the wall of media persons.

Thinking fast, Alya took a garbage bag from one of the youths and walked over to the nearest mound of debris. She picked up a crushed soda can and a hunk of discarded concrete and dumped them into the bag. The teenagers joined the actress in her impromptu clean-up. The cameras went rat-a-tat-tat like machine guns in battle. The awareness drive at Charkop was over in another ten minutes.

༄

Examining her picture on the front page of *City Times* with a crushed soda can in one hand and a garbage bag in the other, standing with a group of teenagers who could easily be mistaken for backup dancers rather than environmentalists, Alya was pleased. Below the picture was an article describing her appearance at Charkop. Danny was mentioned in the last line: 'Dharmesh Pawar, environmentalist and boyfriend to film star Alya, was the organizer of the awareness drive at Charkop.'

Danny understood the power of the media. He didn't seek credit. His aim was to inspire students into becoming eco-warriors and launch a nationwide 'youthquake'. If getting famous personalities involved helped in doing that, he'd take their help and let the media get all over it.

'The event at Charkop was a success,' Jayant said, joining the couple for brunch at Alya's apartment.

'Imagine what an impact it would make if you became brand ambassador for the Wetlands Trust,' Danny told Alya, 'With your clout, the trust could achieve so much more.'

'It's an interesting proposition,' Jayant advised her. 'The biggest stars in Hollywood are spokespersons or brand ambassadors for charitable foundations and trusts.'

'Let's not jump the gun here,' Alya said, giving Danny a sharp look. 'You should be happy I showed up for the campaign. I get paid for making such appearances. I did it for you.'

'I know that, of course, and I appreciate it. What I meant is that if more celebrities showed an interest in social and environmental causes—something close to their hearts—they could achieve a great deal. People look up to them, for better or for worse.'

'What do you mean, for better or for worse? Honey, you couldn't buy publicity like I got you.'

Jayant studied the food on his plate. He shovelled a spoonful into his mouth. It was more than he could chew, and combined with the acrid aftertaste of the conversation he had just witnessed, it was hard to swallow.

14

Thailand

It was five in the morning. Alya brushed, showered, got dressed and blow-dried her hair. Her maid had already packed her bags. The woman knew it all—how to pack for a location shoot or a promotional tour, for a cold place, a hot place or a wet place. The only type of packing she had no clue about was for a romantic getaway because it involved things from drawers that she didn't know existed. Alya was lucky in a lot of ways. She had a roaring career, a good man, lodgings-to-die-for and smart help.

Her driver took her suitcases and put them in the boot of the car. Birkin bag slung over her shoulder, the actress was about to step into her vehicle to embark on another film schedule in a foreign land when she paused and returned to her bedroom. Standing beside the bed, she looked down at the man she was leaving behind, his dense curls forming a halo around his head on the pillow. Her eyes scanned his mildly ripped arms. Pleased that a specimen like him was hers for the taking as and when she desired, she drew a line with a manicured nail on his bicep and whispered, 'Goodbye.'

∞

Women in yellow and pink harem pants strolled along the beach, the sheer fabric of their costumes clinging to their shapely legs. One of them picked up a shell and admired its form.

Behind the graceful nymphets was a harshly paradoxical sight—a crew of burly men heaving a brightly coloured canvas onto a wooden platform. The sand around the men was littered with mechanical instruments. White screens blankly stared at the platform while a gangly crane loomed above it. In front of this stage, there was a semicircular track half-embedded in the sand, with a plank on four wheels with a camera, a chair and an umbrella attached to it.

Stray dogs sniffing at dirty utensils beside people polishing off lunch in a shack nestled in the palm trees created the illusion of this being a regular village—but this was no ordinary settlement. This was Village Bollywood transported to the shores of Thailand.

The whistling of the wind and twittering of the birds on the verdant island in turquoise waters were rudely interrupted by the alien tune of bhangra pop. Hearing the choreographer's boom box, the dancers gathered at the centre of the set. Their guru snapped his fingers and they got into formation onstage, ready for a rehearsal. The cast and crew emerged from the camouflage of the forest. The beach was under siege—its 'Bollywoodization' complete.

A pair of beauties materialized upon the sands and went to their separate tents followed by their make-up artists, hairstylists and personal attendants. The shorter of the two was Alya. Beyond her own reflection and that of the stylist plumping her curls in a handheld mirror, she could see the other girl—Rehana—donning her war paint. Jayant was stretching like an alley cat on a foldable chair in her tent. He was focussed on Rehana out of boredom, a full stomach or in a show of dramatics, Alya could not tell. Together, they watched Alya's adversary admiring her rear in a full-length mirror that had been thrust into the sand.

'Why does she get a full-length mirror and I this crappy handheld one?'

'She's a star child, that's why,' Jayant teased.

'I guess she'll go and tell daddy if she doesn't get her way.'

'Don't even try to stand up to family clout, Al. Not here. Not ever.'

'*Chup reh, Rehana ka dewaana* [Shut up, Rehana's fanboy].'

'I'm no fan of hers. She's a tart.'

Alya squinted at the opposite camp, watching Rehana's make-up assistant airbrush her legs with foundation. Alya was charismatic. She was street smart. She had the 'it' factor. But Rehana had a model's good looks. She was irresistible to men and some women too.

'She's in great shape, there's no denying it,' Alya said. 'I eat three sticks of celery a day and still can't be so lean.'

'You eat three sticks, she eats one,' Jayant pointed out.

'Or she eats two and barfs them up,' Alya quipped. If her hairstylist and make-up artist had heard her—which was likely, since they were close enough to lick her ears—they feigned ignorance superbly.

'Speaking of celery, I'm hungry,' Alya said, watching a man scampering up the beach with a bottle of Gatorade, headphones, a mobile phone and a celery stick clutched in his chubby hands. Huffing and puffing, he entered the enemy camp and delivered the goods to Rehana. He was well-dressed and had an expensive haircut, but the wet patches under his arms and around his shirt collar betrayed those distinguished bearings.

'Just look at the fat bastard,' Jayant said.

'Be quiet, you could learn from him,' Alya retorted.

'We're not doing so bad. What say you?'

'I say, let's keep up the momentum.'

'She's only the supporting actress, Al.'

'For now.'

Jayant took a second look at Rehana's manager.

'Give me my robe, chico. It may still be some time before Dude decides to grace us with his presence,' Alya said.

∞

To rise to the highest rank of the film industry, the director of *Ek Pal*, talented as he was, needed a big-budget bonanza under his belt. It was critical that this movie succeeded at the box office. If that meant keeping his cool until his lead actor arrived on set three hours late, he was resigned to do it. He crossed his fingers behind his back and prayed for the schedule to finish within the estimated time.

The sun was beyond the point in the sky that it should have been for filming to begin when the actor who called himself 'Dude' arrived with his band of yes-men. His arrival had an effect of biblical proportions; moods were uplifted; the atmosphere was infused with energy; the change in tempo testament to the impact of a hero, real or make-believe, on mortal men.

At some point on his journey to superstardom, Dude had developed the tendency of referring to himself in the third person. He had invented choice phrases for himself, like, 'The Dude needs a break;' 'Here comes The Dude;' and 'I know, I'm dude-a-licious.' And to millions of women around the planet he indeed was dude-a-licious. The actor had been voted

Sexiest Man Alive in *People* magazine's India edition for three consecutive years.

Passing Alya's tent, hands cocked like trigger-happy pistols, Dude called out, 'Hey Alya, are you ready for the shot?'

Jayant suppressed a fit of laughter at how cheesy the man was. Alya shot back, 'Ready when you are.'

Passing her competitor's tent, the actor waved at Rehana too. Alya smirked when Rehana sucked in her tummy and pushed out her booty as she waved back at him. That reminded Alya of her cutlets? She called out, 'Cutlets!'

Anticipating a flogging for forgetting those vital accessories without which her mistress dared not be seen on screen, Alya's personal attendant dashed to her side with the spongy thingamajigs. Alya slipped the inserts, code-named cutlets, into her bikini top and got an instant boost to not just her body but also her confidence.

Flanked by a team of assistants, the director tinkered with the contraption on the tracks embedded in the sand. Light technicians took their posts by the halogens and screens. The crew cleared the platform and made way for the backup dancers, the heroines in sarongs and the shirtless hero. Dude immediately hit the floorboards with thirty push-ups and ninety abdominal crunches.

A group of young tourists, high on Thai stick, watched the scene unfold from afar. They heard someone shout, 'Action!' Was it the voice of God? Was it directed at them? They were baffled. Entranced by the spectacle, they were unwilling, or unable, to move. A recorder blared. The stage erupted in colour. The landscape behind the women dancing in harem pants seemed to throb to the beat of the music, its hot pink path stretching into bubble gum oblivion.

Alya skipped over to Rehana and together they pranced off the stage with their backup dancers, making way for Dude and his bad boys. Oiled muscles glistening, bandana-swathed heads bobbing and hips pumping with a vulgarity unmatched by the raunchiest music videos, they danced in perfect synchronicity.

Then came the command, 'Cut!'

'I'm parched,' Rehana said, stroking her slender neck. A spot boy rushed to her rescue with a bottle of chilled water. The liquid trickled from the corner of her mouth and formed a trail from her bikini-clad breasts to her bejewelled navel. Following the trail with his eyes, the spot boy fantasized about it trickling into his mouth. Rehana was aware of the effect she had on him, but she was unfazed. It may have been different if he were Dude. But there was no chance of that happening. Dude was too busy pumping his muscles or counting calories on his watch to notice anyone or anything.

Alya's stylist was powdering her sweaty face and spraying her flyaway hair as they waited for the director's next command. She glanced at the dancers standing idly around her—one was chewing on a protein bar, another was picking her nose, quite naturally, and the rest were shuffling impatiently. It was then that she felt it. Leaving her hotel room that morning, she had discovered, to her dismay, a spot of blood in her underpants. Now, at 3.30 p.m., the clot that was oozing out of her signalled that the super-sized, super-absorbent tampon she had used to plug her menstrual flow was saturated.

'Crap!' Alya exclaimed.

'Yes, Madam, what can I get you?' her attendant asked.

'Um, nothing. Just go about your business,' she responded.

She approached the director, with the intention of asking for a break so that she could cover the half-a-kilometre on the burning sand to her trailer parked in the palms. Jayant was in the crowd surrounding the monitor.

'The take is good… We'll keep it,' the director told his assistant, watching the rushes of the sequence they had just shot.

'That angle doesn't work for me,' Dude said.

'You look superb,' the director reassured him.

'Do another take,' Dude demanded stubbornly.

'We have to move on to the next sequence. It's our last day at this location. We have a lot of ground to cover before sunset.'

Dude called one of his cronies, a stuntman who was always present even when not required. 'What do you think, Munna?' Dude asked him.

'I think there should be more distance between you and the backup dancers. The boundaries are getting blurred. You need to stand out. *Teri body dikhni chahiye, re* [Your body needs to be visible],' Munna commented.

'Correct,' Dude agreed.

Alya was familiar with Dude's tantrums. For an actor to ask a stuntman for his opinion over that of the director was unforgivable. But if she had to pick a side, she'd choose Dude's. She wouldn't risk pissing him off. They say that hell hath no fury worse than a woman scorned; but an actor scorned, or an actor who perceives himself to be scorned even if he hasn't been, can become unforgiving.

'Sir, excuse me, may I take a short break?' Alya asked the director.

'We're doing the next sequence right away.'

'We'll retake the last sequence after it, in that case,' Dude said.

'We won't have time to fit in a retake of the previous sequence. The light conditions later in the day will change too drastically for a retake to be feasible,' the director explained patiently.

'You'll find a way,' the actor said, nonchalantly, and returned to the stage.

For the next segment of the song, Dude had to spin on his heel and give Alya a come-hither look after which she would run towards him and leap into his arms. The sequence was to conclude with the hero lifting the heroine off her feet.

'Action,' the director exclaimed. Dude did his bit and Alya did hers, with one thought going through her mind: *I hope my sarong doesn't get stained.*

'Cut!' the director yelled. The actors returned to their original positions.

'Action!' the director repeated. The moves were redone.

'Cut! We'll go for another,' the director instructed. Dude liked to give many takes from which the best would be selected. It gave him more scope to look good. Alya, however, was worried, imagining a red archipelago forming on her blue sarong.

'Action!' the director called again. The actors repeated the routine, but this time Alya's distress became manifest. She half leapt at and half slammed into Dude and, in the ensuing collision, something happened—something exquisitely amusing for Rehana and terrifically embarrassing for Alya. A thingamajig popped out of her bikini top and sprang into the air. To a mortified Alya, it appeared to be moving up in slow motion.

'Cut!' the director yelled, pretending he hadn't seen a thing. Everyone pretended they hadn't seen a thing, *the* thing, except Rehana.

Jayant was sitting in the shade of an umbrella, sipping on pineapple juice when the incident occurred. Even in this heat, everything on the set froze—everything but the cutlet that had fallen back down and was bouncing on the stage. Snapping out of inaction, Alya's assistant picked up the cutlet and put it in her bag. Jayant didn't know how to react—the event was unprecedented. Then, he felt Alya's phone vibrate in his pocket. Grateful for the intervention, he too snapped out of inaction and took the phone to Alya. Speaking to a friend, he was sure, would provide her the comfort she needed. 'It's for you,' he said. Alya put the phone to her ear.

'Hi babe, how are you doing?' the voice on the other end of the phone said.

'Monica, this is not a good time. I'm in the middle of a shoot,' Alya said.

'I was at The Gauntlet and guess who walks in?' Monica continued, ignoring Alya's response.

'Can it wait?' Alya asked, still dazed. 'Call me tonight.'

'You have to hear this.'

'Who walked in?'

'Danny.'

'And?'

'He was with a pretty young thing.'

'Huh?'

'They were enjoying a meal, just the two of them, alone.'

'What nonsense, Monica.'

'Girlfriend, would I lie to you?'

Things with Danny had been going in the direction Alya had wanted. Now, she would have to deal with this snag in her well-planned progress. Why was the universe conspiring against her? *Why, oh why, is this happening to me?* Alya questioned herself, looking at the indigo sky.

∽

15

(No) Piece of Cake

Stacks of books rose to the ceiling of the café like wallpaper, halting only to make way for posters of the giants of literature such as Tagore, Dickens, Christie and Poe. This and the staff dressed as literary characters serving coffee and cake to melodies from movies based on books was what made Café Wormhole a popular destination for Mumbai's literati.

Reena and Malini sat at a table beside the iron stand draped with newspapers from *The Wall Street Journal* to the *Tokyo Times*. Malini was sipping on a mint-flavoured mocha and Reena was contemplating while staring at her chocolate tart.

'What's up, Reena? You seem a little low today,' Malini commented.

'I'm getting sick of socializing,' Reena responded.

'What do you mean? You hardly socialize.'

'I'm getting sick of being forced to meet men over coffee. Yesterday, my parents hooked me up with another South Indian Brahmin fellow as if I haven't met enough already.'

'You sure have, I can vouch for that.'

'His family got to know of me through the community grapevine and contacted my parents. To cut a long story short, we met. Malini, he was wearing a lungi and black rubber slippers and his forehead was smeared with ash. The only thing missing was a topknot.'

'Gosh, that's hilarious.'

'His get-up wouldn't have been a problem for me if he had been the cheerful type, you know? Cheerful enough to toss his lungi with his cousins during the climax of a Rajinikanth film. But the stick jammed up his butt made tossing of any kind impossible for him. A stiff stick that should've been in the front rather than up his rear, a stick that'll accompany him to his funeral pyre, a stick his future children will be glad was one stick less for the burning.'

'What rage! I didn't know you had it in you, Reena.'

'He asked me if I'd ever touched alcohol.'

'That's classic.'

'Then, he asked me if I could sing Carnatic music.'

'At least he didn't ask you if you were a virgin.'

'My father received a mail from him this morning listing the qualities he didn't like in me. If I was ready to correct them, he wrote, he would reconsider his rejection of me.'

'What an asshole!'

'I've had coffees with so many jerks that I've lost my taste for coffee.'

'Maybe your dad should stop looking and just leave it up to you.'

'About a month ago, I was introduced to this nice enough guy, considering he was forty-seven and still on the market. But who am I to judge, right? I was ready to accept that he had a stutter and was the same height as me—you can imagine how short our kids would have turned out. What I couldn't accept was that he had been jobless for five years and had been living with his parents and off their money.'

'No, of course not. You can't accept that.'

'Today, he's off the market and I'm still on it.'

'Don't be so harsh on yourself, Reena.'

'Why not? I mean, think about it, even vertically challenged men with speech impediments who live with their parents find partners and rubber-slipper-wearing tight-ass guys reject me. There has to be something wrong with me.'

'There was this chick I knew from high school who married a handsome, educated, well-settled guy. When she was pregnant—and this I got to know through mutual friends—her seemingly exemplary husband made trips to Thailand with his buddies to sample the local flavours, not of the culinary type but of the infamous two-legged variety. When the baby arrived, he made a resolution: he would no longer indulge in Thai prostitutes but local Russian ones instead because that would keep him closer to home.'

Reena was least expecting this salvo.

'She was living in ignorant bliss, clueless that she could contract HIV because of her husband's dangerous liaisons; ignorant, till her flesh started to peel off her body. So, tell me, do you want to trade places with her because she's married and you're not?' Malini questioned.

Reena remembered the expectant father she'd shown a flat to. 'Lie there and let me pleasure you. I'll do whatever you want,' he had said. What if she had gone along with it? She, too, could have contracted a killer disease! The idea made her suffer a small paranoid convulsion.

'You have to be careful when choosing a partner. People are not always what they appear to be,' Malini told her.

'How can anyone *really* know another person?' Reena asked.

'One must get to know oneself first, then one must make an effort to understand one's partner and then decide what one wants from a relationship,' Malini elaborated.

'Sounds complicated,' Reena replied.

'The topic of gender equality has always interested me. Humankind can achieve it, I believe so, but only if both sexes contribute equally. Men, for example, will have to be more tuned into their feminine side; be sensitive and patient with a woman when she's menstruating or going through menopause. Women, on the other hand, shouldn't have unreasonable expectations men can't fulfil,' Malini paused to wipe the creamy moustache on her lip from her mint mocha and continued, 'When people understand how to work as a team with their partners, fill in each other's blanks, become one, they can understand the oneness of the universe.'

'I'll leave finding oneness in the universe to the mystics,' Reena said, resting her head against her arm on the table, 'I'm only interested in finding "the one".'

'Weigh the pros and cons and choose the best you can, that's all.'

'For me, there is *no* choice. Look at the candidates I have before me.'

'Personally, I think when chance and intuition align, one meets their match, and it usually happens unexpectedly.'

'I hope you're right.'

'Enjoy your own company. As a working mom, I can tell you this, time for myself is a luxury I wish I had.'

The waitress serving them—a pretty young woman with a silver stud in her eyebrow and a navel piercing, which was showing from under her crop top—overheard their conversation and said, 'I'm sorry to intrude on your conversation but I couldn't help myself. I don't see what all the fuss is about. I mean, who cares? Men are not a need women can't do without.' Upon hearing this fresh perspective, Reena sat up to better hear the waitress, 'My marital status doesn't define me. If I don't get someone who, as my favourite track puts it, roles with my agenda, I'll be fine. A financially secure woman is a master of her destiny—she creates her own happiness. That's how I see it,' the waitress concluded.

Reena took a closer look at the waitress, convinced she was Lisbeth Salander from *The Girl with the Dragon Tattoo*. What a splendid state of independence she had just described. The waitress then left them to their conversation.

'She is damn right,' Malini said.

'Yeah, well…' Reena muttered.

'There's this couple I know who met and fell desperately in love when they were very young. They eloped a week after meeting each other. It has been forty years since and they believe they're still in love, but the truth is that they actually hate each other,' Malini said.

'How do you know them?' Reena asked.

'I like that poster of Terry Pratchett up there,' Malini said, distracted, pointing at the wall behind the cashier's desk. 'I'm going to see if they have more for sale,' Malini continued, pushing her chair back to get up.

'Wait a minute, tell me about that couple. Who are they?' Reena insisted.

'My parents,' Malini said distractedly as she walked towards the cash counter while looking at the poster.

Reena watched Malini talking to the cashier, smiling, waving her hand as she spoke. She tried to imagine what it must be like to be the child of parents who married young for love and went on to hate each other.

Could it be why Malini spoke in such an analytical, almost clinical way, like somebody who had chosen not to be a part of what's going on; someone who had detached themselves from the world around them only to observe it objectively? Reena brooded over the unsettling possibility that her friend had been neglected or unloved as a child. Or was she reading too much into it? Malini's manner of speaking could simply come from her being a nerd—one that Reena was so fond of and one who kept her amused. As she watched Malini writing something on a piece of paper, possibly a link or an email ID, biting down on her lower lip with her slightly buck teeth, a faint picture formed in Reena's mind. The image of a little girl huddled in the corner of a room sucking her thumb while reading stories about the gods in *Amar Chitra Katha*. Reena urgently wanted to know if her intuition was right but didn't know how to string the right words together to ask. Reena had bared her soul to Malini, but Malini had revealed little about herself to Reena. She wondered if Malini sharing something about herself today had been spontaneous or intentional.

'How did your parents meet?' Reena asked Malini when she returned to their table.

'In the air,' Malini replied.

'What?'

'On an intercontinental flight.'

'That's cool.'

'It goes to show that people meet in the unlikeliest of places, doesn't it?'

'What do you think? Do opposites attract or do people with a lot in common attract each other?'

'The more critical question is, do you have a safety net to catch you if you fall?'

'What do you mean?'

'Compatibility, longevity, marital bliss—there are no formulas for them. If there were, wouldn't that make marriage a breeze! What happens when a marriage fails? If the woman has been a housewife with children and no money, how many parents and friends are willing to help her get back on her feet? I don't know the statistics on this but I'm guessing very few. To have nothing and nobody can break the strongest person. It can make them vulnerable to exploitation and abuse. What they need is kindness, empathy and, most importantly, financial security—a safety net.'

'I have enough money to see me through life and a family that loves me,' Reena quipped.

'Then you have nothing to worry about,' Malini said.

'Are you happily married?' Reena probed.

'My husband's not wealthy but he's an affectionate, hardworking and sincere man. I respect him for that. I also find him charming, attractive and loads of fun to be around. We do what we must to make the house a home. The returns have been worth the investment—the struggles, adjustments, compromises—especially the emotional returns,' Malini replied.

'So it can be found—a pot of gold at the end of the rainbow.'

'Only if you accept that you can't have everything your way. You can't have your cake and eat it too.'

Just as their conversation was winding up, Reena's eyes fell upon the chocolate tart on the table in front of her. Comfort food. *Yes*, she thought. She wanted it. She needed it. Her fork dug into the tart seemingly on its own and went into her mouth. The confection pleased her taste buds. She didn't want to remember, or to be reminded, that it was fattening. She wanted to enjoy the result of her action without taking responsibility for it, just as she wanted to fantasize about marriage without considering its implications. She cherished each decadent bite, trying to ignore the niggling thought: *you can't have your cake and eat it too*. But the effort at ignoring it made it stronger, driving it deeper into her belly with every bite. If only she could get a husband without having to make choices; if only she could enjoy the tart without gaining the inevitable calories; if only she could get a husband without having to make changes; if only she could have her cake and eat it too.

16

Sea Rock

Abandoned. Broken. Ill-reputed. Hotel Sea Rock had been devastated by serial blasts. Back when Reena had been in Goa, a deeply indoctrinated persona non grata strolled into the hotel and planted a bomb on its eighteenth floor.

The explosion had caused not only the closing of the hotel but also an illustrious chapter in Hindi cinema. Located at the edge of Bandstand, Sea Rock had been synonymous with the film industry. Exalted figures of the seventies and eighties had whisked through its lobby as often as gusts of wind from the sea. If the kimono-clad Japanese girls peering out from the murals of the revolving restaurant on the top floor, Paris of the Western Empress, had broken their silence, they would have told outrageous tales. The geishas had witnessed adulterous romances, indecent proposals, artistic rivalries and ruthless smear campaigns. It may have been why they had to be silenced, permanently.

Since its devastation, Sea Rock had been a festering eyesore, blocking the view of the Arabian Sea from Taj Lands End across the street. The hotel had nothing to lose, and so its managers decided to host the rave called Sundown on its premises. It was an annual gathering religiously attended by trance aficionados—an event too risqué for conventional hotels to risk their reputation on hosting. But Sea Rock did what it had to do to survive after the explosion.

The sea-facing exterior of the hotel had a deck and swimming pool on one side and a bar on the other—an ideal site for a rave. The roof of the bar had been converted into a makeshift VIP area. If Bollywood personalities were to come, which they did, this was where they went. More impressive than the celebrities attending the event was the general crowd: wearing beanies, baggy jeans, maxi frocks, sporting dishevelled or fabulous hairdos, dressed to their own liking and geared to dance.

The celebrations that night were to be a double whammy. Sea Rock had been recently sold to the Taj Group, so this was to be its last Sundown, and Paul van Dyke was invited as the guest DJ. Lasers tore into the night sky like a rebel's yell, proclaiming the world-renowned DJ's presence in the city and commemorating Sea Rock's legacy and also its imminent rebirth.

Reena couldn't stop moving to the music while her sister, who was on holiday before beginning her Master's programme at Stanford, couldn't stop ogling at the eclectic collection of men at the rave. That she was receiving a favourable response from them was no surprise to Reena; Keya was a good-looking woman. In actuality, the sisters looked alike. But, somehow, unlike Reena, Keya managed to attract attention from the opposite sex. *What's wrong with me? What vibes do I give out?* Reena wondered, wishing she knew. 'To hell with it,' she said, and cutting through the mass of moving people headed to the DJ's console.

There he was, Paul van Dyke, the dishy Dutchman. He was the reason she was here. He had real power to heal. His energy was contagious. Those hands, graceful as a classical dancer's when they moved to their own music, were spellbinding. The ravers were an orchestra and he was their conductor. Solace was to be found in his benevolence. Upon arriving at the console Reena saw the only other person, aside from the DJ, who could make her feel better, who made her feel comfortable in her own skin—Jackie Funwala. Wearing high-heeled boots, a blonde Afro wig and edible eyewear, she was gyrating uninhibitedly in front of the speakers and having fun. To be in the presence of someone who didn't give a damn about the constructs of society was reassuring to Reena; and that the society gave a damn about Jackie's views was more reassuring.

Reena wasn't sure Malini would make it tonight. She had a husband, children, in-laws, housework and a career. Her parents did not support her with any of it. They didn't approve of her marriage—they didn't approve of much of what she did. When Malini reached Reena through the crush of dancers, they embraced and jumped up and down, with Jackie's blonde Afro bobbing behind them. Free of her self-deprecation, Reena merged with the present in a way that she hadn't since plunging into the waters off the coast of Goa, near The Tree.

Just then, Alya entered the rave on her businessman beau's arm; striding past the jumble of jiggling bodies, eager to bask in the attention she was accustomed to getting. But this was not that kind of party. Immerssed in their own realities and illusions, no one noticed her.

Instead, she was drawn to someone she recognized in the crowd. *Is that Malini dancing over there with those girls? I wouldn't be caught dead with them! Her standards have certainly taken a nosedive. Talk about stepping down in life,* Alya thought. Before her train of thought could trundle further, it was derailed by an observation. Malini was a girl who had had everything—looks, intelligence, amiability, wealth—how could she end up leading an ordinary life and be content with it? Alya was confounded by this. Revolted, even. And yet, for some reason that she couldn't understand, she begrudged Malini for it.

Finally coming up to Malini, Alya asked, 'What are you doing here?'

Why? Do you own Mumbai? Do people need your permission to be here? Reena wanted Malini to reply. But, instead, Malini said, 'Alya, you know that I live here, and that I've been living here for quite a few years already.'

༺༻

Alya and Malini had bumped into each other a number of times since the latter had moved to the city. On each occasion, Alya had asked Malini to call but whenever she did, Alya didn't answer. Finally, three years after Malini had moved to the city, Alya—stuck at home because of a sprained ankle from attempting to do her own stunts—had decided to call Malini.

'Come over, let's watch a chick flick, chat and drink wine, whatever,' she had said. Malini had obliged but when the visit had translated into her having to wait for two hours in an adjacent room while Alya attended an 'unscheduled' film narration, it had become clear that the invitation had come less from Alya's need for companionship and more from her desire to show-off her sprawling sea-facing apartment. Those had been tough times for Malini, but it was Alya who lost something invaluable that day, something irreplaceable, something she had a way of losing—a friend.

'Karan, this is a friend of mine from Delhi.'

'What's up?' Karan said, pretending not to notice Malini's good looks.

'We're headed to the VIP area,' Alya said, pointing to the roof of the bar, 'join us.'

'We're fine down here, thanks,' Malini said.

'Come on, you must,' the actress insisted, glancing at the women with Malini. To her horror, she recognized one of them. She had met this woman in Delhi, at Eisha's wedding.

'Alright, we'll join you in a while,' Malini said. She had been caught unawares by Alya, but the blonde bombshell dancing behind her was not. Although her waxed and sparkle-smeared back had been turned to them, the foremost eavesdropper of Bollywood had heard everything. She had swiftly read above, below and between the lines. Jackie's bulb was lit. There began the scheming.

The lovebirds, as Funwala was to refer to them on the next episode of *Read My Lips*, ascended to the area reserved for the most important people. Their entourage joined them. Bobby and Monica hopped onto an armchair and began making out while Jayant lit a cigarette and viewed the party from above. The only one who noticed Alya drop Karan's hand was the man himself. 'What's the matter?' he asked, rubbing her shoulders, 'Don't tell me you're still angry with me!' Alya shied away from his touch as he continued, 'She's an old friend from university. You can't expect me to stop talking to friends that happen to be women.'

Alya turned to him and said, 'The way you both tumbled out of the loo at Abbas' house could have fooled anyone, even

Flapjack.' Thanks to the tequila shots she'd done at The Hacienda before coming to Sundown, she was finding humour, sardonic as it was, in the affair. 'Gosh, that Flapjack, he's worth his weight in gold! If he weren't so damn expensive I'd buy him in a New York minute.' In their six years together, Karan had never seen his girlfriend be so cynical. 'I'll have a Sex On A Robot,' she told the attendant at the VIP area.

'Do you mean Sex On The Beach, Madam?' the attendant asked, confused. Sex on the beach she'd had so many times, and on so many beaches, that it had lost its novelty.

Karan knew he was walking a tightrope. He had to be careful. He asked his disgruntled girlfriend, in the soppiest voice he could muster, 'How do you think I feel watching you romance other men on screen?' It was a clever strategy that succeeded in throwing Alya off.

Jayant, who could overhear their conversation, was less convinced. 'What a load of crap,' he said, a wisp of smoke leaving his mouth with the words.

'You know that you're the only one I want,' Karan went on, 'let's not ruin the night.'

Alya left him and went to where Jayant was standing, overlooking the deck. She spotted Malini and her friends talking to the guard stationed at the bottom of the stairs leading up to the VIP area. Malini waved at her. Alya pretended not to have seen her. Jayant was embarrassed and ashamed by her behaviour. They had all been friends back in Delhi. That it had been a long time ago didn't warrant such nastiness. Then again, he had seen Alya change so much over the years that it wasn't all that surprising.

Alya had invited Malini up. She had insisted on it. But now that Malini was trying to come up, her passage was being blocked. The security guard was not to blame; she and her friends could have been obsessive fans trying to gain access to celebrities. Neither had he been informed to allow visitors up nor had he presently been instructed to let in those who were waiting.

The scene below irked Alya, but it also aroused her. To see Malini being denied entry gave her pleasure. She allowed it to happen. She willed it to happen. It was empowering to be reminded of her superiority when she was feeling so low. She was the privileged one now. She could befriend people, use people, block people and behave as she pleased. She was a star. What reason had she to despair?

17

Clarity

'Happy Birthday, sis,' Alya's brother said.

'Thanks, Vishal,' Alya responded.

'Soni made this for you,' he said, handing her a box wrapped in scribbled paper.

'How is my angel?'

'She's good. Come and visit us. We've added an extra room and a plunge pool to the house.'

'Hey, check this out,' Karan called out to them.

'What is it?' Vishal asked.

Crouching with Karan over a UFO-like machine, Bobby replied, 'It's a state-of-the-art gadget—part TV, part computer, part art.' Karan's technicians had removed the wood-carved relief Alya had bought from Bali to install the main component of the apparatus on her living room wall. Karan pressed a button and watched the wall transform into a screen.

'Have you seen anything like it in Australia?' Bobby shoved Vishal playfully.

'He couldn't have,' Karan said. 'It's not in the market yet.'

Jayant entered the house as the boys were tinkering with their toy.

'Hey, chico,' Alya greeted him.

'Hello,' Jayant responded.

'Come over here,' Alya beckoned to him.

'Alya, we need to talk. It's urgent,' Jayant said.

'Okay, shoot.'

'Abbas Ali is interested in doing a film with you.'

'Yes, I'm aware.'

'And you know that Dude is keen on doing his next movie with you too?'

'I do.'

'Pops wants to cast you in his home production.'

'Is he acting in it?'

'No, he's not. He's producing it.'

'Want something to drink? I've got these wonderful tea buds. When you put one in a cup of hot water, it blooms into a flower.'

'I'll have one,' Vishal said.

Alya asked her maid to bring biscuits and the tea.

'As you can see, there's a conflict of interest here. You'll have to make a decision, Alya, and soon,' Jayant told her.

'I've got a superb idea,' Bobby interrupted their conversation, stopping his head banging to the rock music playing on the surround sound system. 'Let's play, A Voyage into Trance.' Karan tapped his smartphone and the Oakenfold musical extravaganza began playing, lighting up the wall with graphics.

'Epic,' Bobby said.

'Look at how the visuals come alive to the music,' Karan said.

'Yeah,' Bobby agreed. 'It's like some kind of a living being.'

'Spectacular,' Alya said.

Jayant was lost. 'Alya, please, listen, we have to tread carefully,' he warned her. 'We're walking on eggshells. We can't afford to hurt any egos here.'

Sensing the tension in his voice, Vishal got up and went to the adjacent room.

'You know how it is. I've gone over your dates and'—Jayant said.

'Don't sweat it, Jayant. It's under control,' Alya reassured him.

'We should make a statement, today.'

'Take a chill pill, chico.'

'What a spectacular audio-visual experience!' Karan interrupted Jayant and Alya again, pulling the latter towards him.

'Yes, it's amazing,' she agreed.

'Sis, come quick,' Vishal called her from the other room.

Alya and Jayant went to him.

'Paul van Dyke was here in our city, under the sky by the sea, at Sea Rock's last hurrah,' Jackie Funwala was saying on the TV screen in the room. 'It was a fabulous night.' Vishal turned up the volume of the TV set as Alya entered the room. 'My pulse raced and temperature soared as I watched B-town's hottest couple walk in, hand-in-hand, birds of a feather, white-on-white. I'm *still* breathless from seeing them,' Jackie fanned her face with an Oriental paper fan. 'If you haven't guessed already, sugar plums, I'm talking about Karan and Alya.' The spectators dropped one by one onto the couch, starting with Jayant. 'Speaking of birds, a rare one tweeted a tune about the actress today. It seems our spunky girl has let the cat out of the bag by leaking the name of the leading man in her next film. And the winner is Dude. But if industry buzz is to be believed, she had already committed to doing Mr Ali's film.'

Jayant was taken aback. He looked at Alya as Jackie continued to dish in the background, 'Pops too was showing a keen interest in her acting chops. Have you read the legend's tweet today? We all knew that Pops is a closet poet, but today's ode to Alya was unusually…descriptive.'

Jayant held his head in his hands and sighed. Putting the cat back in the bag was going to be a picnic in hell.

'Alya, darling, it looks like you've got a whole lot of explaining to do,' Jackie said, peering into the camera in a way that made Alya cringe.

'*Ek Pal* did win me the Filmfare award. People say Dude and I have great on-screen chemistry. You did too,' Alya said to Jayant, trying to justify her decision while trying to partially blame him.

'I wish you had discussed it with me before taking a call, and certainly before releasing it into the public domain,' he said, with a palpable sense of betrayal.

'I didn't exactly let it out,' Alya replied.

'In that case, you've been played by Dude's camp.'

Vishal switched the TV set off and returned to the living room.

'You can be labelled as belonging to Dude's camp, and also, Abbas may think you blew him off. The same goes for Pops. These are people you don't want to mess with, Al. I would have handled it for you, tactfully.'

That last word hit her like a bullet from one of Dude's imaginary guns. Staring at the greyness of the TV set, she said, 'Dude is as big a star as any, right?'

'Yes, but if this next film with him bombs at the box office, he will drop you like a pile of bricks and move on to the next big thing.'

'You mean the next young thing.'

'You said it.'

'There's no loyalty here,' Alya said. The remark was ironic, considering what she had just pulled on Jayant. Paying little attention to it, he continued, 'I'm concerned, Alya. If this movie doesn't do well and Dude's camp drops you, where will you stand with Pops and Abbas?'

'In the doghouse?'

He raised his eyebrows.

'That's not going to happen,' she declared, marching off to the living room. 'I won't let it happen.'

Outside, hugging her boyfriend, she said, 'The visuals are brilliant, marvellous.'

Vishal looked at the flower in his teacup. From a bud that had bloomed in hot water into a glorious flower—spreading fragrance and flavour to its hostile environment—it had wilted once the water had been emptied out, its petals clinging to the porcelain base for sanctuary. He saw Jayant watching him. They both saw the signs; their expressions attested to their clarity—crystal cruel clarity.

18

Paradoxes

With its ancient structures and crisscrossing lanes, at their generous best, permitting passage for a single cycle rickshaw, Chandni Chowk is a monumental city within a city. It is a Matryoshka doll of a place—the further in you go, the smaller, tighter and quainter it gets. A 400-year-old living relic of structures perishing with love of recipes possessively preserved and of trades and traditions traversing generations. Chandni Chowk exists in a broken piece of time: suspended, out of sync, defying the general continuum. And yet, by assimilating modernity into its diversity, it thrives.

Here, one can find specialist bazaars peddling common and crazy commodities, in stark contrast to each other, side-by-side: hoofs, horns, artificial limbs, copper wires, lace, leather, safety pins, pickles, acid and essential oils. Parallel to one of these bazaars is a street lined with food joints, including the legendary Old Famous Jalebi Wala. This place sold its first star attraction, a bright orange syrupy squiggle called a jalebi, in 1884, and has since fed prime ministers and film stars.

Alya, the latest addition to its list of illustrious patrons, had no clue about its legacy. She was acutely aware of the giant confection she was holding in her hand not because of its flavour or history but the repulsive realization that the thousand calories she was about to consume would find their way to her waistline by nightfall. There were no toilets around either, at least none close enough to disappear into and chuck up the jalebi before it could cause irreversible damage. Chandni Chowk, for Alya, was just another film location—the type she most dreaded.

In this movie, Dude and Alya's second one together, a dilapidated and bustling street was required for a scene. The film's location scouts had selected a spot not much different than most in Chandni Chowk—cluttered and teeming with odorous humanity—a no-go zone for imperious urbanites, especially celebrities. The pushing and shoving that went on while filming gave rise to an unmoving crowd in which the heroine's security personnel were plastered to her like surgical gloves.

A third of the day's schedule still remained, but it was still too much for Alya. Crowd aside, a petulant itch under her short wig was slowly starting to torment her. She couldn't remove the accoutrement not only for the integrity of the scene but also because it was her just defence against mortal danger. A cobweb of wires was hanging overhead, a matrix of inexpert wirework so elaborate that it barred sunlight from reaching the narrow lane they were in. One drop of water on the web could trigger an electrical firestorm, sending any creature within striking range—dog, human or rat—to the afterlife.

The actors were caught in a mass of bodies moving as one, all to the left and then all to the right—a brew of humanity muddled with polluted air, honking cars, screaming vendors, bleating goats and bawling religious bravado. That a rider of a rented cycle rickshaw—who spent his days pulling weights of varied sizes along the slender lanes of Chandni Chowk and his nights on the pavement with stray dogs curled up against him—owned a mobile phone, made Alya wonder if there was anyone on this planet of nearly eight billion people that didn't have one. The pathological human need for connectivity confounded her. Especially since, in that moment, she was more connected to humanity than any sane human would wish to be.

People are closer, physically, than they've ever been owing to their sheer numbers, so why are they suffering more than ever from an aching need to be connected emotionally? Alya thought. Her contemplation about the contemporary quandary was interrupted by the cursed wig. So intolerable had it become that she simply wanted to chop off her head—a thought she shouldn't have been having, not when around the bend from Gurdwara Sis Ganj. This was the famous site where Emperor Aurangzeb after inflicting weeks of unimaginable tortures upon Guru Tegh Bahadur, the ninth Sikh Guru, ordered his beheading for refusing to convert to Islam. Alya's deeds were none so noble as to deserve such martyrdom. She decided it best not to behead herself. She had worked hard for the crown.

The director's sudden cry made his team forget their itching, bitching, contemplation and procrastination to see what had upset their captain so. The culprit was a passing mongrel, a starving creature that had mistaken the director's foot for a suitable place to empty the contents of his weary bowels. The team pretended not to have seen the offence, it being too humiliating and foul-smelling for a sensitive filmmaker like their captain to withstand. He declared, 'It's a wrap.'

By the time Alya's car arrived, the crew had gone to dine

on Tandoori Bakra at Karim's. On returning to her suite at the Taj Palace Hotel, she ordered a peach iced tea and got into a bathtub with lavender-infused water.

Rejuvenated after the bath, she checked for mails and messages on her phone. It started ringing. Hearing the voice on the other end of the line, Alya said, 'Hey, chica! When did you get in?... What a day I've had!... Really?... But I'm going back to Mumbai tomorrow... Fine, I'll stay an extra day, for you.'

∽

Eisha's parents had moved into a bigger house after their daughter had given birth to a son. Passing the baroque sculptures at the entrance and arriving at the bar stacked with bottles of the finest liquor, Alya appreciated how far they had come.

Eisha embraced her.

'How are you? How are the children?' Alya asked.

'They're alright, they're with their nurses,' Eisha replied.

'You popped those kids out fast, chica.'

'Bam bam, one after the other,' Eisha said, dropping slices of tangerine into their vodka tonics for zing. 'My three-month-old is a funny looking thing. She can barely hold up her head. It wobbles on her tiny neck...like this,' she said, imitating the infant.

'Can I see them?'

'No the maid is putting them to sleep right now,' Eisha replied, handing Alya her drink.

'So, where are we going?' Alya asked.

'We're going to Malini's pre-wedding bash for her brother and his fiancé.' Eisha replied.

'I also got an invite for that.' Alya said, sipping her drink.

'I'm going because I know many people who're going.'

'But isn't Malini a close friend of yours anyway?'

Eisha's lips contorted as she tried to remove a shred of the tangerine that had gotten stuck in her teeth.

'You mentioned we were going somewhere else after that,' Alya continued when she got no response to her comment.

'That's a surprise,' Eisha said, spitting the shred into a napkin.

Alya wasn't big on surprises but her boot camp exercise regime and rigid work schedules were getting tiresome, even boring. She could do with a little unpredictability, she reckoned.

'How's Jayant?' Eisha asked, offering Alya pistachios.

'Um…he's fine.'

'I miss hanging out with him. He still works with you, doesn't he?'

'He worked *for* me.'

'Yes, of course.'

'He was my manager, but I've become very selective about my films. He only handles my endorsements now—that's where he makes his commission. I decide which movies I'm going to do,' Alya clarified just as Eisha's mother entered the room with her furry pooch in tow. He had grown totally grey but for the rhinestone collar around his neck that brought out the blue in his eyes. Eisha's mother chatted with Alya briefly before leaving the two friends alone.

'Travelling long distances with two children is a hassle. That's why I come to Delhi only once a year,' Eisha said, when her mother had left the room. 'It took me a while, at first, to get used to Los Angeles, but I've found ways to make it home.'

Alya wondered what ways those were. 'India's getting so damn expensive. Eating at a decent restaurant in Delhi costs as much as it does in LA. And it's not just eating out.

My niece was over yesterday and when I told her that I was going for a wax, she begged me to take her along. I was like, "No way, you're thirteen, too young to get your pubes waxed. They're probably not even all there yet." But then she told me her friends from school were doing it, so I figured, what the heck, and took her with me. It was amazing. The salon had all sorts of shapes on offer, like in LA.'

Alya knew of places in Mumbai that went further, offering the equivalent of facials devised specially for the vulva, but she kept mum about them; she wasn't as candid as Eisha.

'I just had a thought,' Eisha continued her ramble.

'Oh no,' Alya sighed, anticipating more on the subject.

'With the temperatures reaching 45 degrees in the summer, what a whiff the beauticians must be getting from between all those legs!'

'That's a sick thought.'

'Sweaty puss-puss!'

'Gosh, no.'

'Just imagine.'

'I don't want to imagine.'

Eisha drew in a deep breath.

'Stop!'

'But I can't do without it. If I don't get waxed down there, I end up with an adolescent beard—patchy and scratchy.'

'Are you done?'

'I get freaky where the sun don't shine.'

Evidently, a semblance of Eisha's old humour was still intact, although much else was gone. She was a different woman after marriage as predicted by her groom. Gone were the idiosyncrasies that endeared her to her friends, which also brought her joy. But she wasn't grieving the loss. It was the price she had willingly paid to become a rich lady.

'As I was saying, it costs as much as it does in California,' Eisha continued.

'India is changing, chica,' Alya responded.

'Not for the better.'

Alya wasn't sure if she agreed with her.

'Everywhere you go, you find trash.'

'Somebody once told me that America is home to four per cent of the world's population but counts among the five largest producers of trash,' Alya retorted. That somebody had been Danny. Alya was surprised that she remembered the statistic. She was usually diplomatic, but something about the new Eisha wasn't sitting well with her.

'Robin couldn't believe you stayed at some dinky hotel when you came to LA. We expected you to stay at the Chateau Marmont. That's where celebrities stay when they visit the city,' Eisha said, lighting a Vogue cigarette. 'Want one?'

'No, thanks,' Alya said.

'How about some nose candy then? I have a baggy.'

'Maybe later,' Alya replied.

'Come on, one line for the road.'

'No, chica.'

'Why not?'

'Alright, if you insist. We have a long night ahead of us.'

19

The Tuxedo

Alya had visited Malini's farmhouse once, before Alya became a star. Tonight, it was unrecognizable. Guests had to go round the pond that, on quieter nights, offered refuge to ducks from the Yamuna. On the other side of the water body, which was aglow in blue-green lights that gave its islands of tall reeds an otherworldly quality, they arrived at an opening in the wall of plants. Going through it, they came upon the party. Backlit slabs of ice stacked fifty feet high were dripping into a black granite pool. Mannequins with snow boots and goggles huddled around a fire to keep warm. A velvet snow leopard lazed on the wall, gazing at the tundra of a thousand itty-bitty disco balls dangling from dry branches and beams; like snowflakes on steroids, shooting sparks of light where there was darkness.

Alya hesitated on seeing the number of people at the party. She wasn't sure she wanted to be around so many humans after her day at Chandni Chowk. But this was an altogether different assemblage. It was what made her country unique. One could go from a place like Chandni Chowk—inhabited by people from a bygone era, sheltered, steeped in tradition—to a place where one can find oneself rubbing shoulders with princes, politicians, artists and freaked-out night birds at a tundra-themed party, which could have easily been in Moscow or Minneapolis.

Malini was greeting her guests at the opening in the green wall. 'I was in the city shooting for my next film,' Alya told her as Eisha walked past them. 'I was meant to return to Mumbai this evening but stayed an extra day to attend your party.'

'Thank you, it means a lot to me,' Malini said.

The Mamgai siblings had tagged along with friends of the bride-to-be. 'Remember me?' Ranjita asked Alya. 'We were introduced at Eisha's wedding.'

Alarmed at seeing the family pet mingling with the guests, Malini called out to him, 'Labowsky!' The dog came running to her, drooling as he begged for titbits. 'You should be in Pa's bedroom, naughty boy,' Malini chided fondly. He licked her hand, his tail wagging vigorously. Malini held the dog by his collar and asked one of the domestic workers to take him into the house. 'Labowsky's very social,' she told the sisters. 'You have a golden retriever too, don't you?'

'He's dead,' Ranjita said.

'I'm sorry,' Malini said. She was convinced that heartbreak must have killed the dog. She had gone to their house once for lunch, when she still lived in Delhi. The handsome retriever had been tied to the gate by a chain. Sensing his sadness, she had wondered why people kept dogs only to chain them outside their homes. The same went for Persian cats and parakeets, put on show like medals and fancy cars. The sisters were aggrieved by their single status. Malini imagined bachelors visiting their house, seeing their pet and bolting, fearing that they too would wind up like the chained beast if married to a Mamgai.

Eisha returned from the bar and, handing Alya her drink, whispered in the Mamgai sister's bejewelled ears, 'I'm sure you have tonnes of gossip for me.' Getting closer, so Malini wouldn't hear her, she added, 'I can't wait for the other party!'

Just then, Malini left to receive the last of the guests. She was a fine host, Alya noted. She even looked the same as when they had met for the first time at Jayant's house eight, or maybe ten, years ago. More intriguing than her vigour, though, was her fortitude—how she managed to live separate lives. One out here, hosting grandiose parties at her parent's house and the other, back in Mumbai, where she was an anonymous nobody. How she led her dual lives of abundance and austerity intrigued Alya.

'Come on,' Eisha said, grabbing Alya by the arm, 'let's meet old friends.'

Later on, Malini joined them at the bar. Alya noticed a nondescript female shuffling rabbit-like behind Malini's imposing frame. 'This isn't champagne!' Eisha erupted, tossing her drink at the bartender. 'You fools should know the difference between wine and champagne.'

'I'm sorry, Madam, there's no more champagne,' the bartender told her.

'No more champagne!' Eisha screamed, on the verge of a hysterical fit. 'It's only 1.30 a.m. What kind of shit party is this?'

'I'm sorry,' Malini said. 'My brother invited more people than planned.'

'Gatecrashers!'

'We were gatecrashers too…as teens. Remember?' Malini reminded her.

Eisha was mortified that Malini had said that in front of so many people.

'Let's go to my room for a bit,' Malini said.

'Why don't you come with us?' Alya asked Eisha, trying to pacify her. Eisha bluntly refused to go.

'Alright then, lets go without her,' Malini said, cutting across the lawn. As they descended the grassy knoll leading to Malini's room, Alya suddenly remembered who the shuffling girl behind Malini was and where she had seen her. She had been with Malini on both occasions—once at Eisha's wedding and the second time, she couldn't recall. But she did remember her name—Reena.

∽

Candelabras, carved boxes, singing bowls and Tibetan Thangkas dotted Malini's subterranean room. The opulent monastic flourishes gave Alya a sense of both peace and abandon. Malini passed her a hookah. The women partook of it and when the room was filled with the sweet scent of Moroccan cherries, and Alya had loosened up, she embarked on a monologue divulging the pitfalls, perks and necessity of stardom. The show came to a premature end when something hanging from a cupboard caught her attention. The hookah pipe fell from her hand as she stared at it—a little tuxedo, complete with coat tails, trousers, silk shirt, bow tie and cummerbund.

'That's for my two-year-old son,' Malini said, seeing Alya's interest in the ensemble. 'He's wearing it to my brother's wedding.' Alya's eyes burned from holding back tears. Malini recognized the pure emotion, shining brightly—pain. The sight of the little tuxedo had powerfully stirred something in Alya. Malini turned the other way, not wanting Alya to feel more vulnerable than she already was.

'I want to go outside,' Alya managed to say, her voice

cracking. Malini rose and unlocked the door to the garden.

Outside, a man on a motorcycle was making rounds of the pool. 'So it's true what they say, full moons make men rollicking mad,' Alya commented, having regained her composure.

'Oh well, I'm glad my party's a success,' Malini responded. The glacial blocks of ice beside the pool were dripping and the water was overflowing while steam rose from it towards the firmament.

'Look,' Reena joined the conversation. 'That guy over there is dancing with a doll.'

'They're mannequins,' Malini corrected her.

'Same difference,' Alya said. 'The man's fallen in love with a mannequin.'

'It's not uncommon,' Malini mused.

Just then, Eisha decided to leave the party. Malini made no attempt to stop her, the aromas wafting from the Laksa counter too tempting to resist. She and Reena went and helped themselves to the food.

'Are you leaving?' Alya asked Eisha, catching up with her.

'What else am I to do? This party sucks,' Eisha complained.

'Does it?'

'I tried finding you.'

'I was in Malini's room. Didn't you see us go?'

'No, I didn't. That woman gets on my nerves.'

'Where are you going?'

'To the next party, of course,' Eisha said. 'Ranjita and Romila are already on their way there. It's a girls-only affair.'

'What do you mean?'

'It's a bachelorette party.'

'Eisha, I'm not sure I want to go.'

'Come on, you'll have fun.'

'I think I'll head back to my hotel, if you don't mind.'

'You have to come!'

It would take more energy to argue with Eisha than to go with her, Alya surmised, so she went along.

'I went to Lebanon on holiday with some friends,' Eisha told her on the way.

'Why Lebanon?' Alya asked.

'Do you notice something different about me?'

Alya had noticed a lot of things different about Eisha.

'Lebanon is the Mecca of plastic surgery,' she said. 'It's the most lucrative business in Beirut. There are five women to every man out there. Can you imagine how hard it is for a chick to get hitched there?'

'Desperate times call for desperate measures.'

'Whatever work you choose to get done costs you a quarter of what it does in America or Canada. The Lebanese tourism ministry offers travellers three-day packages that include a procedure, a day of sightseeing and a night out in town.'

'How did you come to know of this?'

'A friend of mine went on one of these package holidays. Can't blame her—she's single and looking to mingle.'

'Does Robin know about the purpose of your trip?'

'I told him that we decided to go on holiday to the Middle East after watching the second *Sex and the City* movie.'

'He took the bait?'

'Babe, we're Beverly Hills housewives. We can get away with anything.'

Alya knew about Eisha's post-wedding rhinoplasty. She, too, had gotten a nose job done ten years back. 'So, chica,' she said, curious, 'what did you get?'

'I got my lips plumped and cellulite removed from my

thighs. The fat removed from my thighs was banked.'

Alya was visibly surprised. She had never heard of banking before, at least not of the type that stored flesh.

'It's the latest technology in cosmetics.'

'Are you telling me that they've preserved your fat in an actual bank?'

'Yup, like cash, jewellery, eggs and stem cells, people can bank their fat now. Once the fat is removed from your body it's shipped to a bank where it's preserved in liquid-nitrogen vapour. If you bank your fat cells now, they can be injected into your face later, to fill wrinkles, replace volume and regenerate skin.'

'Impressive,' Alya said. More impressive was how a woman who hadn't touched a book since the eleventh grade had managed to acquire and retain such intricate knowledge on a subject as complicated and invasive as cosmetic surgery. Eisha knew her fats and cells, pumps and plump down to the minutest detail.

Alya was also ready to go to the ends of the earth to preserve her beauty if it helped promote her career. But, for now, she was satisfied with her Mumbai surgeon. The photographs of celebrities, like Kim Kardashian and Dolly Parton, pinned on his clinic board were inspiring. So were Parton's quotes. 'As long as I've got the money, if I see something sagging, dragging, or bagging, I'll go get nipped, tucked and sucked', was Alya's favourite. Another was, 'God didn't make plastic surgeons so they could starve'. Dolly Parton had a fantastic sense of humour, apart from an incredible body and phenomenal talent. It was the combination of these factors that earned Parton her Grammys and her millions. It was why Alya admired the grand old dame.

'Didn't Robin notice something different about you when you came home?'

'I told him that I'd lost weight on the camel safari,' Eisha said. 'Dehydration from being in the desert can create a good illusion.'

20

Dystopia

This part of Delhi was flatter than a disc. The sloping driveway going up from the gate to the building took hundreds of tonnes of dirt to build, merely to demonstrate affluence. Ascending the driveway, Alya saw a square structure that looked like a gelatine cube dropped on top of an artificial precipice. They heard laughter coming from the glass and steel house. As they drew closer Alya saw the women inside. They were posh and most of them, Alya presumed, were married with children.

'Don't be nervous,' Eisha told Alya, taking her hand. 'You'll fit in perfectly.' Eisha strictly cavorted with her own kind but an exception was made for Alya because she was a star; everyone wanted to be in the company of a star.

The women were chatting noisily inside the house. They smiled at the actress. A few introduced themselves to her to make her feel at ease. The hostess brought her a flute of champagne from the porcelain fountain flowing with the drink. She pressed a few buttons on a concealed control panel and canvas shades descended from behind pelmets on all sides of the spacious room. The lights changed to shades of pink and blue and the speakers played, 'Push It'.

'What's going on?' Alya asked.

Ranjita and Romila squealed.

'You'll know soon enough,' Eisha replied.

A couple of women came out of the washroom together.

'Let's go in before someone else does,' Eisha said.

'Where?'

'To the loo.'

Alya understood what that meant. She figured she could do with a boost of energy to see her through the night. She snorted a white line off the corner of the sink while Eisha inhaled the rest of the contents of her baggy, rubbing the plastic on her gums to avail of the last of the snowy particles.

Returning to the living room, they saw that the ladies had formed a circle. 'Preeti, darling,' the hostess said, making a toast to the prospective bride, 'here's to your last day of independence.' The lights went out as the host screamed shrilly, 'Let the hen party commence!'

A spotlight came on. 'What the...' Alya began, but no one heard her. They were under the pheromone spell of a pharaoh striking a pose in the spotlight. Alya gawked at the gathering. She, the celebrity, the heroine, had become a non-entity. The only celebrity in the room was the munificent pharaoh flown in from Giza on a magic carpet. Sore from his journey, he was thrusting his pelvis forward and back to relieve a stiff muscle. The Mamgai sisters, watching the energetic pumping, twisted into a knot that made it difficult to tell them apart. The ladies went for refills to the porcelain fountain—that, too, had become an object of magic for its endless supply of champagne. Others began to dance.

The pharaoh removed an item of his clothing with each step he took towards the women. He flung off his chest plate, his armbands, his headgear, until all that was left was his bottom, into which an ample woman thrust a thousand rupees. Another lady, emboldened by liqueur and ice, did the Lambada with him. Goaded by the cooing, squawking and squealing coming from the circle around them, Lady Lambada stripped off the pharaoh's bottom—leaving the muscular male's royal appendage with nothing but a miniscule G-string covering it. Mass hysteria spread. The women reached for the brushes and bottles of paint laid out like pretty mementos on a nearby table. They dipped the brushes into the colours and swiped at the man's glistening skin. 'Funky Cold Medina' started playing at that very moment, adding a lyrical twist to their sexual spell, doubling its potency. Someone brought Lady Lambada another flute of champagne—not the wisest idea. Further emboldened, she yanked off the pharaoh's G-string, leaving him buck naked, streaked with paint and sporting a Viagra-induced erection.

'You tell me, which party was better, eh?' Eisha asked Alya, the white powder making a ring around her left nostril like icing sugar. Alya made a sign for her to wipe it off.

The squawking was replaced by a collective gasp. Lady Lambada was on her knees with her hands encircling the pharaoh's manhood, stroking and tugging at it as if it were a plaything. 'Honey, let's go for some food,' the hostess interjected. 'I have delicious grub laid out in the lawn.' The offer came too late. The grub in Lady Lambada's tummy came racing up and spewed all over the pharaoh's manhood.

Looking at himself, spattered with puke, the hapless stripper stopped a gag reflex. Never before had something like this happened to him in his brief but illustrious career. He had made countless house calls. Delhi's Prithviraj Road was the unlikeliest of places from across the world where he expected a woman to first adore and then vomit on his most precious organ. The hostess tossed a napkin at the dumbfounded entertainer, who covered himself and made a discreet—albeit extremely embarrassing—exit.

Amusing as this glasshouse dreamscape was, Alya wanted out. 'You should have told me you're leaving,' Eisha said, following her as she walked out of the house.

'You were having so much fun, I didn't want to bother you,' Alya replied.

'It's just some harmless fun, you know, girly fun.'

'I need my bed. I'm exhausted.'

'Please don't think ill of me,' Eisha said, descending the slope. 'That lady in there has three children from a cheating husband. You can't blame her. She's wasted. She doesn't know what she's doing. She probably won't remember tomorrow—'

'Eisha, go back to the party,' Alya interrupted Eisha without looking at her, afraid that the profound emptiness she was sure she'd see in her dilated pupils may be contagious.

The chauffeur was awaiting his passenger with the door open. Alya got inside and said goodbye. She had always admired Eisha's presence of mind. She was one to quickly recognize an opportunity and take it unhesitatingly. When an ideal candidate for marriage came her way, she snatched him off the market in no time. This gave her a life of comfort and privilege without having to slog, sweat and allow herself to be humiliated for it. Granted, she lacked fame, something Alya wouldn't trade for the world, but Eisha had a husband, children, social status and loads of cash to burn. Alya had secretly envied her for it, until now.

As the driver readjusted his rear-view mirror, light from the car behind them reflected off it and struck Alya in the eyes making her involuntarily look at herself in the small rectangular mirror. *No. Not me*, she thought as she glanced at her reflection, but her certainty quaked. She had achieved everything that she had ever wanted, and more, yet she still kept wanting. And she couldn't tell what it was that she wanted. *Should it not be the other way around? Shouldn't I have more answers and fewer questions at this stage in my life?* She asked herself.

21

A Resolution

'Am I speaking to Ms Reena Subramaniam?' a sombre voice said on the phone.

'This is Reena,' Reena responded.

'I'm sorry to inform you. Your father is dead.'

'Excuse me?'

'My name is Sailesh Gupta. I am the manager of Sirius Tower in Colaba. Mr Subramaniam is lying on the ground in the lobby. He has no pulse.'

'Have you called for an ambulance?'

'No.'

'I'm calling for an ambulance right away. Stay with him till it arrives.'

Colaba was an hour's drive from Reena's office in Bandra on a regular day—but this was no regular day; it was tempestuous and sodden. In a city built where a city shouldn't have, upon a tropical coastline, began Reena's living nightmare. She called Angel Hearts Hospital—the closest medical facility to where her father was—as her driver dodged vehicular snarls and inundated roads in the monsoon rain, cutting through back alleys to negotiate the shortest distance to the tower.

Despite every effort to stay calm, Reena's very core was

trembling; manifesting, first, in a single hiccup, then in an involuntary sigh and, ultimately, in profuse, uncontrollable sobbing. 'This is my fault,' she cried. Her father was not supposed to be meeting the manager of Sirius Tower. It was she who had made the appointment. He had gone in her stead, giving her the day to laze at home, reading and watching videos.

Mr Gupta phoned Reena and informed her that the ambulance had arrived and that the paramedics were examining her father.

'I'll be there in five minutes,' she said, getting a hold of herself. *Could dad be gone?* The thought reduced her to a fraction of her recognizable self; as if her father were intrinsic to her existence, as if his absence was her absence. But somewhere inside her, she refused to believe he was dead.

Paramedics were loading Mr Subramaniam into the ambulance when Reena arrived. Raindrops fell on her father's flaccid face as they fell on hers as she leapt from the car and into the van. She held her father's hand, kissed his cheek and placed her fingertips on his forehead. It was clammy. This man, who had pestered her about marriage and criticized her constantly, had gone quiet and cold. His nagging had caused her pain, but the prospect of his demise was now causing her such unfathomable agony that it made that other pain seem like an anaesthetic. 'No, Dad,' she whispered, 'you cannot go.'

Leaping and lurching like a ship in a storm, the ambulance ploughed towards the hospital through lashing rain and gale-force winds. A paramedic pressed a stethoscope to the patient's chest, straining against the siren and nature's outrage to listen for a heartbeat.

When Reena saw the paramedic mouth something, she

leaned forward and asked, 'What did you say?'

Squinting, the medic repeated, 'I detect a faint pulse.' The second paramedic checked and confirmed, 'Yes, the heart is beating.' He removed the oxygen mask from Mr Subramaniam's face and inserted a blood-thinning tablet into his mouth. Reena's shoulders slumped and head fell forward. It was her turn to go limp from gratitude.

Mr Subramaniam was whisked away to the ICU upon reaching the hospital. By the time Reena was done filling the paperwork, her mother arrived at Angel Hearts, tears of surrender streaming down her face. Reena hugged her mother. She, too, looked diminished. Now, Reena was certain that departing souls took with them fragments of those to whom they were dear; the taken pieces vanishing forever.

They sat in the waiting room for the longest hour of their lives until Dr Nagar, the chief cardiac surgeon, emerged from the ICU and informed them that Mr Subramaniam urgently needed a triple bypass surgery. 'Your father has suffered a heart attack,' he told Reena. 'The angiography shows blockage in three main arteries of the heart. In one artery, the blockage is 100 percent. In the second artery, it's more that 90 percent. In the third, it's 60 percent.'

'How could this happen? My father avoids fried food and sweets. He goes for a swim thrice a week. He is a healthy man,' Reena demanded.

'Several factors cause blockage in the arteries. Lifestyle is just one of them. The others are smoking, genetics and stress.'

'When will you perform the surgery?'

'We need to conduct further investigations and get clearance from the anaesthetist.'

'Thank you, Doctor,' Dolly said.

'Don't worry, we'll do the surgery in the next two days,' Dr Nagar assured them.

'Can we see him?' Reena asked.

'You may see him briefly and from a distance. Please don't touch anything in the ICU to avoid spreading infections. The patient's condition is fragile.'

⚬∞⚬

Dr Nagar's statement about genetics and stress contributing to a person's likelihood of having a heart attack was playing on Reena's mind while she waited the ICU outside during the five-hour surgery. Her mother was at home, praying in the family shrine, and her sister was on a flight from New York. Recalling the occasions when she had caused her father stress—there were many—she was tormented by guilt, making her wonder if she was the cause for his collapse. A stretcher with a body covered with a white sheet rolled past her. *Oh, no. Please don't be dad,* Reena thought desperately. All the sounds around her—machines bleeping, people talking, nurses calling, doors swinging open and closed—seemed to go silent. The only sound she could hear was the turning of the stretcher's rusty wheels. Walking alongside the stretcher with a hand on the body was the old man from The Tree. The silvery strands of his hair were moving of their own accord, extending out, reaching like glowing tentacles into the air around his head. The live halo swayed and then resettled as he turned his head to give Reena the same sublime smile he had given her when they first met in the forest. He entered an elevator with the stretcher and the doors closed behind them.

Dr Nagar emerged from the operation theatre in medical overalls. Reena braced herself for the worst. 'Ms Subramaniam,' he said. 'The surgery was a success. The blockages have been bypassed.'

Reena closed her eyes and thanked the Almighty. Her days as a wild child were behind her. She would manage crises and shoulder her mother's fear along with her own. Her gratitude gave her strength. It made her resolute. She remembered the waitress from Café Wormhole, the one who told her, 'A man is not a need a woman can't do without.' Those words couldn't have been truer in that moment. Reena knew it. *I am a strong woman. I am no less than Atlas; I can carry the world on my shoulders*, she thought determinedly. She vowed to not have low self-esteem. *I'm not going to beat myself up, not anymore.* Never again would she allow her emotions to hold her hostage. She rejected being a slave to her circumstances. Nearly losing her father made her see her own worth, it gave her a fresh perspective.

22

A Discovery

The Act India Forum invited thinkers and achievers from around the globe to create awareness about the problems confronting our planet and to propose solutions for them. Sponsored by a major Indian news magazine, *Indobe*, the event hosted former presidents, prime ministers, business leaders, authors, activists, athletes, spiritual luminaries and celebrities from the entertainment industry. It was held every November at a fort in New Delhi, under a sky filled with twinkling stars that no one ever saw because of the smog obscuring them. Representing the Indian film industry at the event this year were Abbas Ali, Pops, Jackie Funwala, Alya and Rehana.

Alya and Jayant were placed at a table with the head of a pharmaceutical company, his spouse and an Ayurveda guru. Past the slick tan shoulder of the guru swathed in robes, Alya saw Rehana, her competitor. She was sitting five tables ahead of her, next to Abbas Ali. Abbas had been so put off by Alya deciding to do a movie with Dude over him, that he chose Rehana over her to play the leading lady in his upcoming magnum opus. The decision had also been based on ruthless realism—the nubile actress was fast gaining popularity.

Noticing Alya gaping at her made no difference to Rehana. Her expression showed steely confidence in soon outranking the reigning queen of Bollywood. Alya looked away only to find Pops in her line of vision, glaring at her with disapproval. *Is there anywhere I can turn and not chance upon something or someone disturbing?* Alya thought, as she debated the wisdom of accepting the invitation to the forum. The Spanish Inquisition would have been more pleasant.

Just then, *Indobe*'s CEO and editor-in-chief started making his opening remarks, much to Alya's relief. He introduced the first speaker, '...without further ado I invite Mr Dharmesh Pawar to talk to us about environmental conservation. He has pioneered important legislations for the protection of endangered species, such as the rhinoceros, the gharial, elephants, tigers and bear.'

Alya looked for Danny at the round dinner tables. Jayant pointed with his chin at the dais. Danny rose from his chair and approached the podium, as the CEO said, 'I present to you the man on a mission.' The fort resounded with applause.

Alya was impervious to the spike in her former boyfriend's popularity. She was busy with her own life and career. Danny's activism had spread from Mumbai's mangroves to the entire subcontinent. For people who gave a damn about the dwindling wildlife in the receding forests of their country, he was a reason to be hopeful.

'You may think the key words of our times begin with the letter "I"—iPad, iPhone and individuality have become the axes of our existence. But no "I"—small or big—can survive outside of our earthly environment. That makes the key words of our times the ones that start with the letter "e"—environment, economy and ecology.'

Alya appreciated Danny's good looks as he delivered his speech onstage. She had always found him attractive, even when they had been together, but didn't remember him looking quite so dashing.

'India is losing roughly 330 acres of forest land every day to industry, housing and mining. What makes the loss so tragic and unacceptable is that few places on earth have the rich biodiversity we do. That makes it our responsibility to secure our forests, not just for our children but also for the world. To achieve that, we need an effective leadership—"effective", another word beginning with "e", a word that our leadership needs to understand far better.'

The intelligentsia laughed at this jibe at the political establishment, very typical of him. Danny continued, 'Poachers are similar to cross-border terrorists: they hide in forests for days to make a kill. With their crude weapons, they inflict excruciating agony upon the animal before killing it. Forest guards have to receive military-type training in guerrilla warfare to counter them and the guards have to be armed. This is a war; it's time we see it for what it is.'

While Danny made his powerful speech, the only thing Alya was seeing were X-rated daydreams of him. She was aware only of her animal instincts. Jayant could see her attraction developing, or rather, redeveloping, towards her former flame. However, there was no way of guessing which way it would go—land her in a mess or trigger a momentous change.

'Tiger parts from India are sold to buyers in China. Elephant tusks from Africa end up there, too. Rhino parts go to Vietnam. This is a global trade. Diplomatic means must be used to incapacitate it,' Danny said.

I could poach you right now, Alya thought before reeling

herself in *No, stop Alya. Pay attention to the speech.*

'If we give wild species space, isolation and protection they will flourish without human help. That is why human settlements, ideally, should be kept outside protected forests. Who else do forests need protection from but humans? Let's learn from African countries like Rwanda, Kenya, Namibia and Botswana. They offer the world's finest nature experiences while promoting sustainable tourism practices that benefit both wildlife and local communities. When governments and private enterprises come together great things can happen, like the founding of institutes for specialized veterinary medicine, which are so desperately needed in a country like ours—that is rich in wildlife but poor in the numbers of specialized veterinarians to treat animals,' Danny paused for a sip of water, more to emphasize his point than to moisten his throat.

'We can no longer afford to waste time on debating and delaying—those small "d"s are for dodos—a bird long extinct. The time has come to get the youth involved and force change, before elephants and lions become mere memories stored as emojis on their next-gen phones. Act, NOW,' Danny concluded emphatically. Alya missed most of what Danny said but not how he said it. The man was on fire. She wanted him more than she had ever wanted him.

When Monica had called Alya on the sets of *Ek Pal* and told her that she'd seen Danny with another woman, Alya had found it funny at first. But she had eventually started believing the ugly story, or at least that's what Danny had thought. She had shouted at him and called him a cheat, even when he had tried telling her that the woman had been a co-worker, nothing more. Alya had refused to listen to him, and the reason for it was that she had already decided to end the relationship. Monica's story had merely presented her the excuse.

Alya had broken off three years of love and friendship with the sensitivity of a butcher. News of the end of his relationship had reached Danny through rumour, speculation and worse, through the tabloid media. She had never discussed the matter with him, and she had never looked back, until now.

∞

A bestselling author spoke after Danny, followed by an international athlete, and then Pops. His was the longest speech, characterized by controlled voice intonation, subtle and grand hand gestures, shifts of feet and swells of tears. The legendary actor did justice to his reputation. The audience was enthralled.

When the first half of the programme ended, guests were directed to a rose garden with sandstone columns and gurgling fountains. The CEO of *Indobe*—a media mogul—was in the habit of playing his favourite songs from the seventies and eighties during the 30-minute break while his guests savoured kahwa, spring water and wine.

Alya saw Danny, leaning against a pillar, watching her. The music in the background revealed the unsaid,

> I heard it through the grapevine, not much longer will you be mine [...] Oh I'm just about to lose my mind.

The emotions Danny had felt and wanted to express to Alya when they had separated were pouring out from the jukebox.

I know a man ain't supposed to cry, but these tears I can't hold inside.

There was nothing standing between them except some random people and pillars.

It took me by surprise, I must say, when I found out yesterday.

Guilt crept over Alya.

You could have told me yourself [...] honey, honey.

The lyrics had spoken Danny's mind. There was nothing more to be said, unless Alya said it.

Jackie Funwala tapped Alya on the shoulder. She looked at her with tenderness, like a friend or a mother, and nodded in Danny's direction. Alya was smart enough to understand what Jackie was trying to convey, but she couldn't get herself to do it. She couldn't admit to Danny that she wanted him back. She couldn't admit that she had done him wrong. A part of it was because she feared rejection. The larger part was the prospect of change. She was used to getting her way; shifting her perspective could make the mental machinery that she had meticulously built malfunction.

A gong sounded. The second half of the forum was to commence. People strolled back to their seats.

'Hey, Al,' Jayant said, sensing her disinterest in the remainder of the programme. 'In five days, we're off to Cannes.'

'Ready as always,' Alya responded automatically.

When the forum ended, she left the venue without speaking to anyone. She was scheduled to return to Mumbai the following morning but couldn't stand another hour in

Delhi. Bruised on the inside, consumed by despair so deep it reminded her that she was alive, she took the red-eye flight back to her city of dreams. She needed to touch, grasp and be held. *I need someone. A man. Karan. Yes. Karan. A man can remedy the pain caused by a man*, she thought.

―

Alya arrived at Karan's house past midnight, restless, craving to be held, intent on dousing her misery in carnal pleasure.

'Madam, your arrival is…inopportune,' the head servant said, alarmed at seeing her at the front door.

'What do you mean?' Alya demanded.

'Sir is…indisposed,' he responded, fumbling to block her way into the house.

Alya brushed past him thinking, *why is he so nervous?* She got her answer in the bedroom, where the master of the house was hopping about with his jeans wound around his knees. She watched him pull them up to his waist, only to see the zipper get caught in the worst possible place, causing his smooth face to turn anguished. Alya felt as though she was watching a mime.

The room looked like a scene from a crime novel—the curtain was ripped, the bed was crumpled, a glass had fallen to the ground. 'What's going on here?' she demanded, embarking on a search of the room. She opened the cupboards and looked behind the curtain. She pulled the feather blanket off the bed and discovered a pair of twisted pink panties. On the Spanish tiles was a black bra with pink trimmings. Draped on the armchair was a nylon dress that reeked of cheap perfume. The crux of the matter had to be reached or the plot to this crime novel would fall apart. *No way am I going to lose the plot*, Alya thought as she went into the bathroom. There she found what, or who, she was hoping she wouldn't—a dusky beauty crouching naked in the shower.

Alya marched out of the room, her footsteps seemingly admonishing her, telling her what a fool she had been. The tapping of her heels counting the weeks, months, years she had wasted on this man.

'Alya, wait,' Karan scrambled behind her, his fly unfastened. 'I can explain. I was just, just—'

'You were just…what?' Alya demanded angrily.

'She means nothing to me.'

'That's worse.'

'Please, Alya. You can't leave me. We're a rocking couple.'

'It's over, Karan. No discussions. No explanations. We're through.'

'This isn't happening.'

'This *is* happening. It should have happened long ago.'

23

Black Gold

Seasoned celebrities often succumbed to the shakes when walking the red carpet at Cannes but Alya, wearing the limited edition Diva by the uber-luxurious watch brand, Genesis, floored spectators with her joie de vivre. The masterpiece on her wrist, with its 300 baguette-cut and 200 brilliant-cut diamonds, was receiving tough competition from its wearer. Alya was dazzling. The managing director of Asia operations for Genesis was proud of his choice. When justifying selecting Alya as the Indian ambassador for the brand, he had told his boss, 'Alya embodies the brand values of Diva. She is modern, spirited and free. She knows what she wants.' Her demeanour was impeccable; her English, superb; her gait, confident. The director had hit the bullseye. Alya was the complete package.

Outside the window of her room at the Barrière Le Majestic, a coquettish pink sky was flirting with its reflection on the surface of the Mediterranean Sea. Inside, Alya got dressed for her last official appearance at the Côte d'Azure. To soften the impact of the minimalist, masculine decor of the suite—

with its bias towards geometric shapes in copper, beige and ebony—white orchids had been placed in select spots. This gave the junior suite the touch of femininity it needed to cater to a wider range of sexual orientations. The hotel, after all, was a preferred accommodation for celebrated artists and entertainers when visiting Cannes. Alya was expected at the Genesis promotional party at the Pommery Champagne Bar in less than an hour. She flung the Marchesa gown she had worn for a previous engagement aside and slipped into a dress by Falguni Shane Peacock, custom designed to complement the platinum watch she was to wear for the occasion.

A French stylist touched up her make-up while Jayant read from a document from the sponsor: '…Genesis had a billion dollar turnover last year. Their growth in India was a hundred per cent…' Alya was largely uninterested in the information, but for a few select phrases, like 'pure white gold', 'blackened rhodium' and 'precious sapphire crystals'. The remaining terminology, such as 'moon phase complications', 'minute repeaters' and 'perpetual calendars', went past her, through the window to sink in the pink sea. An elegant French woman entered the suite and informed them that they had five minutes to go. She was Alya's escort and translator, assigned to her by the watch company.

'You don't have to stay more than an hour at the Genesis party,' Jayant whispered to Alya as they followed the French woman up the corridor.

'Why not?'

'I've been told about this club at the opposite end of the Croisette from the Palais des Festivals called Baoli. Tonight, it will be packed with the type of people you want to meet.'

'Then we must go.'

∽

Baoli was a glittering nightclub that smelled of cigars, strawberries and expensive cologne. It was the kind of place that did justice to the phrase often used to describe the south of France: 'playground for the rich and famous'. If you had less than ten million dollars in your account, you might as well not try getting in.

Alya was a well-travelled woman. Even so, the sight of a topless bartender pouring half a bottle of alcohol along the length of the bar and striking a match to it left her dumbstruck. Manes swished and beautiful bodies glistened in the glow of the blaze.

The President of Genesis led the actress and her manager to a barricaded area at the back of the club, where a man wearing a monochrome headscarf fastened by a black cord sat at a private table with an arm draped over the couch—relaxed as a buzzard amid the buzz of the club. On the sleeves of his white shirt-dress was a pair of emerald cufflinks the size of Alya's earlobes. Over the shirt-dress, he wore an embroidered waistcoat and a finely wrought gold belt. The watchmaker greeted the gentleman and he, in turn, put his hand on his chest and bowed. The Frenchman proceeded to introduce the Indian actress to the man, 'Mademoiselle, this is Sheikh Adnan Ahmad Bin Sultan Al-Ibrahim.'

The sheikh stood up and bowed, saying, '*Ahlan beechi* [Welcome]!'

'I'm Alya,' she said, taking her attention off the international celebrities in the club with effort and redirecting it to the Sheikh.

Jayant introduced himself. The Sheikh's nostrils twitched. He raised a hand to signal to his commandos concealed in the shadows, faintly discernible by their blue and white headscarves. One came forward and asked Alya what she wanted to drink. Jayant let out a sigh of relief—relief at the fact that the Sheikh hadn't called to remove him from the VIP area, thereby separating him from Alya.

Alya looked at the mojito the size of a beer keg on a nearby table with ten straws, each a meter long, sticking out of it. A bevy of beauties were sucking on the straws with vampiric thirst. 'They're probably the kids of some Greek shipping magnate,' Jayant told her.

'I'll have a mojito,' she said.

'Same here,' Jayant added.

'Oh. My. God,' Alya exclaimed. 'That's Angelina Jolie!'

'Al, don't look now, but the tall man standing behind the Sheikh is Leonardo DiCaprio.'

Alya stole a look at the actor and quickly went from a star to a star-struck fan. DiCaprio was as striking as in the films, and he was talking to none other than Frida Pinto, one of the first Indian actresses to successfully break into Hollywood. Alya had seen her at Andy Garcia's pre-festival bash earlier in the week. Alya's PR machinery had to work overtime to get her an invite, but Frida was a sought-after sensation; she was invited everywhere. Alya would have felt a pang of envy if she hadn't known how the cookie crumbled. In her native land, she was a star and Frida a non-entity. Frida had played her cards right on the back of her first international film project, packing her bags and relocating to New York. A decision like that took courage and conviction. Alya respected her for it. She was also contemplating a similar course of action—that was why she was here. But Alya was forgetting one stinging fact. Frida had been young and raw when she had left. She had paved the way for others, and they had followed and succeeded. For Alya, it would be difficult to begin again and look for work or run a new rat race. She was used to being pampered. Then she saw the world-renowned mega model, Naomi Campbell, infamous for throwing her phone at assistants who pissed her off [which didn't take much to do]. Wearing a collar so crammed with solitaires, that it could intimidate a pit bull, she swept across the room; her bodyguards pushing aside people who were coming in her way. 'What power,' Alya said. 'Maybe I should be like Campbell—marry an oligarch and rule the world.' Then she saw DiCaprio shaking hands with Adnan Ahmad bin Sultan Al-Ibrahim. *Who is this Sheikh?* Alya thought incredulously.

'Do you know who that is, Alya, coming this way?' Jayant said.

'Who?'

'That's the director, Jack Anderson. He's in the same league as James Cameron, Christopher Nolan and Steven—'

'I know who he is,' Alya interrupted Jayant.

The director shook hands with the Sheikh, who introduced him to the small and unassuming gentleman sitting beside him on the couch.

'*Al-tabeeb*,' the Sheikh said. 'Meet Mr Anderson.'

'*Salut*, I'm Ives,' the man next to the Sheikh introduced himself.

'Call me Jack,' the director responded.

The Sheikh introduced Alya to the Hollywood director. She felt so nervous that her tongue started drying up and got stuck to the roof of her mouth. She reached for the tray of oysters and Beluga caviar on the table and swallowed the contents of half a shell. It was the first time she had eaten an oyster. The crustacean slipped down her throat like a gobbet of phlegm or a freshly dead slug. *Ew, that was gross*, she thought. Thankfully, her acting chops helped her save face. She took a swig of her cocktail, smiling cheerfully.

'Adnan, I want to meet you to discuss my next project,' Anderson told the Sheikh, leaning towards him. 'You have far greater knowledge than befits your years. Your insights will be invaluable to my film on the Middle East.'

'Jack, forty-five is not young, not where I come from. Tell me, what can I do for you?' the Sheikh asked.

'I'm making a film comprising four short stories, all of which unfold in Saudi Arabia. I want my Saudi characters to be authentic, believable—'

'I'd be honoured to provide you with the information and support you need,' the Sheikh said, his voice smooth as a Havana cigar. 'Please join me on my boat for lunch tomorrow. We can talk at length in quiet comfort.'

Alya inched closer to them.

'Thank you, Adnan, I look forward to it,' Anderson replied.

The Sheikh turned to Alya, bowing, '*Asayida*, I'd be delighted if you joined us tomorrow for lunch on my boat, *Black Gold*.'

'Thank you for the invitation,' Alya said, trying not to appear too enthusiastic. Seeing Jayant staring at her, she added, 'We'll be there.'

∞

'What I really wanted to do was spend my last day in Cannes lounging by the pool at the U-Spa,' Alya complained.

'Hey, no complaints, Al,' Jayant responded, their speedboat bouncing off an azure wave. 'You wanted a chance like this more than anything, and now you have it.'

'You're right.'

'I looked up the Sheikh,' Jayant said, pulling out a piece of paper with handwritten notes from his pocket. 'Sheikh Adnan is the Chairman of the Caliphate Luxury Group of Hotels, with properties in Riyadh, Casablanca, Istanbul, Beirut, Muscat, Cyprus, Athens, Abu Dhabi and Alexandria. His hotel in Abu Dhabi has gold-plated windows. The group is worth over a billion euros,' he read. 'The Sheikh is also involved in large-scale power projects in Saudi Arabia. He operates desalination plants along the Red Sea coast. He is into construction and oil rigging.' Jayant looked up at her and said, 'Ask not what the Sheikh is into. Ask what he is not into.'

'That explains why the President of Genesis was sucking up to him.'

'The Sheikh must be purchasing 50 watches a year to gift to members of his inner circle, which consists of politicians, royalty and global celebrities. He may even own shares in the company.' The Barrière Le Majestic's speedboat dropped off a wave with a thud, forcing the piece of paper out of Jayant's hand and into the waters—the same waters upon which, a kilometre away, bobbed another boat named *Clandestine*.

The Indian contingent at the Cannes Film Festival was growing ever larger each year. Wherever celebrities went, the media followed. Publications dished out generously for pictures of Indian stars frolicking in the French Riviera; magazines such as *Tell All* and *Glitz* had started going as far as hiring European freelance photographers to shoot lurid pictures of Indian celebrities in compromising positions overseas.

Clandestine had two occupants. The young one, with a moustache, was a true-blue renegade with a singular aim—to be an icon of Indian paparazzi. The other one, short and stocky, was his European counterpart. They were waiting to take pictures of Alya from the piddly boat, equipped with pathological patience and a SIGMA150-500 MM F5-6.3 APO DG OS HSM, which in layman's terms, is a camera with massive telephoto zoom capability. The apparatus, though heavy and cumbersome, could take pictures of subjects as far as a kilometre away, especially when attached with a 1.4x tele-converter as they had done. The duo had come with an express agenda: to expose what the newly single actress was up to in Côte d'Azure.

The speedboat bumped against an island-like yacht. Creating the illusion of the yacht being an island was its white hull, which was crafted to look like waves lapping against a shore. Furthering the impression was the swimming pool on the upper deck, chequered with guest cabanas and miniature palm trees. Topping it all off was an artificial volcano with a stream gurgling out of it and into the pool. Familiar with their stunned expression, the boatman explained to his passengers in his French accent, 'Everyone who sees *Black Gold* for the first time has the same reaction. The vessel is one of a kind. The Sheikh had it built according to his requirements. It has bulletproof windows, a helipad, a mini submarine, a missile defence system and a Ferrari 458 Spider.'

'I wouldn't mind having specs like that,' Jayant joked, nudging Alya.

The speedboat pulled up to the vessel's beach deck, looking like a tin pot puttering against a steamship. A combined crew of Arabian and French women and men were waiting to receive the Sheikh's guests. The French crew members were dressed in white t-shirts and blue shorts. Their Arabian counterparts were wearing black overalls with blue and white woven headscarves—the same as Alya had seen the night before, at Baoli. The guests were taken up a flight of stairs and into an enormous salon ensconced in full-length windows, offering sweeping views of Massif de l'Esterel, the Mediterranean coastal mountain range. The decorations in gypsum on the ceiling, Turkish marble in the woodwork and rugs from Afghanistan were giving the salon a royal feel. A dining table inlaid with coral and mother-of-pearl was its pièce de résistance.

Sheikh Adnan Ahmad bin Sultan Al-Ibrahim opened his arms in welcome, the tassels on his ivory *thobe* flapping. The host's grace and amiability was rejuvenating, especially after the sensory onslaught of his boat. A valet offered the guests cardamom coffee and dates stuffed with crushed walnuts and pistachios. Alya noticed a large man, his skin smooth and dark like espresso and his body swathed in white fabric, seated atop a tiger skin spread on the couch. He was leaning on a silver cane with the head of a duck scowling with its ruby eyes at all it surveyed. The man's age was hard to guess, almost impossible, but his identity, and some would say profession, was betrayed by the beads around his neck. He was a swami.

The Sheikh introduced the actress and her manager to his other guests, starting with the most esteemed, His Holiness Chand Baba.

'You met Mr Anderson last night,' the Sheikh said.

'Only briefly,' Alya said. 'I'm thrilled to meet you, Mr Anderson.'

'Good afternoon, Sir,' Jayant greeted the director. 'We in the Indian film industry hold your work in the highest esteem.'

'Are you a director?' Anderson asked Jayant.

'No, Sir, I'm Ms Alya's manager. She's one of our country's biggest stars.'

'A pleasure to meet you,' Anderson said. He introduced them to the woman sitting beside him, 'This is my wife, Amber.'

'Amber Ambrosia, I'm a big fan,' Alya told the Hollywood siren, who was now facing the misfortune of being called a 'former siren' by the American tabloid press.

'Thank you, young lady.'

The Sheikh introduced Alya to the gentleman he called *al-tabeeb*, which she later learned meant doctor. Monsieur Ives was the Sheikh's chiropractor. The host urged his guests to mingle and went over to the other end of the salon. *What's he doing there? Is he crooning? Why would he leave his guests to go and croon to himself in a corner?* Alya wondered curiously. She had to find out.

It was when she reached him that she noticed the striking beast perched on a wooden log fixed to the side of the boat, a Saker falcon. The raptor-like bird of prey was as beautiful as the peacock, she thought, but its beauty was markedly different. The peacock was graceful, colourful and majestic, but there was also something goofy about it, especially when it ran, which it did often, since it spent much of its time foraging on the ground. The falcon, though smaller in size, exuded enormous strength, not only in body but also in character. Wearing a black leather veil with gold tassels sprouting from its crown, the bird was standing on its perch like a proud monarch. The veil was there to protect the falcon from getting startled by sudden movements when not in flight. Veil notwithstanding, the falcon was acutely aware of the Sheikh's presence even before his touch. It was doing a little march of excitement on its perch. The Sheikh stroked the bird on its talons. The white falcon with brown accents on her feathers craned her neck towards him.

The Sheikh called for the bird's keeper and asked, 'Has Barakat been fed?'

'Yes, Khalif,' the keeper replied.

'Good, you may go.'

'He is magnificent,' Alya said.

'She,' the Sheikh corrected her.

'She?'

'Barakat is my white tigress of the skies,' the Sheikh said, without turning to Alya. 'The female falcon is more powerful than the male. She is brave, a patient hunter and copes better under stress.'

'That's fascinating.'

'Barakat and I go into the desert on hunting expeditions together for weeks. She is incredibly courageous, flying out in pursuit of her prey sometimes for days. And when she spots her prey—even if it's a small rat—she dives from a mile up in the sky at a dizzying speed and, with absolute precision, catches her kill.' While telling his story, the chivalrous gentleman of impeccable civility transformed into an animal of raw instinct. He turned to Alya, his glowing eyes rapturous, disarming; his bewitching charisma pulling her in.

'Sheikh, you were saying earlier—' Anderson began.

'Forgive me,' the Sheikh said to Anderson, who had come up to them. 'Let us resume our conversation.' They rejoined the group. Alya was so drawn to the Sheikh's enigma that she almost forgot the reason she was there—to get acquainted with the director from Hollywood.

'If you were to describe what it means to be Saudi Arabian to someone who knows nothing about the country, what would you say?' Anderson asked the Sheikh as they sat down.

'The first thing one has to know about Saudi Arabia is that 95 per cent of it is desert, an area larger than France. It is called the Empty Quarter.'

'If it's so big, why's it called the Empty Quarter?' Amber asked him.

'Sand stretches into the distance as far as the eye can see, but every grain has a story to tell. The desert was a crossroads traversed by explorers, trade caravans, pilgrims and armies. For millennia, all trade going eastward from Europe and Africa had to cross it.'

'In what way has the desert carved the identity of the Saudi people?' Anderson probed.

'In the same way it sculpts sand dunes the size of ships—gradually and naturally. Centuries of trade and pilgrimage caused the inhabitants of the region to become a thoroughly mixed breed of people. The desert is our common mother. She has taught us how to survive the harshest of her moods. Our ancestors, the Nabateans, learned how to create underground aquifers and mastered mathematics, medicine and literature.'

'Ah, yes, it is so,' Dr Ives agreed.

'At heart I am Bedu, as are most Saudi Arabians. The word refers not to an ethnic group but to a lifestyle. We were desert-dwellers, leading a life of liberty and simplicity. Now that most of us live in townships and cities, we are nostalgic about when we used to be free of modern-day cares.'

'And what about Saudi women?' Amber probed. 'Are they carefree?'

'They have the same cares as any. They are concerned about the well-being of their families.'

'Yes, but they're deprived of choice, are they not? They have no choice but to wear the veil which, in a sense, robs them of their individuality,' Amber persisted.

'The *abeyya* worn by Saudi women consists of a *niqab* covering the face, that's correct. But the custom of wearing a veil predates Islam. Bedu women used to cover their faces to protect their skin and hair from the harshness of the sun and desert sandstorms. Habit and repetition made it tradition, which made it the norm, much like what happened with the caste system in India. Saudi women have the right to own property, they decide on how to dispose of their income, and now that they are even actively pursuing political careers, they will soon have more control over the running of the state.'

'So, they are okay with being covered from head to toe?' Amber persisted.

'Saudi people are discrete. We cover up. We satisfy our desires behind closed doors. But is discretion any worse than the overt expressions of sexuality prevalent in the Western world, where images of near-naked men and women are used to sell every product imaginable? You may question Saudi discretion, but a common Saudi can ask what all this exposure to nudity is doing for Western society.'

'No one's complaining.'

'Are you sure? One wonders if the saturation of sexual imagery in the people's everyday experience isn't robbing the act of its mystique. The high rate of divorce in your country may have nothing to do with it. Maybe it's just plain selfishness that makes people get married, have children and then decide that they don't want them. But then again, these things might just be linked. Please don't take my curiosity as a critique of Western culture. I'm the greatest connoisseur of it. What I'm trying to say is that until one gets to the heart of another's culture one is tempted to be critical.' The solemnity that descended on the boat could have blown a hole in its hull.

'Adnan, you're an optimistic and progressive leader of your nation,' Anderson interjected, embarrassed of his wife's directness. 'Thank you for enlightening us about your culture, for your time and patience and, of course, your exquisite hospitality.'

'Since we're here on French waters, let me conclude by telling you what the Saudi people have much in common with the French—we love our dates and coffee.' It was a clever pun that Amber laughed at, but with such rancour that the other guests felt uneasy.

'I'm starving,' the Sheikh said, cheerily, changing the topic.

'Me too, I could eat a horse,' seconded Dr Ives.

'You mean a camel,' the Sheikh kidded.

'That too.'

'Young lady,' Amber said, addressing Alya while getting up. 'Shall we?'

'Absolutely,' Alya, who had been sitting beside her, replied, wishing to remind the Hollywood siren of her name.

Black Gold's kitchen staff, picked from the finest restaurants in Provence, had laid out the buffet in so discreet a manner that no one noticed lunch had been served. The head chef stepped forward to assist the ladies. 'In the appetizers we have Maghrebian couscous, camel kebabs, crayfish, onion compote and foie gras in a glass with crisp toast,' he said, gesturing to the dishes. 'In the main course, there is quiche lorraine, langoustine and Mediterranean rockfish with halves of potatoes cooked to softness in broth laced with saffron.'

Moving on to the end of the table, he said with a flare, 'In Middle Eastern cuisine, we have khouzi which consists of a whole lamb pot-roasted with almonds, sultanas, spices and hard-boiled eggs, served with rice.'

Alya resisted the urge to look at the vegetarian Swami and his conjoined cronies to see what they would, or could, have for lunch. Then, she saw the round table by the window covered with platters brimming with figs, fruit, cheese, baguettes and eggless pastries.

Concluding his tour of the buffet, the chef said, 'In dessert, we have mille-feuille, profiteroles with ice cream, pralines, macaroons, strawberries and mascarpone.' Amber left before he finished. Alya followed Amber. She would have followed Amber to Mars. Amber, according to her, belonged to the elite group of women who knew what it was like to be a goddess; liberated from restrictions, no longer needing to pretend, fight or win. When you made history in Hollywood you lived forever. You had won. You became everlasting.

The men, too, rose from their seats. Pointing to the lamb, the Sheikh said, 'The eyes are a delicacy reserved for the guest of honour. Today it is you, Jack,' he explained, scooping the eyeballs out with a spoon and gently placing them on the director's plate.

'That's just vile,' Amber said, looking away.

'Ms Ambrosia—' Alya began.

'Young lady, call me Amber,' she interrupted Alya.

'You are an inspiration,' Alya told her, 'I have immense respect for you. What amazing performances you've given in your career—'

'I advised Jack not to do this film.'

'Pardon me?'

'I advised Jack not to do this film on these Middle Eastern people, what with their female subjugation, terrorism and lamb's eyeballs…' Amber started as a tall figure in a black burqa glided on the deck outside the windows behind her. Alya made out a fetching female silhouette under the billowing fabric. The part of the niqab over the woman's eyes had been cut out and replaced by a strip of net. Protruding from the centre of the net was a triangular gold ornament, appearing somewhat like a beak. Alya guessed the ornament was there to conceal the shape of the woman's nose or, perhaps, to make it easier for her to breathe under the veil. Entranced, Alya watched the woman who, in turn, was peering into the salon through the windows, watching Alya. The woman was impossibly concealed and, yet, in her kohl-lined, almond-shaped eyes, a fire was burning. Her eyes made Alya feel like a man. They made her want to know the woman under all that shapeless fabric.

The Indian photographer on *Clandestine* saw the burqa-clad figure gliding along the upper deck of *Black Gold* in the viewfinder of his giant camera. This was of no interest to him. He twiddled with his moustache and breathed in the salty air, waiting for his chance to come.

Back on the boat, Amber was still engrossed in drawing her judgments, 'These are not the sort of people we should associate with, I told Jack.'

'I'm sorry, what did you say?' Alya turned her attention back to Amber, away from the enchanting woman on the deck.

'I refused to go to a shrink when my son died of a drug overdose. I didn't take any anti-depressants. I dealt with it, on my own,' Amber said, suddenly changing the subject.

'I'm sorry,' Alya said distractedly, looking at the window again. The woman was gone.

'Did you know that they used super cold mechanisms of brainwashing in the Man Confederation of the Sixty-third Galaxy? They had absolute psychiatric control of their officers.

Ron said, and I'm quoting him, "The psychiatric idea of man is a Godless, soulless piece of meat. A psychiatrist kills a young girl for sexual kicks, murders a dozen patients with an ice pick and castrates a hundred men",' Amber continued.

'Who is Ron?' Alya asked innocently.

'Why, Ron Hubbard of course, the founder of Scientology!' Amber replied, surprised the Indian actress didn't know about him.

Alya's eyes wandered to Swami Chand Baba, chomping contentedly on his fruit and eggless treats. Dr Ives, who was sitting beside the Swami, was trying to communicate something to Alya. He was nodding his head from side to side and giving her a cautionary glance. From what Alya could make out, he was warning her about Amber.

Just then, the old siren noticed the Doctor. 'I don't like that man,' she said. 'Many of the drugs used to paralyze the populace are developed in his country. This Swiss Doctor, I'm telling you, is an undesirable element.'

'Would you mind very much if I joined you?' the Doctor said, approaching the women.

Amber put down her plate and went away.

'Please do,' Alya replied.

Monsieur Ives sat down and said, 'Amber Ambrosia is a scientologist.'

'I don't know much about the religion,' Alya admitted.

'Call it a cult.'

Alya looked around the salon for Jayant. She hadn't seen him in a while.

'What do you know about His Holiness Swami Chand Baba?' Ives asked her.

'Nothing, actually.'

'Would you like to hear an intriguing story about him?'

Alya glanced at the walrus-like man with the two cronies crouched at his feet, busy on their iPads.

'They're his pet astrologers,' the Doctor told her.

'Sure, Doctor, tell me the story.'

'There was a khalif who had everything any mortal could desire. Not a thing was beyond his reach, but one—a son. What good was a fortune without an heir? He cast a net far and wide to find somebody who could help him escape his predicament. Before long, he learned about a crafty man of faith, said to be the only person on earth that could help him. The Khalif sent his fastest jet to India to fetch the holy man.

'When the door of the jet flung open, the Khalif waiting on the tarmac saw a motley crew—the likes of which he had never seen before: astrologers, numerologists, pundits and palmists, of various ages, shapes and sizes—pouring out. Members of the welcome party gasped, but silently, lest the chief of the crew cast a spell on them; shutting their mouths indefinitely.

'The Swami and his troupe were greeted with pomp and pageantry at the palace. But the more the Khalif watched the man in white robes slurping on coconut water, nibbling on traditional treats, the more sceptical he became of his abilities.

'Mademoiselle, would you care for a glass of apple cider?' Dr Ives paused and asked Alya.

'No, thank you,' Alya replied.

'He helped himself to a glass from a waiter's tray.

'The Khalif and the Swami sat on the palace lawns at the edge of the desert,' he continued. "The Swami gazed at the Arabian oryx wandering the distant sands while the Khalif told him about his predicament. Do you know the date, time and place of your birth?" the Swami asked him so suddenly that it seemed he was speaking to the oryx. The Khalif looked at his men. The Swami repeated the question.

'"Yes," the Khalif replied.

'An elderly man stepped forward and, taking a magnifying glass out of the pocket of his kurta, held the Kahlif's hand. As he did so, four commandos pounced out of the dry desert air and pointed their swords at his neck. The Khalif dismissed them, for, though he detested being touched by strangers, in this case, the end justified the means. With quivering fingers the old palmist took the Khalif's hand once again and began reading the lines on his palm. An astrologer, in the meantime, recorded the date, time and place of the Khalif's birth and mapped the geographical coordinates of the location. When he asked for the same for his three wives, it irked the Khalif. Another man speaking of his wives was unacceptable, even if that man were such as the astrologer; frail as a corpse and sterile as one too. Unaccustomed to such blatant intrusions of his privacy, his brow arched viciously at the Swami, as did the falcon standing on a perch beside him.'

Alya was more concerned about Jayant's whereabouts than the ins and outs of the Doctor's tale—until he mentioned the falcon. Monsieur Ives now had her undivided attention.

Dr Ives continued, 'The Swami explained to the Khalif that, according to astrology, the positions of certain stars and planets in the cosmos may affect a person's mood, relationships and circumstances. The placement of a particular planet in a person's horoscope could have a potentially negative effect on that person by creating an obstruction in his or her preordained path. By doing a ritualistic prayer involving certain offerings, he said, the negative energy generated by the troublesome planet might be weakened or neutralized.

'The Khalif was a businessman. He cared little for such mumbo-jumbo. "What needs to be done?" He cut to the point. "When can you find a solution?"

'"Tomorrow morning," said the Swami.

'At breakfast the next day, the Swami declared, "The second of your wives will bear you a son. An obstinate planet in your horoscope is causing the delay. A puja has to be done to minimize its ill-effects."

'"When can this puja be performed?" the Khalif asked.

'"After consulting your horoscope and that of your second wife, an auspicious date and time will be set for the ritual. Tomorrow, I shall return to my country and get to work there. And you, Khalif, get to work here with wife number two," the Swami said with a naughty smile playing on his lips.

'"Nothing happens without a reason," he preached at his last dinner at the palace. "Meaningful coincidences are the essence of the universe. What is meant to happen will happen, be it in a straight line or by way of a winding road. I was brought here as the enabler of your destiny. It is I, Khalif, who had to give it the push it needed."

'"Have a safe journey back home," the Khalif wished him, eager to see the results of his visit.

'A year later, the Khalif's second wife gave birth to a boy and the Swami got a new ashram worth a hundred million dollars.'

'Is Adnan the Khalif?' Alya said.

'Ah, my lady, I cannot say.'

They looked at the Swami. 'Don't let appearances fool you,' Dr Ives said. 'Chand Baba is a shrewd man, dare I say, businessman. He has amassed millions by making predictions for politicians, actors, barons and tycoons. The man has, literally, made a fortune from the stars.'

If only Alya knew of his own rascally nature, this Monsieur Ives. Doctor to the wives and mistresses of the wealthiest men alive—whose tender bodies he attended to with more than his expert chiropractic hands—the moustached monsieur claimed to have bedded 191 women and counting.

'Doc,' said Alya, to the mousey Ives with stories tucked up his sleeves, 'would you kindly request the Swami to grant me a few minutes.'

'Yes, Mademoiselle, I will. He's a friend.'

Ives took Alya to Swami Chand Baba and expressed her wish for a consultation. He agreed. Taking a seat on the carpet beside his cronies while she waited for their guru to call upon her, Alya asked them, if they, by any chance had seen Jayant.

༺∞༻

Jayant had suppressed his bodily urge since boarding the boat. But when he finally got the chance to flee his obligations and empty his bladder, which was stretched to capacity, it was to discover, to his unutterable dismay, that the toilet was occupied by the one person on the vessel in no hurry to vacate it—not until the minutest particle of food in her system was out—Amber Ambrosia.

Nobody saw Jayant leave the salon, mind driven by matter, taking the stairs to the lower deck. There, he came upon a corridor with a set of doors on either side. He opened the second to the left and, bingo, found another lavatory. His need was so dire that he barely managed to unzip his trousers before streaming into its golden toilet bowl. The relief it gave him was incomparable, although short-lived. Days of consuming Mediterranean dishes dowsed in butter and garlic had coagulated into another load in his constitution, a load he'd earlier failed to notice because of that first bodily urge commanding his attention. Jayant resigned himself to the golden throne.

Fascinated by its outlandish curiosities, buttons, mirrors and charms, Jayant succumbed to yet another pressing urge—to fidget. He touched the button beside the toilet roll. Half a metre of paper unspooled and then automatically stopped. He touched the button near the toilet seat. Perfume spritzed into the cubicle. Then, the button on the metallic door drew his attention. When he pressed that, a pixelated image appeared on the door. Jayant covered himself, conscious of the green three-dimensional face staring at him. He pressed the button again to switch it off. But the life-like female face with a sarcastic expression refused to leave. He touched her forehead. She frowned. He touched her mouth. She smiled. He touched her ear. She winked. Deciding it better not to mess with the interactive digital art installation, he looked behind him for a button to switch it off. He found a painting by Picasso hanging on the wall. Impossible. Leaning closer, he read the signature at the bottom corner of the blue painting. *Who hangs a Picasso in the toilet of a boat?* Jayant thought incredulously. Merely looking at the painting made Jayant feel like he was committing theft, as if seeing was paramount to stealing. Picasso scared the crap out of Jayant. Literally. Having emptied what felt like half his body weight, he thanked the dead painter for his posthumous favour and then tapped the toilet paper button for paper, the spray button for a wash and the dry button for a luxurious blow dry for his behind. *It's a full service station!* He thought while washing his hands at the golden faucet under the watchful gaze of the digital damsel. The whole experience made him feel like a child in a playground. He pressed all the buttons all at once and pawed at the digital face, not knowing that what he didn't know could harm him. Engineers from Ships Electronic Services had interconnected the switches of the customized cubicle; the whole module was computerized. Jayant was giving too many commands, driving the system berserk. The toilet roll unspooled, the water sprayer sprayed 'tst, tst, tst' onto the back of his trousers, the perfume spritzer kept spritzing and the golden faucet wouldn't stop trickling. Attacked by the cubicle's personal care products, watching the digital dame's face hideously contort, Jayant feared for his life. The playground had become a prison. It was time to get out. He yanked on the door handle. It was jammed. He banged on the door. No one heard him. At the end of his tether, he screamed, 'Get me out of here, please, somebody get me out.'

∞

Clutching the rail of the deck with one hand and her purse with the other, Alya made her way to the flybridge. She could see Anderson past the windows of the salon, committing a cultural crime of the highest order by feeding Barakat his lamb's eyeballs. The award-winning huntress and pageant queen devoured the edible trophies, making the award-winning actress conscious of the diminution in her own otherwise robust sense of accomplishment—in consequence of Chand Baba's prognostications about her future. She needed fresh air and a fix of nicotine to recover from her session with the Swami.

The occupants of *Clandestine* were beside themselves with joy upon seeing the heroine on the flybridge. The sky was clear, the sun was shining, the rocks were a vibrant red; it was an ideal day to shoot a spy film.

Alya tilted her head towards the sky to feel the wind in her hair and on her skin. The cameraman saw him—Adnan Ahmad bin Sultan Al-Ibrahim—in his viewfinder Approaching her from behind, he wore a smile and an untroubled countenance. They turned to face each other, the actress and the captain of industry. For the men on *Clandestine*, these were not real people. He was a god of meagre men; she, an ethereal being. Together, they made an exceptional picture. The camera shot like an Uzi. 'They're about to kiss,' the stumpy assistant yelped, jumping up and making the boat rock violently.

Still clicking, the camera dropped from the young Indian sleuth's hands and into the sea. 'You bloody idiot,' he yelled, lunging forward to save it. The boat capsized. In a few seconds, weeks of intricate planning, hours of waiting like crocodiles in a creek and thousands of dollars-worth of equipment were drowned.

Back on the *Black Gold*, the Sheikh was speaking to Alya on the deck. 'In the light of this splendid sun, it feels like I'm seeing you for the first time and also as if I've known you forever,' he said. 'What is it about the French Riviera?' he asked with a sweep of his arm, gesturing to the shore and then out to the sea, the white tassels of his thobe flapping. 'These ancient rocks, the ever-changing colours of the sky... They keep drawing me back.'

'You are fond of the place,' Alya said.

'And of you,' he said, watching her with the intent eyes of a falconer.

Alya felt shy, like a school girl. She looked away. 'I heard you have three wives. You are a lucky man.'

'There is room for one more in my heart.'

Alya looked back at him.

'My home is in Jeddah. It is the most cosmopolitan town in the kingdom. According to local legend, Eve died and was buried in Jeddah.'

'Oh, look,' Alya said, pointing at a dolphin couple racing against the *Black Gold*.

'I see,' the Sheikh replied, taking pleasure in her enthusiasm.

They smiled at each other. 'I've seen one of your films,' he then told her.

'What?'

'Middle Eastern people like Indian films. My wives watch them. How many years have you worked in the movies, Asayida, if you don't mind me asking?'

'About ten years.'

'And how much have you earned in those ten years?'

The Sheikh's questions were getting personal. Alya wasn't sure how she should react. 'Around fifteen million,' she heard herself say.

'Dollars?'

'Yes.'

'Alya, I like you. Something about you makes me want to be near you. I cannot explain it, because I don't understand it myself. But we can have plenty of time to get to know each other, if you choose.'

'Sheikh, you are thrice married.'

'I know it's hard for a non-Muslim to understand. I don't expect you to. But business, you do understand. So, here's my proposition. For each year you stay with me, I will deposit five million euros into your personal account. You will have your own apartment on the highest floors of the Burj Khalifa in Dubai, just a two-hour flight from your city. I will take you wherever you want to go. You'll accompany me to prestigious events like the King's Cup and the Qatar International Boat Show. You will not only rule my heart but also my palace, along with my other wives each of whom has an elaborate court of her own. I have hotels in Europe and the Middle East. You can stay in any of them as and when you please and get treated like a queen. We'll visit Paris and be Parisian together. We'll drink coffee amid the Corinthian columns of the Crillon. We'll go for camel safaris and star gaze from a traditional Bedouin tent. Together, we'll sail the Bosphorus.'

'Your proposition is generous and tempting.'

'Come to my chambers later so we can engage in a more comprehensive conversation in private and then you can decide.' Saying this the Sheikh walked away as if there were other pressing matters that needed his attention. Alya also had an important matter that required her attention—Jayant. Flicking her cigarette into the sea, she went in earnest search of him.

Bypassing the cockpit and salon, she went down a flight of stairs. Below deck, she arrived at a narrow gallery. The woody space was filled with the aroma of musk. Daylight streamed in from a series of portholes, illuminating the gallery and highlighting its delicate ivory and beige iconography. Alya heard hushed voices coming from an open door up ahead. Tracking the murmuring to its source, she arrived at a domed room where members of the Arab staff were engaged in *shahada*, the profession of faith performed by Muslims five times a day. Mortified by her own impertinence, she tried to retreat but not before she was spotted by one of the worshippers. 'Madame,' he said, 'we are finished with our prayers here in the prayer room. May I be of assistance to you?'

'I'm sorry to intrude. I have no idea where I am,' Alya said, embarrassed.

'You are in the staff quarters.'

'I'm looking for my friend, Jayant.'

'Allow me to help.'

The crew member led Alya back up the stairs and to the guest cabanas by the pool. No one was there. They went to the salon but Jayant wasn't there either. 'Your friend may have lost his way on the boat or he may have gone to the washroom on the lower deck, below the salon,' said the staff member who Alya noticed, only now, bore an uncanny resemblance to the Egyptian actor Omar Sharif.

On reaching the far end of the salon, they heard a feeble banging. As they descended the stairs to the lower deck, the banging got louder. When they finally arrived at the corridor, it stopped and was replaced by whimpering.

Alya knocked on the second door to the left and asked, 'Jayant, are you in there?'

'Oh, yes, Alya,' he cried, 'thank God.'

'Stand back,' said the valiant Omar Sharif lookalike, throwing his weight against the jammed door.

'No point in doing that,' Jayant told him hoarsely. 'I've tried everything. It won't open.'

The Staff member, with the salt-and-pepper hair, remembering something critical, pulled out an implement resembling a pen drive from his pocket. 'Sir, hold on, I have a master key.' He inserted the device into a keyhole in the door. It opened with a click and out slipped Jayant onto Alya's Jimmy Choos.

'You look terrible, chico,' she said, chuckling.

Drenched, nauseous, afraid, Jayant was now also offended. He wanted sympathy, but the one familiar person that could have given it to him was finding his situation comical. 'Are we ready to go?' he asked her.

'What did you say?' she asked in disbelief. His audacity had crossed the line. She provided him his bread and butter. She decided when they came and went. The man was obviously not in his right mind.

'Allow me to lead you to the upper deck, Sir. You can rest and recover there while I get you a towel and dry clothes,' the stranger said, showing him the kindness he had hoped to get from his closest friend. Leaning against the handrail of the walkway, smoking a cigarette in the warmth of the sun to help him recuperate, Jayant waited in his wet clothes for Alya to say her goodbyes. 'I'll be right back,' she said, rubbing his arm with mock concern. 'Call our boatman and tell him we'll be leaving shortly.'

The Sheikh had invited Alya to his chambers for a talk. The least she could do was bid him farewell. Aware that the master suite was located directly under the crest of the artificial volcano, Alya headed to the pool with the cascading waterfall. From there, she ascended a flight of stairs going up to the suite's private deck, not realizing that this approach was far more intrusive than her gatecrashing the prayer room.

Alya witnessed a scene so extraordinary upon reaching the zenith of the yacht that it would be eternally imprinted in her memory. Beyond the glass doors of the master suite, she saw a rain shower pouring from a sunroof shaped like a cone into a Jacuzzi. Therein sat the Sheikh, smoking aromatic tobacco from a *shisha*. Painted on the wall of the atrium encircling him were the sculpted dunes of the desert. Oryx and gazelle roamed on the foreground and Nubian ibex grazed at the back. An oasis glistened like a mirage where pink flamingos freely fished, unmindful of the Arabian leopard sitting on a mound of rocks yawning after eating a gazelle. From the low-hanging branch of a bare tree, a falcon eyed a flock of demoiselle cranes, mid-flight. Taking a siesta on a walnut bed jutting out from the atrium wall were two lithe creatures more breathtaking than all the animals of the desert. Silver *khanjas* and antique swords hung at the entrance of a wardrobe, alongside a full-length portrait of David Beckham or 'Al-Beckham' as he was known in the Sheikh's country. Beside the soccer star's cleats, on a rug of silky brown goat hair, stood a tall woman in an *abbeya*. The Sheikh pressed a button on the waterproof panel on the side of the Jacuzzi. Arabic music filled the volcano and, as it did, the fabric encasing the woman slipped off her shoulders, freeing her supple breasts as it fell to the ground. Barefoot, wearing no more than an embroidered garter belt, she began to dance, snakelike, moving with an impossible sensuality: her hips leading the way, followed by her fingertips, her olive skin glowing in the sunlight and her face hidden behind a black and gold mask.

Gazing upon this unimaginable scene, Alya was lost to her own presence. However, the ever-alert Barakat cocked her beak in the intruder's direction and screeched. So completely was the falcon camouflaged against the dunes in the mural that Alya had mistaken her as a part of the scenery. The Sheikh flung aside his water pipe and, wrapping a robe around his body, rushed to Alya just as she was about to leave.

'Wait!' he called to her, his arm outstretched. Alya had already reached the top of the stairs and was about to descend. Her heart thumping, she stopped and turned to look at him one last time. Knowing that she would not return, knowing that he would never see her again, the Sheikh placed the palm of his hand on the glass separating them and said, 'May chance be on your side.'

Alya kept going until she reached the walkway outside the salon. From there, she saw Jack and Amber boarding a boat moored to the beach deck. Bobbing beside their vessel was the speedboat with Jayant in it. She raised her arms above her head and waved at Jayant. He didn't see her; he was looking at the shore.

Reclined on a couch in the salon, snoring so loud that she could hear him through the bulletproof windows and over the drumming of her heart, the Swami had been the last guest she had seen before disembarking the ship. When the Majestic's speedboat pulled away from *Black Gold*—from the chance that came, that almost was and that now she was getting further away from—Alya thought of the Swami. Would his prophecy about her future come to pass?

24

A Bittersweet Farewell

Belly full of the tuna kept on the balcony by her newfound mistress, the kitten licked her paw, unmindful that she would soon be bolting for cover behind a potted plant when the children arrived at the house. Arranging a bouquet of flowers, Reena asked her maid to bring the delicacies from the kitchen and make the house presentable. The ceremony was over. Her parents had gone home. The priest was also about to leave.

The kitten's ears perked on hearing a gnomish scraping at the door. 'Maasi, it's us,' a boy called out, scratching the wood with his fingernails.

'Come in, children,' Reena said, opening the door. 'Chutki's made your favourite treats.'

As the boys bolted into the house, the kitten bolted behind a potted plant. 'Behave yourselves, children,' Malini reprimanded them. Then, she congratulated Reena. 'It's lovely, the new place, I'm so proud of you.'

The priest came forward and applied a vermilion dot on the homeowner's forehead. 'Hard work pays off,' he said, blessing her. He did the same for Malini and her children. As he left, the children scurried to the household shrine and began ringing its bell much to the kitten's chagrin. The friends sat down to talk while Reena's maid, Chutki, entertained Malini's sons. They liked her because she was an inch taller than them, and significantly more gnomish. She took them to Reena's room, pinching their cheeks and stuffing their mouths with *prasad*, promising to tell them grisly stories from her childhood in the village.

'It's been a while since we met,' Malini said. 'How is everything?'

'Dad's recovering well from his surgery. Mom is back to her usual state of heavenliness over her godman, Sri Sri. Keya has landed a job at Goldman Sachs in New York, and I... I'm going on holiday to Barcelona next month,' Reena updated her.

'Wow, that's great.'

'I can't describe how relieved I am that Dad has stopped forcing me to meet so-called eligible bachelors. I'm through with the Ramalingams and Shamalingams of the city.' They laughed, and it was genuinely satisfying because the subject of marriage had been no laughing matter for Reena.

'You're not alone,' Malini said. 'So many women are struggling to find a good mate.'

'I wonder why that is,' Reena said.

'It takes a strong and secure man to be with a strong and secure woman.'

'That makes sense,' Reena said, picking a snack from the tray.

'Parents who raise their sons to be secure individuals and teach them about gender equality turn them into men who accept independent females—it's as simple as that.'

Malini's sons discovered the feline. 'Boys, stop bothering that cat.' Malini's admonition gave the kitten a chance to skedaddle.

'I'm at peace with myself. I'm happier now than I've ever

been,' Reena said. 'I may even consider adopting an orphanage.'

'An orphanage?'

'I pass one every day on my way to work and see the children playing in the yard. As of now, they have twenty-five kids. I went in and asked around last week. I'm thinking of helping them out with raising funds and finding adoptive parents.'

'What made you think of it?'

'The need for a larger purpose.'

'You're right, self-preservation and the pursuit of wealth can't be the only things we strive for. We all need a purpose to bring meaning to our lives—a hobby, a charity, a goal to achieve or a problem to solve.'

'Caring for my parents and going to work every day weren't enough of a purpose for me,' Reena said. 'Now that business is going well, I want to give back.'

'You've thrown the idea out there, let it swirl in the empire in the sky. The answer will come to you.'

'I don't care anymore about what people think of me,' Reena said. 'Mom was watching a rerun of one of Jackie's shows before the puja today. I respect that Jackie Funwala. Her confidence and grace are inspiring. She's not a size zero. She's not even a biological female. Yet she carries herself like a queen. Jackie is who she believes herself to be.'

'Reality is subjective,' Malini commented.

'I know how hard it is to hold your head high when you're constantly looked down upon. Loving myself hasn't come easy,' Reena said.

'You love yourself now—that's what matters.'

'A friend once asked me, "How can you get someone to love you if you don't love yourself?"'

'That friend got it right,' Malini said, grinning because it was she who had said it.

'One thing has become clear to me. Our lives mould us to a certain point, but beyond that point it is we who do the moulding. From here on, *I* will be the sculptor of my life,' Reena asserted.

'More power to you,' Malini said.

'It was Dad's emergency that brought about the change in my perspective.'

'So that's what did it.' Malini had been concerned that Reena's sudden sense of conviction may have been coming from frustration or exasperation. But adversity had not radicalized her—the conviction was coming from a place of light.

'Maasi, take us to the park,' the children whined, jumping onto Reena's back.

'Alright kiddos, let's go,' she said, wiping her moist eyes.

'Not today, children. Go back to Maasi's room and watch cartoons,' their mother told them. '*Chutki, bachon ko kamre me le jao* [Chutki, take the children to the room],' she instructed before turning to Reena. 'I've been meaning to tell you something.'

Chutki took the children back to the room.

'What is it?' Reena asked her.

'I'm moving to London.'

'When?'

'My husband just landed a plum position in his company's London branch. And for me, it doesn't matter where I work, it could be Burkina Faso. All I need is a computer and coffee and I'm set.'

'How did he get you to agree to leave? You've always been so bent on living in India. Although I never understand why.'

'I respect my country and its Constitution. We are liberal people despite what our polarizing political figures try to tell us. They box us as Hindu, Muslim, Sikh, Christian, Buddhist, but we're already integrated. We celebrate each other's festivals. We work with each other. We marry each other. It's done. They can't see that. The clock can't be turned back. They're doing a disservice to the nation by playing these dirty vote bank games.'

'Malini, not the history lesson, please.'

'There's so much to see, smell and taste here, and though it can get emotionally exhausting sometimes, it's exhilarating. I feel a sense of curiosity, freedom and adventure here that I don't feel anywhere else.'

'Thank you for the personal input, Malini. I appreciate it,' Reena said. 'I know you feel that way, but I'm still surprised you agreed to leave.'

'We may return at a later date. It's possible. Anything is possible. For now, I have to balance my career and the needs of my family the best I can.'

'Are your in-laws going with you?'

'No, my friend.'

'I don't get it, how in the hell did you manage to live in a joint family for so long?'

'I love my husband, so I did it for him. Besides, we had no choice. His family migrated to Mumbai from Kashmir when he was just seventeen. The exodus left his father in shock—he couldn't start over—so my husband had to work night and day to provide for his parents and sister. Later, when the children came along, the number of dependents increased, furthering his financial responsibilities. We just couldn't afford two homes.'

'Yes, I know the story.'

'This is how I see it. A joint family, in theory, is an ethical and practical system of living, but it can only be successful in practice if everyone's expectations from each other are clearly defined. Each member has to respect the other's privacy. There can be no hierarchy because that leads to discrimination. If even one member is exploited, as is usually the case in a typical joint family, then a system that is ethical in theory can become unethical in practice.'

'What a nerd you are, Malini. Really, one of a kind!' Reena exclaimed.

'The story has moved to the next chapter, we can finally afford to rent an apartment for my in-laws here as we move on with our children to make a fresh start.'

'I'm going to miss you!'

'You mean you're going to miss my jabber?'

'I'm going to miss your encyclopaedic blabber, yes.'

'Huh, what can I say, I'm speechless.' Malini winked at her.

'When are you going?'

'At the end of next month.'

'That soon? What am I going to do without you?'

'What you always do, Reena. Watch movies, go for concerts, exercise, drink wine, read a book, get a massage and make friends—new ones, good ones.'

'You've been there for me in more ways than I can say.'

'You chose me to be your friend—the credit goes to you,' Malini said, kissing Reena on the cheek. 'I lucked out, too, Reena Subramaniam, you're the best friend I have ever had.'

Reena hugged Malini and took time to let go.

'I'm not dying, you silly chick,' Malini said, holding her by the shoulders. 'I'm just moving.'

'I'm coming to see you in London.'

'You'd better!'

The children returned from Reena's room, pleading to go to the park. 'Alright, boys,' their mother gave in, 'let's go.'

'Stay a while.'

'Babe, the kids have pent-up energy that needs letting out.'

'I'll come with you,' Reena insisted.

'Enjoy your day off in your new home,' Malini told her, getting up. 'Let's do lunch on Monday.'

'I'm showing a studio apartment to a prospective buyer on Monday.'

'Then we'll do it another day,' Malini said. 'Nab that deal!'

'It'll be a big score for me if he goes for it—a certain Mr Dharmesh Pawar.'

25

Power Outage

The photographer had held his breath and dived into the waters of the Mediterranean to salvage his monster camera caught between the rocks on the seabed. The pictures of Alya and the Sheikh on *Black Gold*'s sky bridge, digitally re-mastered and cropped, awarded the young paparazzo the prestige he had always wanted among his ilk. Despite the photoshop, the pictures were still grainy; giving them the scandalous appeal tabloid publications made a killing on.

Alya would have seen them as much-needed publicity for her floundering career, if not for the nature of the article that accompanied them. Featured in a leading tabloid magazine, the article titled, 'How to Go From a Millionaire Boyfriend to a Billionaire Boyfriend', came with ten tips written to sound as though the actress had said them verbatim. The most upsetting tip for her brother to read was number five: 'Get fine jewellery, abrasive scrape peels, Juvéderm fillers and bee venom facials.' It came with close-ups of Alya at a ribbon-cutting ceremony: eyes puffy, lips swollen, the skin on her chin scaling. Alya visualized Jackie on *The Jackie Funwala Show*, in a fabulous gown in her swanky new studio set—bigger, glitzier and grander than the one before—displaying pictures of Alya on gigantic screens with graphic arrows pointing at her minutest flaws. Stocked with an arsenal of images, chief among them those of the actress sharing what appeared to be a kiss with an Arabian billionaire—their Lichtenstein dots rendering them ever more clandestine—the screens were flashing picture after scandalous picture.

Vishal tossed the magazine into the wastebasket. Speculation concerning his sister's dwindling career and torrid affairs had trailed him on all his recent visits across India. Rumours were rife, like the one about Alya playing arm candy to the chief minister of her home state. People asked him if she was moving abroad. A mate at his class reunion went as far as asking him if she'd had a vaginoplasty—that was less a rumour and more chauvinistic nastiness. It was getting hard for him to distinguish between fact and fiction.

Vishal wasn't impervious to his sister's gradual transformation into an inauthentic version of herself. It concerned him. But she was a grown woman; she had the right to live her life the way she chose. As her brother, though, it was all difficult to digest. He looked at her sitting across from him and wondered what she was thinking and planning. Would she see this article, too, as a minor setback, the way she saw all obstacles in her path?

Alya knew she'd become a soft target. She regretted replacing Jayant, her former manager-cum-friend, with an image consultant who promised to boost her prospects.

'So what have you decided, Al?' Engrossed in their own thoughts, neither of the siblings noticed Jayant enter the room. 'Are you going to do it?' he asked Alya, taking a seat.

'What are you talking about?' Alya asked.

'The Sheikh's proposal.'

'The Sheikh you met in France proposed to you?' Vishal asked, surprised, though mildly, for not much surprised him anymore about his sister and her shenanigans.

'Yes.'

'And?' Vishal probed.

'And, I can tell you this, I respect the man.'

'You respect the man for asking you to be his fourth wife?' Vishal asked, laughing.

'Yes, I do, because I prefer a Sheikh who puts his cards on the table and is honest with me about his proposal to be his fourth wife than a man who claims his undying love for me only to turn out to be a player.'

'Like Karan?' Jayant blurted.

Alya looked the other way.

'I would have gone for it,' Jayant told her.

'Why didn't you?' her brother cautiously asked.

'There is more for me to conquer here. The best is yet to come,' Alya silenced Vishal. The maid trundled into the room with cups of green tea. A door slammed in an adjacent flat.

'I should be going, sis. I have a flight to catch,' Vishal got up and kissed Alya on the forehead. 'I love you.'

'Love you too.'

Jayant rose with effort and hugged Vishal. 'Goodbye, old friend.'

'See you, pal,' Vishal said, touched by Jayant's emotional farewell, clueless that it would be his last.

'I have something important to tell you,' Jayant said, when he was alone with Alya.

'I have something important to tell you, too. I want you back on the job, and I mean, full-time,' Alya told him, uninterested in what he had to say.

'Barbara and I are moving to Canada,' Jayant casually informed her.

'You'll get a twenty per cent commission on all my projects,' Alya offered, ignoring the gravity of his revelation.

'Ten years in the entertainment industry have taught me a lot and given me even more, and I'm thankful for it. But I'm not getting any younger, Al. None of us are. One can only know what being young is when one is young no more. I'm tired. I'm balding. I'm growing fat. I'm drained. You can call it depraved, but I want my old life back.'

'How morose.'

'I want to play golf, cook, read, practice yoga at sunrise—'

'You might as well check yourself into an old-age home and be done with it,' Alya interrupted him, annoyed.

'I want to spend time with my wife and children. You should think of shifting gears, too, Al. You deserve a break, some fun, a long vacation.'

'Barbara finally got her way, huh?'

'It's not Barbara. It was our decision, together. I want out.'

'Does your decision have anything to do with pay?' she asked him, sipping on her green tea.

'My present earnings don't exactly meet my family's needs, it's true, but that's not the reason.'

'How will you make a living in Canada?'

'Barbara's got a position as a music teacher at a school in Montreal. I'll be joining my brother-in-law in his mini-golf business.'

Alya laughed so hard that drops of tea trickled out of her nostrils. 'What about Mukta, your sister?' she asked, getting a hold of herself. 'Are you going to leave her behind?'

'She's coming with us.'

'You don't have my permission to go. There is work to be done. I need you here,' Alya asserted.

'You know that I've always wanted to move to the West, eventually. That eventuality has arrived. Please, Alya, try to understand.'

'No, Jayant, *you* have to understand. It's not about you.'

Alya's statement confirmed what Jayant had, sadly, begun to suspect of her proclivity. Alya was concerned only with Alya. He was grateful for the doorbell that spared him the effort of fruitlessly defending his decision. The atmosphere got heavier as Barbara entered the room; it seeped through the blinds and begged the windows for release.

'Have you also come to say goodbye?' Alya asked her.

'I've come to take Jayant home. He injured his ankle on the boat in Cannes.'

'Is that so?' Alya asked, surprised.

'I'm not saying goodbye, dear, of course not,' Barbara told her. 'There's plenty of time before we leave. The kids will want to meet you.'

Getting up with his wife's help, Jayant said, 'Will you be seeing Eisha anytime soon?'

'Actually, we're meeting on Saturday. Robin is hosting a party at Hard Rock Café to commemorate his first business venture in India.'

'Tell her I said hi.'

'Barbie, I'm going to miss the children and you and your cupcakes.'

'We're going to miss you, too,' Barbara responded.

'I'm like an aunt to them.'

'You *are* their aunt,' Jayant said.

'You have been a wonderful aunt to them,' Barbara added.

Then, holding Jayant by the arm, she said, 'Honey, you alright?'

'I'm on top of the world,' Jayant replied, the door closing behind them.

Alone in her house with its closed windows, Alya could think not of vicious stories, wicked gossip or unexpected farewells, but of one thing—a toddler's tuxedo she had once seen in her old friend's room.

26

In a Quagmire

Roughing it out on the shadier side of the Sea Link Bridge, Alya would never have guessed that eighteen years later, she'd be living in the age of social media, cryptocurrency and virtual reality, and attending a launch party in a British-era mill converted into a Hard Rock Café.

Time has a curious way of turning things on their heads, she reflected, not only with regards to her own journey but also the lives of the people around her. Upon reaching the venue, she watched Eisha, in her Swarovski-encrusted Dior gown, flanked by Ranjita and Romila, pandering to the newest queen bee of cinema, Rehana. The well-known diamond merchant, Ranjan Hiranandani, desperately desired the nubile actress with a model's good looks and was willing to splurge on her hobbies and whims if that's what it took to possess her. Rehana had diamonds coming out of her derrière and movies lining up round the bend for her.

Laila Ali saw Alya but didn't bother to wave at her. With the strike of a pen across Alya's name, the former reigning actress had been banished by Bollywood's first lady from her annual Christmas luncheon; disbarring her from filmdom's premier address forever or at least until she delivered another hit or married a diamondwala.

'Want to go to the loo?' Monica asked, hollow-cheeked Monica, the last of Alya's entourage, whose longevity too was uncertain, owing to her deadly diet of cotton balls soaked in vodka.

'You go ahead,' Alya replied.

'I can't leave you alone,' Monica said.

'I'll be alright.'

Affected by the pretension she was witnessing, which she had been privy to until recently, Alya went to the bar for a quick fix to bury the discomfiting truths being fired at her so quickly that they were making her feel kind of numb. Waiting her turn at the bar, she admired the rock 'n' roll memorabilia hanging from the rafters and appreciated the eclecticism of the compilation. The man leaning over the counter beside her interrupted her musings. He was not, as she had assumed, ordering a drink; Abbas Ali was busy thrusting his tongue into the bartender's ear. Alya ducked as he turned to leave, though she didn't have to. Abbas was intent on making his way back to his wife who was dancing with her friends.

Dude entered Hard Rock with his latest muse, an Indian–Australian surfer chick he had met on holiday. Alya was sure she'd see this woman in his next film. He had a tendency of doing that, introducing his muses to his world of celluloid. He cocked his trigger-happy fingers at her. It was getting old. It was all getting old. She was having trouble processing how old it had gotten. Then, she saw Eisha gesturing for her to come to the dance floor. Alya recalled their last conversation about nightingale poo facials, the latest wrinkle-busting serum and human sperm selling for 250 dollars a pop at snooty spas in New York. There had been a time when they had talked about other, more interesting things, a time lost, a time they both pretended had never been because it had to do with a slum and a bog.

When Monica returned from the washroom, they downed the tequila shots that Alya had ordered at the bar and, satisfactorily inebriated, embarked on a tour of the party. Going along, Alya picked up shreds of gossip not because it was her intention to do so but because that's what clucking tongues do. She was starting to feel relieved they weren't clucking about her when she heard the name Robin Chauhan. 'We were at the Buddha Bar in Monte Carlo when he met them,' a man said, 'the Swedish flight attendants.' Alya stood with her back against him, curious to hear what he was saying, since he was talking about her good friend's husband.

'Airhostesses,' came a familiar female voice.

'I returned to Villa Chauhan at about three and crashed on the couch.'

'And then what happened?' came another female voice, also familiar.

'I awoke to noises of people having sex. When I peeked from under my blanket, I saw that they were having a ménage à trois.'

'You mean Robin and the airhostesses?'

'He promised them boob jobs from the same place his wife got hers in return for their favours,' the man chuckled.

'And here I thought Robin was a clean-cut guy!'

'Let's go,' Alya said, pulling Monica by the arm. Listening to such slander suddenly felt wrong. 'Eisha doesn't deserve this.'

'Where are we going?' Monica asked.

'To the dance floor,' Alya replied.

'Sure, I'm game.'

As they were leaving, Alya saw that Ranjita and Romila were part of the triad gossiping about their friend's husband while drinking his booze at his party. It had become boring—the predictability of the world she inhabited.

Cindy Lauper's polka-dotted dress, Madonna's red corset, Elton's shoes, Britney's jumpsuit—a solar system of iconic objects was rotating around her as she danced. Men entered her orbit like pitted asteroids pulled in by the gravity of her beauty. Laila and Abbas Ali looked on, nodding their heads at what had become of the former siren. Alya wanted release from the orbit. 'I need to get out of here,' she said. 'You coming?'

'Nope,' replied Monica. 'I'm staying.'

Looking for Eisha, she saw Elvis Presley's white bell-bottoms on the top right corner of the club; the ones the king of rock 'n' roll had worn during his final stage performance in Las Vegas, a week before he famously keeled over and died on his toilet bowl. Seeing the culmination of his celebrity hanging there, like a lifeless thing in a glass coffin, symbolic of the full stop in his illustrious career, gave Alya the jitters.

She stepped outside the club and lit a cigarette, trying to remember where she had parked her car. Her driver had taken the day off at the last minute, citing his uncle's death. Walking past fabulous automobiles arranged in neat rows on either side of her, Alya made her way towards the end of the VIP lot, fairly certain that's where she'd parked her car. It started drizzling, causing steam to rise off the black tarmac and fog the windshields over. Within moments, the rain grew stronger and washed the fog away, enabling Alya to clearly look into the vehicles. She saw figures inside one of them, moving to Prince's iconic lyrics coming from Hard Rock: 'This is what it sounds like when doves cry.' A shirtless man was sitting in the backseat of the car with his head on the headrest. It was dark, but Alya could make out a female form straddling the man. She stepped closer and recognized the man—it was the bartender from Hard Rock. The woman, taking a swig from a bottle of champagne and rubbing her nose, was Eisha. Shoes sodden from the murky puddle in which she stood, clothes drenched, strings of hair clinging to her face like fingers, Alya ran from the site.

27

Natural Light

Working with her father in an office with nothing but a telephone and a calendar at a second-hand desk was showing its results. Reena's solo enterprise—Space Solutions—operated out of Andheri's corporate quarter and boasted of five workstations, a reception, washrooms for male and female staff, a small balcony and a pantry. It went beyond buying old apartments, refurbishing and reselling them. During restoration work, utilitarian features, which saved space while giving the place a contemporary aesthetic, were incorporated into the structures. These features were personally designed and developed by Reena, the director of the company. It was a clever strategy to use in a city like Mumbai, where space was money and aesthetics were almost entirely lacking. The formula was doing wonders for the company's bank balance. Space Solutions had an ever-increasing list of satisfied clientele—a list on which Danny was soon to appear.

The design philosophy Reena had adopted for her most recent project artfully blended the inside with the outside, resulting in an uninterrupted expanse of space drenched in natural light. Her management skills had also improved. Her workers had become more cooperative. Products and materials were now sourced as and when she required them. Consequently, the apartment turned out the way she had envisaged it.

When she had first bought the 2,300 square-foot moss-and-moth-eaten wreck of a place, she knew instinctively that the first step she had to take to create a fluid space was to knock down the internal walls. Once the walls were down, Reena tore the roof over the sunniest spot in the apartment and replaced it with glass; creating a luminous, enclosed courtyard for a dining area, nursery or workstation. She made an open-plan kitchen with white, black and red tiles. The reclaimed boards she'd used to make the shelves and cupboards in the kitchen and bedroom, and the hardwood floor running throughout the studio, gave the sleek and contemporary space a touch of earthiness.

Reena stood at the window at the front end of the flat and looked down at the intersection—at its human tides, changing signals and vehicular traffic. She was at peace. The fourth-floor studio was shielded against the chaos of its surroundings by the cheerful yellow blooms of the poinciana tree. Reena had invested much time and energy into this space. She couldn't help herself. She had acquired a taste for creative pursuits. With every apartment she renovated, she made a conscious effort to make it a gender-neutral space agreeable to persons of every age—an endeavour necessitating boundless creativity. Anyone could walk in and buy the apartment. It could be Danny, Jackie Funwala, a Ramalingam, an old geezer or a solo career woman such as herself.

Three knocks sounded on the door, announcing the arrival of the first potential buyer, and it was just as well. Reena was beginning to wish she had installed an armchair in the studio for a more comfortable wait.

His was a recognizable face but she was seeing it for the first time. The man had a solid brow, softened by curly black locks hanging like the tendrils of the tree by the window, drizzling cheery yellow drops. He had a strong presence, his body language was unmistakably more masculine than most men Reena had met—and she had met more than she had wished to because they were so different from the type she wanted to be with. He made her self-conscious. Swallowing, she said, 'Mr Dharmesh Pawar?'

'That's me,' he said with a warm smile.

'I'm Reena Subramaniam.'

Danny stepped inside.

'Mr Pawar, this studio has a lot to offer—' She began her sales pitch.

'Call me Danny,' he interrupted her. His candour made her more nervous rather than putting her at ease. *Reena, don't shuffle your feet. Work it. Crack the deal. You are a businesswoman. Selling is what you do. Be confident. Focus,* she told herself and continued, 'The space is conducive for work, relaxation, entertainment, you name it. It's pliant and can also be remodelled to suit your needs.'

Danny smiled at her, his eyes gentle and gripping—warm and open, like the studio.

'The windows are precision-engineered. They're designed to insulate the home against noise, rain, dust and pollution,' Reena continued as he squinted—not at the sunlight pouring through the windows but at the shuffling little woman before him. The smartness with which she was crafting her sales pitch and the smoothness of her delivery were admirable. Self-assurance was an attractive trait to him. He knew how hard it was to achieve, especially for women in his country who not only struggled to get a job but also to maintain their dignity in it.

'I like how bright it is in here,' he said, going to the bedroom and bathroom at the back of the apartment. Returning, he stopped in front of the wall opposite the open-plan kitchen. 'My friend is a graffiti artist, I can ask him to paint something for me here,' he said, indicating the spot to Reena with his finger. 'I'll fix bookshelves along the length of this wall and use them to frame the artwork.'

'That's a good idea,' Reena said.

'I like the woodwork in the studio.'

'Reclaimed floorboards were used to make the cupboards in the kitchen and bedroom. Fresh timber doesn't have the same charm, does it? If we use the same type of wood for the bookshelves, there'll be visual continuity throughout the apartment,' Reena added.

'You have a point and besides, it's more sustainable,' Danny said, turning to the kitchen. 'Hey, that's a good corner for my neon light sculpture.'

'Yes, that is a good spot for something original.'

'The sculpture is as tall as I am and just as twisted,' he kidded.

'There's a lot of scope in here to accommodate all kinds of tall and twisted things,' Reena said, surprised at her humour and spontaneity, which were generally in short supply owing to her mild anxiety. Danny laughed a real and hearty laugh.

'I like the way the studio is shielded from the bustle of the intersection by the poinciana,' he said.

'Yes, it does have a calming effect, doesn't it? I have to admit, the tree was a major consideration in acquiring the place.'

Reena couldn't help but notice the ease with which their conversation was flowing. For a person to whom ease didn't come easily, it had a calming effect. She relaxed a little.

'I can see you are a nature lover,' she said, guiding Danny to the enclosed courtyard. 'You can make an indoor garden in here if you like.'

'I'd like to have a garden.'

'And what would you like to have in your garden, Mr Pawar?' There it was, the impulsivity that Reena had put a lid on for so long breaking loose.

Danny looked at her, really looked at her, the light from the sunroof illuminating the highlights in her hair. To run one's own business required patience, perseverance and sacrifice. The woman must have seen a lot in life, but she hadn't been hardened by it. She was sincere and straightforward. She was bold and at the same time exuded vulnerability. Her paradoxical personality was like that of the city of Mumbai. She was the city. And Danny loved this city. The harmonious juxtaposition of its contradictory traits was irresistible to him. In the silence that they were sharing, he felt as though the woman standing before him was a kindred spirit. He knew her from somewhere, had seen her, met her or been with her before. She reminded him at once of his mortality and his immortality. Wherever he may have encountered her or experienced her in some existential way, Danny was developing feelings towards this woman.

Reena could see the play of emotions on Danny's face. Shy and surprised, she said, 'Take your time in deciding if you want it.' She went to the window and looked out at the poinciana. Delicate yellow pods were loosening from its tendrils and falling to the ground. One cheeky pod bounced off a pocket of air and landed at the feet of an old man standing at the intersection. Glowing in the glimmer of a fleeting sun, he turned his sapphire eyes up and saw her. Excited, Reena pointed to herself and then back at him, as if to say, 'I'm coming.' Danny was calling out her name, but she didn't hear him.

At the intersection below, the pedestrian signal turned green. People across the street from the old man with the flowing hair and beard started walking towards him. Reena was so engrossed in looking at the apparition from the window that she was insensible to Danny, who had come and stood beside her. She saw the man arriving at the other side of the intersection, and then the pedestrians and old man were engulfed in a haze—it was Danny's breath fogging up the window as he inched closer to it and her. As the fog evaporated, so did the old man. Reena turned to Danny. *Could he be the one?* she thought, looking at his face up close. She had given up on finding *the one*. And yet, here he was in the flesh—Mr Dharmesh Pawar.

28

In a Limbo

Alya's days were hectic, rushing from one appointment to the next. She met the Levitating Baba, then the Silent One and then the Rope Baba. Taking the phrase 'go with your gut feel' to its literal limit, the Rope Baba swallowed nine metres of rope and made predictions for his followers by reading how it coiled on the ground after returning from his innards. Alya left before he could deliver his prognosis, the sight of the slimy rope threatening to make her upchuck her lunch of pan-seared falafel with lemon-tahini dressing. She visited numerologists, graphologists and clairvoyants. She met with crystal healers, tarot card and aura readers. She even did a three-day workshop to learn how to activate her chakras with angels.

It was a Saturday afternoon and Alya was tired. Her overnight stay with a Romanian gypsy in a tent in the dewy woods of Matheran had turned out to be the most strenuous sojourn. The gypsy, a self-proclaimed past life regression therapist, had put her into a hypnotic state and later revealed that many lives ago she had been trapped in a metal container for twenty-six days. In her most recent past life, she said, Alya had been a woman with big dreams who ended up eking out a living from a dusty ranch in El Paso.

Alya didn't know what to believe and what not to believe anymore. The only thing she was certain of was that, in spite of her fortune and fame, she had no work and no man—a predicament she hadn't envisioned in her larger picture. Of all the soothsayers and fortune tellers, the prediction made by Swami Chand Baba on the floating island on the Mediterranean Sea seemed to be taking shape with alarming speed and accuracy.

With no commitments, plans or friends to keep her company, burrowed in her couch, Alya was lingering somewhere between wakefulness and sleep when a spasm caused her leg to jerk and kick the coffee table. *India Today, Bombay Times, Cine Blitz,* brochures, pamphlets and other printed material that had formed a paper tower on the table, toppled to the ground. Alya leant forward and picked up the magazine closest to her foot. Danny's picture was on the cover. Déjà vu. Something like this had happened before. Back then, it had been her brother who had placed the matter before her. Alya wondered who was responsible for it being there or her picking it up this time. She opened the magazine and read the article on Danny's exhibition, titled, 'Leopards of a Concrete Jungle'. Accompanied by a picture of a frightened cub cornered in a kitchen, the article spoke of the buzz surrounding Danny's debut photography exhibition on escalating man–animal conflicts. Tonight was the opening night. *Why should I sit here at home and mope? I'm going to go out there and get him!* Alya thought. Danny would be thrilled to see her at his exhibition. *I'll look ravishing. I'll be irresistible.* Drawing inspiration from one of her two nuggets of wisdom, she'd tell him, 'Let's forget the past. You and I were a great team. We still can be.'

29

Devastation

Alya's driver parked the car across the street from the gallery. While getting dressed, she'd rehearsed what she was going to say to her former boyfriend as she placed her hand on his arm and gazed into his eyes and smiled. She'd apologize if need be.

Just then, Alya saw a jeep pull up to the gallery. Danny sprung out of it. Looking up at the banner hanging from the building with the photograph of the leopard cub from the magazine, he walked around to the other side of the khaki-coloured vehicle. Brimming with excitement, Alya stepped out of the car and started towards him. Just as she was about to reach him, Danny opened the door to the passenger side of his jeep and taking a woman by the hand, helped her onto the curb. Alya stopped mid-step. She watched the pair ascend the stairs to the gallery and merge with other happy people. Danny's companion turned around as if she'd forgotten something in his jeep. Alya got a better look at her: Danny's date was Malini's mousy friend, what's-her-name. She returned to her car. *After me he went for…that? Why would Danny settle for someone like her?* Alya wondered, utterly confused. She visualized herself going up the stairs, holding

Danny's arm. Her vision blurred with tears and she felt dizzy. Reality was striking with brute force; dressing it up in pretty clothes wasn't going to change it. She had herself to blame for losing Danny.

It was all coming back to Alya now—their final row.

∞

'Is everything between us pretend?' he had asked her in their last interaction. 'Are you just playing house with me? Is that what we're doing here?'

She'd started the fight, accusing him of cheating on her while she had been in Thailand. When he had tried to defend himself, she had refused to listen. 'Were you ever interested in my work,' he had said, 'or for that matter, in me?'

'And what exactly is it that you do?' she had shot back at him. 'Aside from chasing birds, cleaning bogs, creating a general hue and cry about the bees and the trees—'

'What do you want, Alya? Do you even know?'

'What are you talking about?'

'I'll tell you what you want—control. You want the world to revolve around you. Alya, you don't need to control every circumstance, every individual and every relationship that enters your sphere of existence. If you must have control, it should be over your ego.'

'Is this a joke? *You* are dumping *me*?'

'Do you actually hear what anyone says?'

'Fine, go ahead. See how you fare without me.'

'If this is going to be your response, I'll take my chances,' he had said.

'Please do,' she had responded.

'Under all those protective layers you've wrapped yourself

in, I hope, for your sake, there's still an Alya worth salvaging. Find her.'

Alya had felt nothing at the time, but the memory of the conversation was poking her in parts she didn't know existed. She watched Danny and Reena enter the gallery, leaving her to study the banner with the image of a leopard trapped in a concrete jungle, staring at her with its haunted eyes. She commanded her driver to take her away, looking at the road ahead of her with the same expression as the cub in the picture—crushed by the fear of an uncertain future.

30

Reformation

Betrayed by her nuggets of wisdom—no looking back and looking at the larger picture—Alya gave into a voracious yearning to wallow in self-pity. Soaking in a milk bath at a villa at the Ananda Resort, she asked whoever might be listening to her thoughts, or hoped would be listening to her thoughts, why her life had stopped yielding to her will.

She had sensed it for the first time after winning the Filmfare award, while locking her prize in the vault. The hole had grown since, sucking her confidence, energy and certainty into its depth. She'd hoped that a retreat in the mountains would rejuvenate her, that walks through a forest of deodars redolent with the scent of pine—capable of penetrating with purity the most resistant of souls—would stop the hollowing inside. But the rebellion within her refused to die. Her mind had become disobedient, obsessively peering into the past. Memories were breaking free, of Minty Bose, of the aspiring actress at Ali Mansion who begged her for her recipe for success and of the story that she had suppressed for all these years—of her childhood. The brainwashing—telling herself that she, Alya the Star, had always been Alya the Star—caved in and crumbled, like that kitchen in the slum where she had once lived.

Watching the Rishikesh valley through her room, clouds hanging low over the winding Ganga, Alya whispered a prayer to the river goddess. As she gazed upon the river, several questions surfaced in her mind: *What is it that you want? You have everything. Why do you still feel so empty?*

She had never considered taking out time for herself, taking what people called 'me time'. Now, with more time than she'd ever had, Alya found herself looking back at her formative years as the daughter of a widow struggling for survival in a deadbeat town. Living fatherless and poor in a community that ostracized families with absentee patriarchs had triggered in her the burning hunger for success. It was then that she had resolved to become the man of the family. Her being was aflutter, and she wanted to stop that fluttering. The longer she looked at the curvaceous river goddess in the valley, the harder and faster came the memories, the tougher the questions got and the stronger her yearning to go to the river grew.

'I want to book a car for tomorrow morning to go to the Ganga,' she told the concierge.

'At what time, Madam?'

'7.00 a.m.'

Alya's night was wracked with dreams of black holes sucking the forest, water, ether and animals into their gargantuan depths. The dreams were vivid and exhausting, like a battle with no end. When morning came, she was relieved to see a mist sailing on the tips of the majestic deodars. She ate breakfast with the peacocks of Ananda vying for morsels of food from her plate and with the monkeys of the mountains. A Korean Tai Chi master practised his art on the neighbouring lawn. A reviving chill infused the air.

The car stopped fifteen minutes before it was to enter the bustling town of Rishikesh. Fighting her way down a slope covered with thick vegetation, Alya arrived at the river. She removed her shoes and walked over pebbles the size of golf-balls along the bank, noticing that the goddess was not at all a sleeping beauty but a beauty racing, rippling and roaring with life. Alya's sense of adventure was awakened. She noticed a boulder nearby, partially hidden by plants, clinging to the hillside. She climbed it and sat with her legs crossed. Drawing in a deep breath, she closed her eyes and as she breathed in and out, repeatedly, rhythmically, her mind quietened. She was aware only of the gushing water. After an hour, she slid off the boulder, eager to walk along the bank again.

Just then, she saw something move on the rocky island in the middle of the river. There was another human being in these isolated environs, where she expected none to be. Alya dove behind the boulder and watched him. Dressed in a black loincloth in the icy morning air, his bony limbs and matted hair covered in ashes and dirt, he was, what in Hindu lore is known as, an Aghori. Alya was fascinated by the ghoulish mendicant—fascinated at first and then petrified, for he was pulling an object twice his size from the swirling edge of the river: a bloated and half-burned corpse. Cleaning the cadaver as a mother would her child, he pried open its mouth and filled it with flowers, all the while mumbling inaudible chants. He placed a rose petal on each eye and covered the genitals with ferns. The body appeared to be that of a young man. Alya imagined him to be a brave soldier who had been shot and killed fighting the pointless, savage and infinite war along the Indo-Pakistan border. She pictured his parents putting their son to rest into the arms of the river goddess.

Subsequently, to her horror, the phantasmal ascetic sat on the corpse. Ten minutes passed. An hour passed. Deep in meditation, he remained still as a stork. Save for a string of beads around his neck, a staff and a *kumandalu*, or copper bowl, he had no possessions. He was unkempt, possibly starved, and yet at peace with himself. Alya had always believed that if you were unknown, you were as good as dead. But this person had no identity, he moved undetected from place to place, like a ghost. He was nobody. He might as well have not existed. Yet, she envied him because he had something she wished she had: satisfaction.

Alya's tendency of micromanaging her life and relationships had made it difficult for her to be spontaneous and trusting. The answer to the questions arising in her since the day she had won her award was one: *there can be no love where there is no trust.*

Just like that, it came to her. The Aghori got off the corpse and released it in the Ganga. He took a dip in the frigid waters, grasping the same rock the corpse had been caught on from whence he had freed it. He climbed up a jagged cliff and, reaching the top, looked out at the great big world. Alya emerged from behind her boulder. She stood beside the river, and said, 'I am responsible for who I am, who I've been, and who I will be. I surrender my fear, the poison I allowed in me, to the currents of this river. Wash away. Wash away.'

The black hole that had been swallowing everything up had been her salvation. After crisis comes catharsis, after destruction comes life. Alya picked up one of the countless white pebbles on the shore, an egg of a pebble, and tossed it into the river. The pebble hit the water with a splash, bounced off it and, getting caught in a whirlpool, began sinking to the muddy bottom to lay there with other fallen stones. But that was not to be. A powerful current originating from the glacial source of the river swept Alya's pebble up and took it, tossing and twirling on towards the open sea.

31

A Blossom

'Ah, Reena, you're here?' Dolly asked.

'Yes, Mom,' Reena responded.

'Nice surprise,' Dolly told her daughter, sitting on the bed.

'The pest control people are fumigating my house.'

'Do you want something to eat? Are you hungry?'

'No, Mom,' Reena said, applying make-up in front of the mirror in her parent's room.

'What's this?' Dolly asked her about the torn package on the bed.

'Malini sent a gift for me from London.'

'What is it?'

'Dad mentioned that Sri Sri's coming to town tonight,' Reena said, trying to divert her mother's attention.

'My friends and I are going to receive him at the airport.'

'Really?'

'I had the gardener pluck me a rose in full bloom from the building's garden to give him.'

Reaching for the pancake foundation, Reena decided, upon second thought, to give it a miss and go for a light compact powder instead. She applied rouge on her cheeks and tinted gloss on her lips.

'Sri Sri is returning from a world tour. He'll be in Mumbai for a day, and then he's off again to Bengaluru. What a hectic life he leads...'

Reena wore her favourite pearl earrings, brushed her hair and slipped on her new peep-toe heels.

'...I was thinking of visiting his ashram in Bengaluru. People say it is the most peaceful place on earth.'

Running her hands over her dress, Reena stood up and said, 'I love you, Mom,' planting a wet kiss on her forehead.

Mr Subramaniam, who was watching his daughter from the living room, was puzzled by what he was seeing. Reena was hovering twice as high as his wife usually did after *darshan* with Sri Sri. If he'd known what was in the package that had come in from London earlier in the day, he would have been more amazed. She was wearing it under her lavender dress. It was the first time she'd worn one—a negligee—and there would never be a better occasion.

'Beta, where are you going?' Mr Subramaniam asked his daughter.

'Dad, have you taken your vitamin tablets?' Reena responded.

'Yes.'

'You must take one every day.'

'I do. But wait... Where are you going?'

Reena pinched his nose and said, 'Father, I am off on a date.'

'A date?'

'Yes, dear father, I have a date.'

32

Swan Song

Reena floated through the galaxies of yellow buds, whipped up by an ebullient wind on Poinciana Lane, towards the house that she had built. This was her first visit since Danny had furnished it. The wall to her left, she noticed as she entered, was lined with bookshelves save for a square of graffiti, drawing its viewer into a multicoloured tunnel leading somewhere, nowhere or anywhere—depending on the viewer's perception and state of mind. Reena saw the recess as an opening to a dimension abounding with inspiration, mystery and delight. She went from spot to spot, appreciating Danny's personal style, observing his objects and the character they gave the studio. 'So this is it, your neon flex light,' she said, stopping at the installation in the corner of the kitchen. 'It's really cool. Where did you find it?'

'I got it in Hong Kong,' Danny replied.

A Qutub Minar of copper plates rose from the kitchen counter while pots, pans, bottle openers, tea strainers and cups dangled from a pan hanger above it.

'Would you like to have tea?' Danny asked her.

'Yes, I would.'

'Earl Grey or Jasmine?'

'Jasmine.'

Danny heated a pot of water on the electric stove while Reena removed her shoes and stroked the carpet with her feet. She tried out the couch, scrutinized his book collection and touched knick-knacks on shelves; pleased they aligned with her sensibilities.

'Would you like to see the nursery?' Danny asked her, handing her a cup of steaming Jasmine tea.

'The nursery?'

'I installed a garden in the glass enclosure.'

'I can't wait to see it.'

They went to the glasshouse with their cups of tea. The enclosure was rimmed with the most bizarre potted plants—peach orchids, poison ivy, cacti that smelled like vanilla, prickly bulbous orange pods sitting like a family of porcupines on the glass shelf, an ancient bonsai and a cherry tomato tree. Beyond the transparent ceiling, day had turned to dusk, giving Danny's cornucopia of exotic plant life relief from its own dizzying botanical drama. The sounds outside were also quietening.

Reena and Danny sat across from each other on stools set against a stone-topped table in the middle of the biosphere. When Danny lit the candles on the table, the shadows of the fauna around them came alive to the flicker of the flames, looking like pagan beings dancing wildly. The lovers' eyes met, making no effort to conceal the desire in their hearts; entranced by each other—man and woman—their energies mingling with the incorporeal dancers and vapours of jasmine tea. Danny removed the cups and candles from the table. He came around to Reena and cupped her head in his hands. He kissed her softly, slowly and for long. The passion that brewed, bubbled and overflowed inside her by the power of that kiss took on a life of its own—like an animal breaking free from captivity. The lovers undressed each other, Reena's lace negligee playing no role but slipping off her shoulders and dropping to the floor with her silk dress. Danny lifted her onto the table. Goosebumps rose on her flesh—not from the cold stone but from the touch of his bare skin against hers. When their bodies merged into singularity, it felt natural, inevitable. This was the first time Reena was making love. Sex, she knew, but love she had never known.

Her heart unchained, released from its self-imposed shackles, Reena guiltlessly enjoyed pleasure. She watched the moon rise past the glass ceiling and the flickering shadows on the walls put on robes of stars. It was as though her whole life had conspired for this moment—the whole world had conspired for this moment. Everything came together and made sense. Her flights of fancy, her exploits and exploitation, her self-esteem and lack of it—her innumerable struggles had not been for naught.

They had all been a means to her resurrection. And what a resurrection! Reena's swan song surged forth: her shriek, her submission, her epiphany, her full-throated cry to the moon launched her tribulations in a fiery blast to the heavens. Her knots unravelled, she was free, released from the binding repetitions of her past, freed by love—by that distillation of mortal experience—ultimate, orgasmic, liberating love.

Acknowledgments

I want to thank my children, Ronin and Ryan, for being patient and forgiving me over the eight years it took to write this book, at a time they were very small.

I also want to thank my friends and all the men and women who have inspired the real and complex characters in *Unchain My Heart*.

I owe a debt of gratitude to my literary agent, Suhail Mathur of The Book Bakers, and the team at Rupa Publications for enabling this book to reach the discerning reader.